MW00527234

RICHARD WOLD

Rich Wold Publishing

Stan
Copyright © 2013 Richard Wold
Published by Rich Wold Publishing

For more information please contact Rich_Wold@yahoo.com.

Book design by:
Arbor Books, Inc.
www.arborbooks.com

Printed in the United States of America.

Stan
Richard Wold

1. Title 2. Author 3. Fiction

Library of Congress Control Number: 2013907363
ISBN 13: 978-0-615-80592-4

To Mike, Steven, Lynsey, and my wife Betsy.
Follow your dreams and they will come true.

*Even though I walk through the valley
of the shadow of death, I will fear no evil.*

ONE

Standing at the edge of the bridge, he looked up. Eyes questioning. Waiting for permission from someone who wasn't there. Behind him cars sped by, screeched, and stopped. Voices shouted for him to get down; others told him to jump. He closed his eyes and hummed to himself to drown them out.

And suddenly it all made sense. He felt resolute, sure of his choice. He had a feeling that peace was near. A new life. Enough of this bitter city and its sour people. Opening his eyes, he looked down again, into the abyss. He wanted to see everything that would happen to him.

He took the first step and began to fall.

Through layers of darkness and light, gas and dust, cosmic particles and black holes, he hurtled in what felt like open space. Was this the end of his life or some new beginning? What awaited him at the end of the drop? More emptiness or a new creation? He wondered if he'd made the right choice.

But he knew he had. And pride in what he'd done replaced his fear of it. *I am wise*, he told himself. *I determine my fate. I will create a new life. I am, I am, I am.*

In a flash the earth consumed his view, blotting out everything around it. He smashed through the atmosphere. The bridge's majestic arches and gleaming steel sparkled against the dark, rippled surface of the water. Gravity, velocity, and acceleration pulled and pushed him, farther and faster.

Though he hadn't expected it—*Too cliché*, he thought, *to be something that really happens*—his life flashed before his eyes.

Faces mostly. Many in anguish. Bared teeth and bulging eyes. Spitting as they cursed his name. They hated him. He could feel it radiating all around him. Damnation. Recrimination for all he had done to them—and to everyone else. The absolute loneliness and emptiness of it was overbearing.

But there was no time for that now. No room for thoughts of the past. Everything was moving again, the earth coming into focus fast. Then came the impact. A loud *crack* sounded as his body broke the surface of the river and hung in suspended animation below. His limbs curled up to his body, returning to the fetal position, retracting from the pain. Like fire and needles being jammed into his nerves, like his flesh ripping away from his bones.

He held his breath, and when he couldn't do that anymore he blew it out in huge bubbles, eager to get rid of the last vestige of this mortal life. He watched them float up toward the sky and took one last look at the light. He smiled. It still called to him.

Stupid light, he thought. *Let me go already.* Then he closed his eyes and let the blackness bring him home.

"Buddy. Hey, guy."

The voice came from above. Not booming from the heavens but quiet and calm. Soothing.

Whoever it was stood next to him. He opened his eyes to look but squeezed them shut again. He was surrounded by white light, searing and literally blinding.

God, he thought, pressing his palms into his eye sockets. Something nudged him, and a dull ache ran through his thigh and down to his foot. His body cringed in pain, rolling to the side, but he found he could only make it halfway. Sharp gravel tore into his cheek; sand stuck to his lips. He exhaled slowly once more, blowing the grains away, then sucked them back in. He was breathing.

"Maybe he's a jumper." A second voice. Closer, like someone bending over him. "Doesn't look too hurt, though."

"I don't think so." The first voice again. Deeper, calmer, older. "Never in my thirty years on the job have I seen someone survive a jump from the George Washington Bridge. Not once."

He opened his eyes then. So it was true. He was alive. Squinting, he trained his gaze first on the ground before him, on the rocks and dirt and meandering seagulls. They chattered and squealed as they fought over bits of rancid trash discarded by the traffic above.

He looked up. From below, the view wasn't anywhere near as impressive as it had been on the way down. Here it was all seamy underside, all bolts and wires. The stink of the river and noxious exhaust fumes. His stomach roiled. He pushed himself up on his elbow and vomited. Nothing but bile. Bucketloads of bile.

"Oh, man." The first voice again. It belonged to a cop. Dark-blue shirt and pants, shiny gold badge. Gun in a hip holster.

His partner—just a kid, and so white he was almost transparent—laughed nervously. His uniform hung off him like a funeral suit on a skeleton. He pulled a wadded-up tissue from his pocket and handed it over. "Sorry, it's all I got."

The flimsy bit of paper did nothing to remove the taste of the Hudson from his mouth no matter how hard he wiped. "You're cops?" His voice was raspy, his tongue like sandpaper, and the words felt foreign on his lips.

"Yeah. Officer Reeves," said the older one as he fiddled with something on his utility belt.

The kid crouched down and held out the gold shield pinned to his shirt. "Officer Penn. You got a name, pal?"

Did he? He blinked slowly. Stared out across the water,

remembering the weightless feeling of the current dragging him down. Almost longing to experience it again.

"Stan Foster." The words tumbled off his tongue without connection. But he was certain that was his name.

"Okay," said the younger cop. "Did you jump, Stan?" He leaned in close, shooting a quick look over toward his partner and then back. "You can tell me."

Stan looked up to the bridge again, tried to picture himself—this man he was—standing up on the edge of it. Ready to take a swan dive to end it all.

But there was nothing. "I don't remember that."

A shot of feedback pierced the air. "Dispatch," Reeves said into his walkie-talkie, adjusting a knob to quiet the squelch. A woman's voice replied that he had gotten through.

"Yeah," the cop went on. "I need a bus under the GWB. We got a guy here, 'bout six foot, one-fifty, dark blond, early thirties. Possible injuries—some contusions and scrapes, maybe sprains or fractures, I don't know. He's alert but not moving around much."

"Are you in any pain?" Penn asked Stan.

"Yeah, my right leg. And my ribs hurt." Stan put a hand up to them and felt his heart beating. Strong and steady, the hum and thump of humanity. "But I think I can get up."

And with the officer's help he did so. Each took a hand and pulled him up.

"Alright, we'll get you to St. Luke's," Reeves said. "Get you checked out."

Penn stepped close to Reeves. Dropped his voice to a whisper. "Why didn't you say he jumped?"

"Because he didn't," Reeves replied, sounding two months overdue on his retirement.

"How can you know that?" Penn sounded just as frustrated that his partner never listened to him.

"He's had firsthand experience." The air stood still for a moment, closing in tightly around Stan's words. He turned his body around to look at the cop, wincing with each step. When their eyes met, he felt that old, familiar rage and saw the faces again, their agony and misery. One stood out this time: a woman with black hair, red lipstick, and haunted green eyes. She fell too. Dress billowing out around her, painted lips in a silent scream. She hit the water feet first; it didn't even splash. But her body was ruined beyond repair.

"I don't know who she was," Stan offered, "but she was beautiful. And young. It must have been a very big loss for you."

"How do you know that?" the older man replied, his voice full of terrified wonder. He shrugged Penn's hand off and slowly moved closer to Stan, shaking his meaty forefinger at him. "How—how the fuck do you know that?"

Stan looked at him for a moment longer, trying to think of something to say but only drawing a blank. Worse, a blackness. Like a hole in his memory, something he should have known but couldn't put his finger on. There was no explanation for what he'd said. No reason he should know it.

He turned to the water, wondering what other secrets lay down in the deep.

TWO

"If there's a hell, I'm pretty sure this is what it looks like."

Stan looked up as the orderly pushing his wheelchair spoke. Half dozing, half staring at his lap, he hadn't even noticed his surroundings. Now he wished he still hadn't. Blinking fluorescent lights, puke-green walls, cracked linoleum floor that hadn't been waxed since the '70s. Mysterious stains. Hard, plastic waiting-room chairs. No pictures, no plants, none of the decorative touches you'd see at larger hospitals. Just crosses and crucifixes, everywhere the suffering of the Lord. And in every crevice the rotting smell of death. Stan wasn't sure which was worse.

"Not far off," he said absently, then tugged on the hem of his too-short hospital gown.

"Here we are, Mr. Foster." The orderly brought the wheelchair to a stop in front of a high desk. A nurses' station. He popped the brake, then came around and stood next to Stan. Young, dark hair, bags under his eyes. He looked tired, haggard. As if he'd been through a lot in his short life. Bad things. The sort of things that made people turn away from the God that hung on the walls in this place.

"Foster," the orderly said to someone behind the counter, handing over a blue binder containing all Stan's paperwork. He turned to Stan and looked him in the eyes. "This is where our journey ends. I wish you luck here."

"Thanks." Now that he could see the guy's face, Stan understood it better. The attitude. He wasn't a bad person. None of those things that had happened to him were his fault. He was just worn down. Too many figurative kicks to the head, and maybe a few literal ones. He understood the feeling. "Thanks for your help. I really appreciate it."

"Alright, Mr. Foster," said a nurse as she came from behind the desk. She wore scrubs with cartoons of little cats on them. Holding syringes and stethoscopes and pill bottles in their tiny, hairy paws. Stan found them remarkably creepy but would try not to hold that against her. "Let's go to your room, shall we?"

As if he had a choice. But he smiled and nodded anyway. This nurse spoke gently; her serenity was genuine. A quintessential nice lady. He could see it in her watery-blue eyes.

She got behind his wheelchair, and they continued down the hall. This was a different ward now; he could tell by the color of the walls. They'd changed to sunny yellow. A happy, carefree shade. The kind that could make you forget your troubles even if you were in a psych ward. Even if you had no idea who you were. At least that was what the powers that be were going for.

"Here we are," the nurse announced, pushing him through a doorway. Thankfully, a private room. "I have your chart, so I won't bother you with a bunch of questions." She put the brake on the wheelchair and started to lower the bed. "You're free to get up and walk around. Use the bathroom whenever you need. You'll have activities and therapy to attend, but those orders haven't come through yet. I'll let you know when they do." She glanced at Stan. "We have a community room at the end of the hallway with a TV and some games. Some of the other patients like to spend time there, so maybe you can make some friends."

Her expression was hopeful. He didn't have the heart to tell her that all he planned on doing was curling up in that uncomfortable-looking bed and disappearing. She took his silence as a good sign.

"I'll leave you to it, then. Your lunch will be here in a little while." She patted him on the shoulder then left, closing the door tight behind her.

The stiff curtains on the window across the room were drawn, leaving the place in a comforting, shadowy darkness. Again, thank that God in the pictures around here. One of them hung to the right of the bed, a big reprint of a painting of the trinity: Jesus, his cheeks as white as his heavenly robe, rising from the cross as his majestic, bearded dad up in the sky looked on proudly. Between them was some sort of mist, the Holy Spirit as smoke from an unfiltered cigarette. Stan closed his eyes and rubbed them. The next three days would last a lifetime.

That was how long he'd been told he'd have to stay for observation. In the ER they'd determined he was relatively okay physically, though they had a lot of questions about his state of mind.

"Join the club," he muttered, then hoisted himself up out of the wheelchair with one thrust. He had tape across his fractured ribs, a splint around his sprained right ankle, and a prescription for enough Vicodin to put down an elephant. But that was about it. No snapped back, no shattered bones, not even a little bit of whiplash. Nothing that screamed, *Hey, I just tried to kill myself!* If anything, he looked like he'd been in a fight. Probably on the winning side.

He hobbled the six steps to the window and pushed the curtains back, just enough to see the world outside. It was still bright. God, it was *so* bright. Like he'd never seen the sun before.

Maybe I lived in a cave. Or in a submarine. He didn't think he'd ever know, so he might as well make something up. He closed the curtain and headed for the bathroom.

"Ooooohhhhhh." Apparently he hadn't taken a piss in a good long while either. Letting it go was practically orgasmic.

He flushed and washed, then stood in front of the mirror and examined his face. Maybe seeing it would change things— would help him remember who he was. Blue eyes; short, brown-blondish hair; full lips and a straight nose—he wasn't ugly. But he was a stranger in this body. Something about it didn't fit quite right. He gave it a few minutes, but nothing came to mind. Finally he touched the bruise on the left side of his forehead. Angry indigo and violet, still very fresh and sore. Maybe that had knocked it out of him. His identity. He thought about banging the other side on the sink to see if anything came back.

"Hello?" Someone was in the room. A woman.

Stan stepped out from the bathroom. "Hello."

The woman carried a tray with his lunch on it: a paper plate full of soggy food, a Styrofoam cup of coffee, a plastic spoon. Nothing sharp or hard, nothing dangerous to his well-being.

Stan's stomach growled. "Just leave it there, please."

She put the whole thing on the bedside table, then stood there as if waiting for an order. Behind her the Jesus painting loomed, Christ's arms out to her sides as if ready to embrace her. Or maybe hold her back.

Stan shook his head. Clearing out the cobwebs. "That's just fine, thanks." But suddenly he didn't feel hungry anymore.

THREE

Bodies.
Bodies *everywhere.*

Stan stood at the edge of a huge pit, the edges rough as if an army of shovels had hacked angrily at the earth. It was deep, twice his height, and wide as a lake. And it was full of them. Bodies. Some writhed in pain—no, in agony. Their skin torn, their flesh gouged and deeply cut. Some missing legs, arms, hands. Some with no eyes. Others with no heads. Fat ones, thin ones, young and old. There was no discrimination. Everyone was equal in suffering and death.

And they bled. The pit was a lake of blood and tears. With slick, naked skin, the bodies slipped against one another. Trying to climb out. To get away. Stepping on the dead ones like they were logs, clawing at the crumbling walls that enclosed them until their fingers were raw, their nails broken off.

Looking down at them, Stan felt something like pity. These people didn't want to be here. Together in their suffering but eternally alone. No one to help them, no one to care. No love. No God. No escape.

Still, they tried. The eternal hope—or maybe stupidity—of the human race. Stan shook his head. People were so self-centered. They didn't think about one another. They didn't think about their place in the grand scheme. What about their fellow man? The poor, the sick, the lonely? What about God?

None of it mattered. People only looked out for themselves.

Only wanted what they could do and be and get. The rat race, they called it. Unbelievable what an apt description that was.

And this is where it gets you, Stan thought as a woman's fingers creeped above the edge of the pit. They felt around for a hold—a rock, a branch—but there was nothing on the vast plain surrounding the hole. Only Stan. The rest was barren, burning ground as far as the eye could see. He absently watched the hand, the thin arm it was attached to, the head of blood-matted hair that barely peeked over the rim. Eventually her weak grip caught his foot. "Help," she rasped, her throat too dry to cry out. She raised her face. Her lips were cracked. Blood streamed from her blinded eyes like tears. "Oh, God, help me."

Stan just looked at her, no emotion on his face. The woman simpered and begged, but her fingers began to slip, leaving bloody, sweaty tracks along the bridge of his bare foot, down the length of his toes. Her arm retreated across the dusty, red ground. Her body slunk back into the pit, landing with a wet thump against the others.

"Sorry," he said to her. But really he wasn't.

Jesus stared at him. Or, rather, looked right through him. Stan hadn't noticed it before, but the savior's eyes in the painting were completely white. Zombified. Like a cat caught in a camera flash. A deer in headlights.

Stan sat up in bed. His ribs ached; he laid a hand on his side to comfort them. Still squinting at the picture, he used his other hand to wipe the sleep from his eyes. Maybe he was seeing things. But he swore Jesus hadn't looked like that when he'd checked in.

He swung his legs over the side of the bed with a whimper. A moan of pain and remorse. A sound just like that woman had made.

Oh, God, help me.

Her words came back to him now, making his head rush. He ran a hand through his hair and closed his eyes tightly. In the black of his mind, he saw the bodies squirming and twisting like worms in a bath of their own filth. He saw the pit and the endless, burning land. Misery filled his senses—the smell of fear, the taste of blood, the touch of her icy hand on his hot skin.

And he remembered how unfazed he felt. How all this torment meant nothing to him. Was that how he really was? Devoid of emotion, lacking in empathy? How could he see all that suffering and not feel even a little moved by it?

But, then, it was just a dream. *Had to be,* he thought. He'd been heavily asleep, adrift on a pharmaceutical ghost ship. Pain meds, psych drugs, he didn't know what all they gave him. A nurse came in every so often with a little white cup and stood there as he swallowed the cocktail. She didn't trust him—or any of her other patients. If she turned her back for a minute they were dumping their pills into the toilet, palming them to save and sell in the rec room.

But Stan took every one of his. They made him feel better. They made him forget what little he knew of himself. He thought this was probably a good thing.

Because the dream. Or was it a memory? It had seemed so—

He looked back over his shoulder at the painting. Jesus watched him still, his eggshell eyes, his arms outstretched. Beckoning. Or maybe pushing him away.

"Well, which is it?" Stan asked. "Yes or no? Real or not real?"

He looked at God in the painting. No answer from him either.

"Typical," he muttered, then reached over the top of the bed and hit the nurse's call button on the wall. A voice replied—faraway, staticky, bored. He asked for painkillers. Not for his ribs but for his mind. He wanted to lose himself again. He didn't tell the nurse this. She said she'd send someone in.

Stan lay back down and closed his eyes, trying not to see the scene anymore. Not to hear the screams. Not to feel the heat of that place, wherever it was, on his skin. But it was hard. These were the only images he had.

FOUR

"Just tell me what you remember."

Sitting behind her desk in her small, windowless office, Abigail crossed her legs and adjusted her skirt as her newest patient—Foster, Stan; suicidal, amnesiac—stared her down. He seemed like an intense guy. Nothing like her usual schizophrenics and borderline personalities. They were eccentric, paranoid, narcissistic. More likely to talk to the voices in their heads than to her.

Stan was a different beast. He was clean-cut, real movie-star good looks. In good health. At least he appeared that way. He was young, tanned, muscular. Wore a tight-fitting, white undershirt, black dress pants, and a pair of hospital slippers. Very different from her usual patients. Usually she was lucky if they tied their gowns closed. Or even put them on at all. Her colleagues at the hospital—two other overworked, burnt-out psychiatrists like herself and a fairly useless social worker—always pushed off the real crazies on her.

Stan wasn't one of them. He was articulate. Philosophical. Intelligent. In the last half hour they'd talked about the state of health care in America, politics, religion. "If you're a lapsed Catholic," he'd asked, "why do you work in a religious hospital?"

She didn't have an answer. Or, rather, she had too many of them. Her relationship with God was so complicated she felt like it could never be untangled. So she never talked about it. Not with anyone. Not even herself.

15

Besides, her beliefs were not the issue here. Stan's mental state was. Maybe he was crazy, but she couldn't help finding him intriguing. He knew all this stuff about the world at large but nothing about himself. He was an enigma even to himself. A puzzle for her to solve.

"I remember the two cops. The ones who helped me." He paused for a long moment, gazing at the picture hanging on the wall to his left.

Abigail glanced at it too. *Birds of Joy and Sorrow* by Viktor Vasnetsov. Took up most of the tiny wall. On the left a black bird sitting on a branch, its shoulders and head a raven-haired woman's. Sunken eyes, gold crown, face downcast, mouth open in anguish. On the right was her opposite, a white bird whose human face was upturned and smiling.

The image intrigued Abby. The dichotomy, good versus evil, light against dark. It didn't fit in with the hospital's Jesus theme, but no one had complained yet. She'd hung it a few weeks earlier. The only adornment in the claustrophobic space.

She cleared her throat and tucked a lock of her blond hair behind her ear. "What else?"

Stan sat back in his chair. "That's it. I remember what happened *after* that. The ambulance and the ER and everything. But anything before this?" He shook his head.

Abby looked down at her notepad. "Mania?" she'd scribbled as he'd talked earlier. "Autism? Freakish attention to detail. Possible God complex. Schizophrenia?"

In the end, she'd scratched them all out. She had no idea what his diagnosis was. Not yet, anyway, and usually she did by now. You work in a psych ward for what, eight years? You get good at reading people's issues as soon as you meet them. A facial tic. A shrug of the shoulders. The words they say—or don't say. It all means something in therapy land.

"Do you remember jumping?"

He blinked. "I remember falling."

Abby smirked. He was a quick one. "But not jumping."

He smiled too. Like they were in on the same joke. "But not jumping. Look, Doctor—" He leaned forward, craning to see the badge hung on a lanyard around her neck. She grabbed it self-consciously. What an awful picture. Her blue eyes, fair complexion, and sharp, delicate features were just a washed-out blur, as if she'd been snapped by surprise in the middle of a hurricane.

"Dr. Petrus," Stan went on. "I don't know how much clearer I can make this. I don't know who I am. I don't know anything about my life. If I did, I would tell you. Don't you think I want to figure—"

He stopped again. Now his eyes seemed far away. Somewhere in his head a wheel was turning.

"Stan?" Abby put down her notepad, leaned forward on her desk. "What's on your mind?"

Another beat and he shook his head, coming back to reality. "Nothing," he muttered, shifting in his seat. "Just a dream I had before. It was…" He ran a hand through his short hair, making it stick out in all directions. "It seemed very real."

"Well, dreams can sometimes show us what's in our unconscious mind," Abby offered. "Things we worry about. Things we keep inside. Freud said—"

"Freud was a pseudo-scientific, misogynist asshole." Stan shook his head. "He'd probably tell me I can't remember who I am because I'm afraid of my deep, yearning desire to have sex with my mother. Whoever she is. Anyway his theories are bullshit. Even he thought so after a while. Didn't he leave psychiatry to go research diseases or something?"

"Cerebral palsy," Abby replied. "And aphasia."

"Right. So don't talk about him, okay? Don't tell me what he thinks about my head. Dreams are fantasies. Just pictures your brain gives you to look at while you sleep to keep you entertained. That's all it was. This dream I had didn't mean anything."

"It certainly sounds like it did. It seems to have gotten you pretty worked up. Why don't you tell me about it?"

Stan let out a long sigh. His closed his dark eyes. "Alright. I was standing in front of a pit of bodies. Some of them were dead. Some were alive, but they were all mangled. I don't know what I was doing there… If I *put* the bodies there, or if I *witnessed* something…"

"And why do you think you dreamed this?" Abby asked the question calmly, gently. He didn't look like a mass murderer, but just in case—

He leaned forward. Eyes blazing. Voice down low, as if he was letting her in on a conspiracy. "You know what I think? Maybe it's not a dream. Maybe it's a memory."

Abigail cleared her throat, uncrossed and recrossed her legs. She picked up her notepad and wrote down "Delusional."

"So you feel you might be a violent man." Her voice came out thin, afraid.

Stan sighed again. "I don't know what to feel." Now he sounded defeated. "I'm just telling you what I see in my head. Who knows what it is?"

"Bipolar," she added, and underlined it twice. He was definitely bipolar. Enigma solved.

"What else do you see, then? Let's explore this."

She spun around in her chair to a small bookshelf behind her. Picked out the DSM-IV-TR and thunked it onto her desk. The book weighed about as much as she did. Flipping through the pages, she looked for the diagnostic code for what she believed his particular malady to be.

"I see a dark-blue shirt. The kind mechanics wear. It's covered in grease and blood. On the white tile floor of a bathroom."

Abby raised her eyes. Finger poised above the book, about to run down a list. "What did you say?"

Stan leaned forward, resting his arms on her desk. Pushing back the pen cup, the inbox over-stacked with manila folders, the small, framed picture of Abby and her sister, Lily, when they were young girls. Abby was older but by only two years. They'd been so close growing up. Now Lily was the only family she had left. But they hadn't talked in so long. Not since—

She put her hand down gently on the face of the book and breathed deeply. The air in the room felt like fire in her mouth, a burning she hadn't felt in so many years. She exhaled. "And what do you think that means?"

"I—I don't know." He sat back slowly. "I'm sorry. I don't know why I said that."

"It's okay," she replied, returning to the book but keeping him in the corner of her eye. *He couldn't know*, she told herself as she flipped pages, her eyes darting for a moment to the photo. Her and Lily. Lily and her.

He can't know what we did, she thought. *But then how did he—*

She slammed the book closed. Folded her hands on top of it. Stan was a short-termer; she wasn't really supposed to help him. Just meet with him once, diagnose him, and medicate him so hospital administration could push his uninsured ass out the door. And she had half a mind to do it, just to get away from him. What was he, a stalker? One of those fake psychics like you see on TV in the middle of the night, picking up on details and using them against her?

"Mr. Foster, I'm afraid our time is up. But I'd like to see you tomorrow for another session."

She wasn't sure what he was. But she felt deep down in her soul that she had to find out.

FIVE

The Hippocratic Oath says nothing about a doctor getting personally involved with a patient. Still, Abigail felt like she might be toeing the line. Trying to figure out his identity—that really wasn't her responsibility. That was up to the cops who'd brought him in, or the hospital's useless social worker. She was just his shrink. Simply there to listen and to medicate.

But something about Stan got to her. He had a look in his eyes. He had fire most of the other patients didn't have. She couldn't just let that go to waste.

Sitting at her desk, she gave her Rolodex a twirl. The little index cards ticked like a roulette wheel as they spun. Even with all the electronic gadgets, she still used the old reliable Rolodex. She watched for one labeled "NYPD." She'd marked it at the top because she knew she'd never remember the detective's name. He'd given her his number a few months earlier when they'd met at a bar downtown, next door to her favorite art gallery. She'd just come from an opening. Installations constructed of glass and wire. A statement on the fragile beauty of post-9/11 New York City. She'd needed a double scotch straight up.

He'd seemed like a nice guy. Worked out of the Seventh Precinct, lived somewhere nearby. Obviously he'd been hitting on her, but she'd had no interest at the time. Not just in him but in anyone. She hadn't been on a date, let alone had a boyfriend, in longer than she could remember. In the last few years, just the thought of intimacy had begun to scare her. Not sex—that

21

was still a good thing, even though she'd been without it for a while too. But being close to another person. Sharing thoughts. Talking about feelings. None of it sat right with her. And the longer she was alone, the more it felt like her natural state.

But those aren't things you say to strangers. "Can you have my number? Sure, if you like antisocial freaks." She'd taken his just to be polite but knew there was no way she would call him.

Well, things change, she thought. Now she needed him. Professionally, at least. After her monumental blow off, she hoped he would talk to her.

"Ah," she said, pulling a card off the wheel. Detective Jameson. The name brought an image of him: average height, graying hair, working-man's suit. Very polite. All in all he'd been harmless. He was just trying to meet people. Another lonely soul in a city full of them.

Abby held the card in one hand as she turned to her ancient desk phone and picked up the receiver. She dialed nine to get an outside line but paused, glancing at Stan's mug shot, paper-clipped to his file on her desk. All the patients here had them, in case they became accidentally misplaced. Stan's was better than most. Stylishly messy hair, half a smirk, bedroom eyes. This guy might be crazy, she mused, but he was deep crazy. He knew things. About psychology, history, society. His insight into the human condition was complex and fascinating. During their session he'd quoted Kierkegaard, *The Hero With a Thousand Faces*, the theory of everything. He'd talked about Magritte, Dali, surrealism, and hidden meanings. All high-level concepts, and he'd spoken of them as if they were baseball scores. All the while his eyes burned into her. His body was animated. He had a need to be understood. To have his thoughts heard. That much he'd shown her.

Then there was that…premonition. Or whatever it had

been. She glanced at her picture of Lily again. At their dad's arm draped around her shoulders, leading off into nothing. Abby had cut him out of the photo long ago. But she still remembered that afternoon. He'd smelled of gas and grease. His blue shirt stained with them, leaving smudges on her pink dress.

Turning back to the phone, she finished dialing. One ring, then two.

"Jameson," a voice said on the other end of the line.

"Detective." She tried to make her voice as bright as possible. "This is Abigail Petrus. We met at RBar down on Bowery?"

She could almost see him leaning back in his creaky desk chair and thumping his big, black shoes up onto the desk, TV-gumshoe style. "Sure, I remember." He had a nice phone voice. Soft and comforting. He was probably good at telling people their loved ones had been shot. "Caucasian, five foot ten, one twenty, light-blond hair, blue eyes."

"Yeah, that's me. Listen, I'm sorry to bother you, but I'm having this—dilemma at work. I remembered you gave me your number and thought you might be able to help."

She closed her eyes, hoping it didn't sound like an excuse. Like she was actually interested in him and just looking for an excuse to call. She only wanted what his badge could get her, not a date. Not a relationship. Not anything of the sort.

"Well, I'll do what I can." His voice was still unbelievably gentle. "What can I help you with?"

Abby exhaled. Maybe this wouldn't be as painful as she'd imagined. "Thanks, Detective. So, I'm a psychiatrist—"

"Mm-hmm. I remember."

"And I work at St. Luke's. We have this patient who came in early this morning, and he has no idea who he is. No ID either, so we have no address. I've tried all the databases but with so little to go on…"

She glanced at her open laptop. Several browser windows were open: the NamUs Missing Persons Database, the FBI's Kidnappings and Missing Persons, the Doe Network, the NYPD Missing Persons page—anything Google could turn up. Not one of them had a thing about Stan. She'd already spent hours going through listing after listing, looking at pictures, descriptions, anything that might identify him. All she was left with at the end of it were tired eyes and a sick feeling in her stomach. There were so many missing people in this country. Mothers, children, the elderly. Where did they come from? Better yet, where did they all go?

"How'd you get him?" the detective asked, breaking into her thoughts.

"Oh, uh, he jumped off the GWB. At least that's what we think. A couple of patrol officers found him on the shore. He doesn't remember jumping, but he was soaking wet and has injuries consistent with impact."

"And there's nothing online about him?"

Abby shook her head and sat back. "No. No hits on his name or physical description in this location." She stuck out her bottom lip and blew some strands of hair away from her face. She sat back. "I don't know… I guess I thought maybe you'd know some other place I could look."

She wasn't quite sure what to ask now that she had him on the phone. She waited for him to reject her request—politely, but still—then hang up and hope she'd never call again.

But that didn't happen. "I've got some friends in missing persons. Let me see what they can scrape up. Can you fax me his vitals?"

Abby breathed out again, this time in relief. "Sure. Give me your number. I'll send it right over."

To be nice, she chitchatted a little with him about work and the city and the weather. As they talked, she stared absently at the picture of Stan. Resisting the urge to doodle on it. Draw a mustache, a black eye, big, pointy horns. She shook her head to clear it, then made an excuse to get off the phone. Yes, Detective Jameson was nice. Yes, he was doing her a favor. But that was where her relationship with him ended. She had no desire to play verbal footsie with him. He got the hint and graciously bid her goodbye.

Standing up, she collected her things, more than ready to go home for the night. On the way out she would stop at the nurses' station, where the unit's ancient fax machine lived, to send out Stan's info. With her bag on her shoulder and her laptop in hand, she bent over to grab his folder. But she stopped short. Was the picture really scowling at her? Maybe she'd been working too much. Or not sleeping enough. Either way her mind was playing tricks now. She closed the folder and opened it again. Stan's enigmatic smile was back.

Abigail shook her head again and turned out the light. Stuffed the folder under her arm. Her high heels clicked as she headed down the hall.

SIX

Stan jammed the pillow around his head, then threw it off again. Nothing helped. The endless drone of wailing and crying pelted his mind. The voices begged for help, for mercy, for relief. As if he were the jail keeper. As if he could escape.

He shoved his fists against his head, kneading his temples to silence the screams. Rising from the bed, he paced the room, his prison cell. Glared out the window, then at the wall. Then the painting, as always, drew his gaze. The air stilled. The voices stopped. Void. Stale. Dead. The silence terrorized him, and he quickly looked away from the picture. Then the voices returned. The humming of a thousand invisible flies he couldn't swat away.

The noise was a welcome relief. There was something familiar about it. No, deeper than that. *Inherent*. Stan more than understood this misery. He felt it on a core level, as though hopelessness and despair pumped throughout his body instead of blood, black cells like the bottom of an abyss. No love in his heart. No feeling in his soul. He inhaled this wretched world, and it filled his body with hatred, waste, and destruction. It made him feel useless. Just a vessel to cause more unneeded pain.

Stan closed his eyes and rubbed them. Let out a frustrated moan, joining the chorus. It all made him so tired. He didn't want to feel this way. He wanted what he sensed in others: Hope. Love. A good soul. Whatever that was. If it even existed.

A knock brought him back to earth. "Stan?" A gentle voice as the door cracked open. Abigail's face appeared. "Can I come in?"

He cleared his throat, pushed his hair back, though it popped right back up. Checked to make sure he had his pants on. Stan had been sleeping so much—or at least trying to—he'd lost track of day, time, and whether he was presentable for company.

"Sure." He moved the chair away from the window, where so often he sat and stared at the sky. Positioned it next to the bed, then offered Abby a seat.

"Thanks." She smoothed the back of her skirt as she sat down. "I just wanted to touch base with you, let you know what I've been working on." She smiled at him. "And of course see how you're doing."

Stan had the bed remote in his hand, lowering the mattress so he could sit opposite her. The bed moved painfully slowly, its dead hum ringing in his ears. He looked at Abby. "I'm doing okay. How are you doing?"

She shifted in her chair, her eyes looking down briefly. "Um, I'm alright too. Thank you for asking."

Finally the bed was low enough where Stan could be eye to eye with her. He sat down and leaned forward, resting his arms on his upper legs. Clasping his hands together in front of him. "Any news about who I am yet?"

Abigail's posture loosened up a little. "Sorry, no. I've been searching all the online databases, but I haven't found anything. I even called up a contact I have in the NYPD. He's looking into your case for me."

Stan nodded, squinting his eyes against the dull light coming in through the window. Falling on the doctor's back, casting her face in shadow. Hitting him right in the eyes. Making his brain pound harder in his skull than it already did.

"Don't give up hope yet," Abigail added. "We'll come up with something. Still a lot of stones left to turn."

He moved his head to the side, and the sun hid back behind the curtain. He got a better look at Abby. In her office the previous day, where they'd met for his first session, she'd been clinical, a little stiff. Her brow always lowered in thought, lips constantly pursed. She took her job seriously, that much was obvious, but Stan knew there was more to it. Something about him had put her on edge, made her nervous in his presence. She'd never said as much, but she didn't have to. It was written all over her.

Now she seemed more relaxed. Maybe she'd gotten used to him. The hour-long conversation they'd had yesterday—on art and literature and philosophy, which Stan apparently knew a lot about—might have helped some. Shown her who he really was—not just an amnesiac jumper with no known address, but an intelligent human being. Not a lost-cause head case like her other charges.

Or maybe it was just that now they were sitting so close to one another. No desk between them. No glaring fluorescent lights. Stan kept the room dim at all times, only letting the natural light in during the daytime. He preferred the shadows; they made everything softer, more agreeable. He looked Abby up and down. She wasn't bad-looking. Quite attractive, really. Tall and thin, silky hair, everything about her pale. White skin, pink lips, crystalline eyes. He wondered how she'd feel if he reached out and touched her.

He sat up straight. "To what do I owe this visit, then, if you haven't found out anything about my identity?"

"Well," Abigail began, "I've been thinking about you since we met yesterday. About the dreams you're having, and that, um…well, the thing you said. About the dark-blue shirt. It—it sounded like something that belonged to my father." She let out a breath, pushed her hair back behind her ear. "I'm just concerned about you, Stan."

The words hung between them in the still air for a moment. Stan let them hover.

"Don't be," he said at last. "I'm as okay as I can be, given the circumstances."

Abigail smiled again. It was a sweet gesture. Gave Stan a warm feeling in his chest. But then a cloud passed over her expression. Like she had changed her mind about something. She stood up.

"So, listen, it's activity time in the day room. Do you think you feel up to it? Maybe you could go down and introduce yourself to some of the other patients. I'm sure they'd love to meet you."

Stan didn't want to make friends, but maybe being around people would drown out the noise in his head. Stop those voices from screaming. Besides, he couldn't sleep, and the TV bored him. Abigail seemed pleased when he agreed to go, then excused herself to get to an appointment. Stan went in the bathroom and washed his face; he put on his dress shirt and his tie. Even in this hellhole, he wanted to maintain some dignity. Show he wasn't like the others. At least he wanted to believe he was different.

Down the hall, the day room was misery central. Full of psych-ward inmates in various stages of awareness. Society's rejects draped across furniture and pacing the floor. Most wore pajamas, bathrobes, slippers. Like they were Hugh fucking Hefner and this was Sunday at the mansion.

Stan took a seat at a long table with a handful of other patients. He looked at them one by one, trying to figure out what each of them was in for. Were they insane or just lost like him?

"Stop staring at me!" the old man beside him hissed, grabbing Stan's arms with his bony fingers.

Stan looked at him sharply. The guy's pupils were like planetoids, huge and easy to see into. In a flash Stan saw a young girl, this man hovering over her. His pants down. Stan didn't want to see any more.

"Sorry," Stan mumbled, lowering his eyes to the table. His brain was throbbing. Too much medication, or maybe not enough. Even his own voice was like a hammer to the skull. This room full of chatter and nonsense threatened to crush him.

The guy leaned closer. He smelled like mouthwash but not enough of it. "Not you." He raised a trembling finger and pointed across the table. On the wall there was another painting. The son of God in close-up, beaming like a glow stick. His crystal-blue eyes looked heavenward; his silky, light-brown hair fell over his shoulders in waves. He was solemn but friendly, serious but welcoming. The perfect blend of teacher and savior. Compassion and justice. *Look into my eyes*, he said. *I'll show you the way.*

The guy was right. Jesus *was* sort of gawking.

Another patient came by and dropped a packet of stuff in front of Stan, then gave one to his neighbor too. A brightly colored folder; inside was construction paper, crayons, a small bottle of Elmer's glue. Safety scissors, the kind made for toddlers. A tube of gold glitter.

Arts and crafts, Stan thought. The daily activity. Like they were in preschool. Is this what his life was about? Amusing bored nurses by playing with crayons? It felt so demeaning.

His neighbor nudged him. Held up a drawing he'd started. Green crayon on blue paper, almost invisible.

"Nice use of color fields," Stan offered, avoiding the man's eyes. "Very abstract."

The man smiled toothlessly. Stan looked back at his packet. So this was what it had come to. Amnesiac, homeless, and now forced to make macaroni art with the clinically insane. He took out the construction paper, the scissors, the glue. *When in Bizarro Rome*, he thought, and spread out the supplies before him. He fanned out the paper. He rolled the tube of glitter back and forth, then picked up the scissors and snapped them open and closed a few times. He put them back. He closed his eyes and drew a long breath. For a moment the noise in his head stopped.

Then he reached out again. His fingers caught a piece of paper and held on to it, rubbing its coarse, crude surface between his thumb and forefinger like a fine piece of silk. The tactile sensation sent an image to his mind. Not of the things before him but of what they could make. Of what they could be. He didn't know quite how to translate the message, how he would form what he saw in his mind out of the items before him on the table. But he knew he could do it. What's more, he was compelled to do it. Driven to create. The urge was stronger than anything he'd felt since he'd jumped—or fallen—off the bridge.

And that was the heart of it, wasn't it? That feeling of falling. It never quite left him. As he picked up the first piece of paper and tore it into strips, he allowed himself to remember the weightlessness of his body as it hurtled somewhere between heaven and earth. Or somewhere beyond them. As he'd fallen, couldn't tell up from down, left from right, even where he was in the universe. He'd drifted to infinity, toward an end that was nowhere in sight, a future as blank as the clear, blue sky.

When he'd shredded all the paper—and some of his neighbor's—he began the tedious task of piecing it back together, not as it had been but in a form wholly new to it. Slathered in glue, the strips stood on end, strapped one another together, twisted and folded to create the vision in Stan's mind: a great, multicolored phoenix not rising from the gold-glitter ashes strewn around its feet but mired in them. No, *reveling* in them. It was a bird that no longer had the desire to fly, yet its enormous wings stretched out, their ragged paper feathers hanging off them like a shroud.

"Stan, did you do this?" The voice broke him out of the trance he'd been in. Dr. Petrus stood at his side. She gestured to the bird on the table. "This is amazing. I was passing by, and I saw what you were doing. I had to stop in to check it out."

Stan stood up. "Yeah, welcome to the preschool open house." He rubbed his chin, looking at this thing he had created. This doomed creature. It was tragic; it was gorgeous. Like something made by a real, trained artist. "I don't know. I just picked up the paper, and it sort of made itself."

Abby nodded. "Well, it's actually quite beautiful, especially given what you had to work with. Do you mind if I take a picture of it?" She pulled her cell phone from the pocket of her white coat.

"Yeah, sure." Stan waved a hand at the bird. "Go right ahead."

Abby aimed the phone camera at his creation. "I'm a bit of an art buff. And I've got to say this is one of the most original pieces I've seen in some time."

As the camera flashed, Stan reached out and touched the bird. Soft and feathery, but the dried glue gave it a hard edge. Something felt very right about it. Not just the process but the subject. Not the materials but the muse.

"It felt really natural," he said. "I don't know how else to describe it. My hands just seemed to know what to do." Stan again had that sense of silence. Just for a moment. But it was there.

Abby smiled, steadying her camera to take another snap-shot. "Maybe you're an artist, Stan. Maybe you're remembering something about yourself."

SEVEN

Abigail glared at the string of red taillights beaming at her through the taxi's windshield. Midtown rush-hour traffic in New York City: the definition of hell. Her cab hadn't moved an inch in fifteen minutes; still, the meter steadily ticked its way up. In the backseat she crunched herself up against the door, trying to touch the seat as little as possible, to avoid the stains of God knew what left by previous passengers.

Cab as metaphor for city, she thought, looking at the driver through the bulletproof barrier that separated them. *No human connection, plenty of filth.*

In front the driver spoke rapidly in some other language, the Bluetooth in his ear making it seem like he was talking to himself. Abigail ignored him and let out a heavy sigh, then checked the time on her cell phone. Seven forty-five. The gallery opening was at eight. She didn't want to stay too long, just check out the show, catch up with some acquaintances. *Maybe* have a drink at RBar. Then go home and shut herself off. Alone, like every other night. The way she preferred it.

"Excuse me," she said, tapping on the partition. The driver grunted, eyeing her in the rearview.

"Can you take Second Avenue? Sometimes it goes faster."

The driver nodded and put on his blinker. As if that would help at all. Eventually the traffic moved at painfully slow and short intervals, and he made his way crosstown. To Second, where at least the cars were coasting.

Sitting back again, Abigail watched the scenery drift by as the driver navigated downtown. A hard landscape, all brick and asphalt and metal. The only soft things were the humans, running around as if the devil chased them. Into and out of buildings, jabbering on cell phones, arms full of shopping bags. Shrieking at one another like harpies over the slightest missteps. Over nothing at all.

But not everyone here was evil, not everyone condemned yet. Something Abby always had to remind herself of. See the homeless shelters, the young children playing, the people smiling and laughing as they waited for the bus. There was camaraderie, even if Abby never felt it.

She'd lived in the city her whole life and after thirty-two years still felt like a tourist. Not a part of the big scheme. Another lowly drone, head down, doing her time. Waiting for whatever end would come.

Maybe it's purgatory. The thought came to Abby in a flash, and with it she saw the people outside in a new way. Not furiously hurling themselves toward ruin but wandering aimlessly. Lost. Starving for something they couldn't give a name to. Unaware of how little their woolgathering meant. Still they kept trying.

Shaking her head, she brought herself out of this morbid musing and realized the cab had stopped. Through the windshield she saw a nasty snarl, red taillights flaring up ahead. She checked the time again. Ten after eight.

"The hell with this." Abigail paid the driver, then got out to walk. The humidity of July hit her, and she shed her sweater, a necessity in the ever-freezing psych ward. As she stuffed it in her bag, she looked up, checking the street signs. Fourteenth and Second—in the East Village but not quite as far as she needed to be. She'd take Fourteenth to Third Ave, then follow that south until she hit Bowery. Visualizing the street grid in her head, she whirled around and smacked into a man right behind her.

"Hey, little girl," he said, eyeing her up and down. Older guy, greasy hair, lack of teeth. In need of a shower. Bad breath and a voice like overflowing sewage. He could have been one of her patients.

"Are you lost?" he went on. "I can take you home." He reached out his grimy hand toward her.

Abigail backed away. As a rule she tried never to be offended by people's looks; in her line of work she couldn't be. Given the people she worked with, she had to be immune to the worst. Ungodly aromas, selective hygiene practices, she'd seen and unfortunately smelled it all.

But this guy. It wasn't his appearance that disturbed her, nor his odor. She could even take the nauseating sexual innuendo. It was the deadness in his eyes. Not the normal junkie stare but a vacancy she wasn't used to. Like black holes, nothing but deep space behind them.

"Excuse me," she said firmly while trying to dodge him, faking left then heading right. He moved his bulky body and stopped her mid-stride. She stopped and looked at him; she stood up straight. Enough was enough. Time to put on the Dr. Petrus act. "Sir, you need to—"

"You don't want to go that way." He leaned in when he said it, his voice a hissing serpent, eyes glued to her thin frame.

Abigail felt paralyzed and cold down to her bones. Why did this guy creep her out so much? Maybe he was a rapist. A murderer. Had a hacksaw and a stock of black trash bags back at whatever hovel he lived in. Abby never claimed to be psychic, but her whole life she'd always trusted her instinct. Her intuition. What did it tell her now?

That this guy was a psycho, and not the kind she liked to spend time with. Get the hell away, her gut said. And get away fast. She turned and headed down Second Avenue, her high heels pocking on the concrete sidewalk, blond hair falling over her eyes. From a safe distance, almost down by Thirteenth, she turned and looked back without slowing her walk. The troll who'd accosted her was nowhere. Swallowed up by the crowd, she imagined. Or off in search of his next victim. Much as it seemed he did, he really hadn't disappeared, she told herself. That wasn't possible. He couldn't just have evaporated like some evil, stinking spirit.

At Twelfth Street she crossed her arms and hugged herself as she waited for the light. "Shake it off!" advised a sign in a nearby window, an ice cream shop pushing milkshakes on a hot summer evening. The traffic light turned green, and the little light-up man said it was okay to walk. Abby moved with the throng. Safety in numbers. In case the demon followed.

By Tenth she was pretty sure he hadn't, so she slowed her gait a little. Loosened her grip on herself. Pulling her cell phone from her bag, she checked the time. Eight fifteen, though it felt about a quarter to twelve. How quickly minutes could pass. Abigail remembered moments she would have liked to last longer. Board games with her sister. Baking with her mother. Aunts and uncles, cousins and friends, so many good times she hadn't thought of in years.

And then there was Daddy.

Turning up St. Mark's Place, Abigail heard her own heavy breathing. When had she quickened her pace again? What was she running away from? Slowing her pace again, she let the crowd surround her—the usual punks and tourists, same as when she was a kid buying boots at Trash & Vaudeville, videos and records at Kim's. Her rebellious days. Her artist days. Hands smelling of oils, a sketchbook always tucked in her bag. Friends from all walks of life—musicians, writers, some painters like herself. She'd dyed her hair blue and gotten her septum pierced.

"You look like a fucking bull," her father had grunted at her when she'd gone home, then slapped her so hard it tore the ring out. After that she only got body mods in places where he couldn't see them.

Abigail lowered her head, trying to shake off the black cloud forming around her thoughts. On the sidewalk a sandwich board advertised two-dollar drafts. St. Mark's Place Ale House. Abby stopped and pondered whether or not to go in. Give up on this art stuff. Have a drink instead. Maybe that was what the gods were trying to tell her. *Stop trying to be so intellectual.*

And there it was, her father's voice again. Berating her, condescending. Spitting as he tore up her artwork. *What, you think you're good at this? You think it'll pay your bills? You're wasting your time.* Eventually she believed him.

Abigail raised her eyes, looking deep into the bar. In her mind she was ten years old again, touring the local watering holes to find where her dad was hiding. Not sent by her mom, as he'd always accused, just trying to prevent trouble. The sooner she found her dad and guilted him into coming home, the less he drank, and the shorter the beating her mother would receive. Simple math, really. Abigail had figured that one out quick.

"Can I get you a seat?" Another voice behind her. Abby snapped her head to the side. A waitress, and a tiny one at that. She smiled so cheerily Abby almost felt like giving her a tip.

"No, no, thank you." Abby held her bag tightly under her arm and smoothed back her hair. She felt frantic, like she was coming apart at the seams. "I'm, ah, I'm not staying."

Turning again, she took off at a good clip—only to crash directly into a woman who hadn't been there a second ago.

"Jesus Christ," Abby shouted out of shock and exasperation.

Stops and starts, starts and stops. She wondered if she'd ever make it all the way to Bowery.

"I beg your pardon," said the woman, her voice deep and melodic. Golden-blonde hair in a tight chignon, crimson lips, heavy dark liner around her eyes. Statuesque. Taller than Abby, who stood five feet ten, and wearing stilettos to boot. Black snakeskin to match her black skirt, her tight, sleeveless top with a pornographically deep V-neck.

Abby backed up a few steps. The woman stared at her dead on, arms crossed, light-green eyes afire. Hip cocked as if awaiting an explanation. When she didn't receive one, she merely sighed and went back to what she'd been doing when they'd collided: waving her arms at a man in the store window in front of her.

"I'm, um, I mean excuse me," Abigail stuttered, hating the pitiful simpering she heard in her own voice. This wasn't like her. She bowed to no one. At least not on a normal day, which this certainly had not been. Flashbacks of her father. Harassed by a vagrant. And her new patient, Stan—she just couldn't get him out of her head. Good looks, superior intellect, an amazing artist. If only he weren't—

"Stop!" the woman shouted, holding her palms up against the glass of the shop's window. Her voice was booming, commanding, wholly unfitting with her lithe body. In a daze Abby followed the woman's gesture, glancing at the man in the window, "Lilith Gallery" in black gothic lettering across it. He had his arms around a sculpture, larger than life-size. A bird with feathers fashioned of long, shredded paper, red and orange, blue and green, shimmering metallics and mattes. Its beak pointed skyward, the tops of its wings trailing on the ground below. Into a pool of golden shards that glittered in the late sun.

Reaching into her bag, Abby pulled out her cell phone and brought up the last picture she'd taken. Stan's creation—what he'd made during arts-and-crafts time in the day room. Holding the phone against the window, she gazed between it and the larger bird. Different scale, slightly different colors. More expensive materials, but the shape was distinctly the same. Even to an untrained eye, it would be glaringly obvious.

"Where did you get that?" the woman asked, peering at Abby's phone. Standing so close Abby smelled her musky perfume, felt the heat that radiated off of her.

Abby looked at her. "Are you Lilith?"

"Yes, I am," she replied, crossing her arms again, raising her chin high. Nodding at Abby's phone, then glaring back at her gallery window. "And I'd like to know where you got that picture of my client's undebuted work."

EIGHT

The elevator lurched and jerked its way up, as if it didn't want to go in that direction. Pressed against an undesirable assortment of the hospital populace—a doctor wiping his nose with a bare hand; a nurse who reeked of cigarettes; a patient slumped in a wheelchair, IV cocktail dripping into his veins—Lilith felt right at home. The diseased, the addicted, the painfully stupid, such were the artists she represented. Brilliant as the day was long, but each just a hot mess.

And then there was Stan. Beautiful, fearless Stan Foster. He was new to Lilith's stable, but she'd heard so many good things about him. Focused, driven, in touch with his inner demons, and all the work she'd seen from him was stunning. Grandiose installations on all of art's epic themes: desire, satiation, remorse. Good versus evil, our gods and our monsters. The heart and the mind and the human inability to control either.

The elevator bumped to a stop, gears grinding.

"This is us," said Abigail, looking at Lilith and smiling. Lilith looked down at her. Literally. Also figuratively. The woman put on a hard face, but deep down she was weak, confused. Like a dog who'd been kicked too much, or maybe not enough. Lilith despised the type. She might pity Abby if she were capable.

"Oh, thank goodness," she said flatly, watching the cattle disembark. Finally it was their turn, and she followed the good doctor out into a waiting area. Threadbare rug, chipped paint, drop ceiling with mysterious, spreading stains. Security guard behind a tall desk, flipping through a tabloid. *If you didn't feel like killing yourself before you got here*, Lilith thought, *you would when you arrived.*

"Hey, Gerald," Abby said to the guard. Gerald didn't respond. Abigail waved her ID card at him, and across the room a door clicked. She walked over, Lilith in tow, and pushed its metal release. It opened, and she ushered Lilith through with a wave of her hand.

Inside the ward, not surprisingly, nothing was different. Depressing, downcast, dark, and gloomy, though it tried to seem otherwise: the yellow walls, the dusty fake plants, the shocking number of Jesus portraits that lined the hallways. So primitive. So ugly. Lilith almost loved it.

And the farther she followed Abby into the rat's maze, the more she came to appreciate the place. Passing open doorways, she glanced in at the patients, some sleeping, some pacing, some in a medicated stupor in front of the television. Blue light flickering against their dead skin, eyes like agate marbles. Lilith felt an energy here, an incredible unspoken air of violent psychosis. She closed her eyes and breathed in the rankness of these bodies that no longer cared for themselves. She heard screaming down the hall, then somebody cursing. Metal crashing. An alarm ringing like a prisoner had escaped.

Stan had to be getting some inspiration here. Mental illness was conducive to art, no matter whom it belonged to.

"This is us," the good doctor said again, slowing her pace until she stopped. Laughing lightly, self-deprecatingly, at her own little joke. She put her hand on the knob of a closed door, then paused. "Listen, I just want to tell you again, Stan probably won't recognize you. I mean, he won't know who you are. His amnesia seems pretty severe, and so far there's been no recall whatsoever. He remembers his name, but that's the only thing we've come up with. He doesn't know where he's from, what he does for a living, if he has a family—he doesn't even know how and why he jumped off the George Washington Bridge." She twisted her brow up sympathetically. "And he hasn't mentioned your name once. I'm really sorry."

Lilith leaned a shoulder against the wall and crossed her arms. The girl was trying so hard. To be gentle, to be professional, to soften the blow. As if Stan's inability to recall his agent—whom he'd barely met in the first place—was some kind of tragedy. "It's alright," she said, reaching out to squeeze Abby's arm. It seemed the thing to do. "I'll try to jog his memory. But if it doesn't work, I'm still here for him." She raised her finely arched eyebrows, imitating Abby's gesture. "I'll help him through this. Don't you worry."

Abigail put a hand on Lilith's and gave her a squeeze back. "Thanks. I'm so glad I found you. What a piece of luck, huh?"

Lilith smiled at her, red lips pursed, and nodded toward the door. Abigail smiled back—conspiratorially, like they were girlfriends now—then turned the knob and led the way inside. Lilith looked around. A neatly made bed, a tray of uneaten food. Black suit jacket and white shirt on a clothes hanger, suspended from a hook on the bathroom door. This room wasn't like the rest of the ward. There was no misery, no stink of desperation. But there was a Jesus painting—large and lifelike. It made Lilith uncomfortable.

"Stan," Abby said quietly. He sat in a low chair by the window. Facing out, looking up at the sky, head rested against the back of the chair. The two women went around in front of him. He breathed deeply and slowly, eyes opened but glazed. Like he was in a coma.

"Stan," she said again, bending down a little closer, smiling at his unseeing eyes.

Finally Lilith sighed. She crouched down, her already short

skirt creeping high up her thighs. "Stan." Her voice was loud and firm. She grabbed his hand and brought it up to smack his own face. "Stan Foster, you troublesome mongrel. Wake up!"

Stan started, then raised his head. "Who are you?" He looked her up and down. "What are you doing here?"

"I brought her, Stan," Abby volunteered. She still bent down as well, bringing a hand up to hold her shirt collar to her chest. "This is Lilith. She says that she knows you."

"Sure I do, Stan!" Lilith's lips spread into a wide smile, showing all her gleaming teeth. She slapped his knee gently. "You and me, we go *way* back."

"I'm sorry. I don't know you." His answer was too fast, the way he looked at Lilith too doubting. She saw something in his eyes. Curiosity. Familiarity. Not quite recognition yet, but that would come. She'd been told it would take time.

"It's okay," she said. "I looked pretty different last time I saw you." Out of the corner of her eye, she saw Abby's brow knit again. Lilith forced a laugh. Brought up a hand and waved the doctor's concern away. "Different hair color. I tend to dye a lot."

Abigail nodded, but her gaze at Lilith lingered. Finally she turned her face back to Stan. She placed a hand on his forehead, checking for fever. "Do you feel alright? You were out of it when we came in."

Looking up at her, Stan's eyes softened. Lilith felt a roiling in the pit of her stomach. Ire rising within her. Jealousy maybe. Stan didn't need this woman, not in his life and definitely not in his art. He needed to get back to work, not to get hung up on distractions.

"I'm okay," he said, his voice low, calmer than when he'd barked his questions at Lilith. "I was just…lost in thought."

Abigail smoothed his hair. How very unprofessional. "Did you have another nightmare?"

Stan cleared his throat and sat up straight. He glanced at

Lilith. "Uh, no. No nightmares today. What did you say your name was?"

"Lilith." She held out a hand to shake, spreading her red lips again. Trying to seem friendly. It just didn't come naturally. "I'm your agent. You're an artist, Stan. I represent you."

Beside her, Abby clasped her hands together, her face just beaming. "See? I knew it," she said, putting her hand back on Stan, gripping his shoulder.

But Stan paid no attention. He took up Lilith's hand. "I'm an artist?" His voice sounded far away. Then it came back. "An artist. I'm an artist. Well, I guess that explains some things."

"Well, it certainly explains that picture." Lilith stood up and tugged down her skirt as she nodded at Abby. "I saw your little arts-and-crafts project on that one's cell phone. It looks rough, but I could sell it for a few thou. We'll call it a study—a working model for a larger piece. Do you have it?"

Stan laughed, the skin around his eyes creasing. "Really? It's valuable? Well, it's in the closet." He jerked a thumb back over his shoulder. "I didn't know where to put it."

"We'll just bring it with us, then," Lilith said, striding over toward where he'd indicated. She opened the closet door. Inside was nothing but the bird, sitting lonely on the floor, facing the back wall.

She reached down for it. "Do you have a bag? Something to pack your things in?"

Stan stood now, tucking in his white T-shirt as he ambled around the chair. He glanced back at Abby, looking quite confused. "No, I don't have a bag. And I don't have things." He moved his eyes to Lilith. "Where are we going, anyway?"

Lilith smiled again. Putting it on big. "I'm taking you home, dear boy. Don't you want to get out of here? Get back to your old life?"

Again that maddening look to his doctor for approval. This

wasn't the Stan Lilith knew. Before he'd been so headstrong, so take-charge, in control of everything and everyone around him. Now he was a shell of himself, a mere mortal held down by the weight of his own flesh. By insecurities, by thoughts. By his emotions for this woman. Lilith didn't like it.

"Yeah, I guess I do," Stan said, rubbing a hand across his chin. "I guess…" He looked around, at the bed, at the unlit bathroom beyond the ajar door. Finally at Jesus and the vaporous spirit in the painting. His eyes lingered on it, as if he liked it. Lilith tried looking too, but she just didn't see whatever held his interest. A chill ran through her. She shook it off and went over to Stan.

"Look," she said, her voice low, her back turned to Abigail. "I know you don't remember me. I know this is awkward. But I promise I am telling you the truth. We know each other." Her eyes moved along his body, pausing halfway down. "I'd say rather intimately."

Behind her, Abigail bristled. Lilith could feel it. She looked up at Stan and continued. "So you'll just have to trust me. And you'll have to come with me." She nodded toward Abigail. "Your doctor can come too, if you wish. If that will make you feel safer. I'll show you where you live and work. I'll show you my gallery where your art's displayed. I'll introduce you to a hundred people who will recognize you in an instant."

She walked over and pulled his jacket off the hanger, then the shirt, and held them both out to him. "Come."

Stan hesitated. Lilith waited for the glance at Abby.

"Come," she repeated, shaking the clothes at him a little. "Put these on now, and let's get going."

Without looking back, Stan obeyed.

NINE

At one end of the backseat, Stan pressed his face against the window, peering at the tops of the tall buildings, the patches of sky. Like a tourist as they traveled through Times Square in Lilith's hulking, black Escalade, complete with uniformed driver and wet bar. She sat on the other end, window cracked, cigarette between her fingers.

She looked at Stan. "Anything familiar yet?"

"Not a thing," he mumbled, feeling a little mesmerized. This city was so shiny, so moving. Everything shimmered and glowed. Gave off an aura Stan felt he could see, especially on the people. Around them, like entities of their own. Some had light shooting out of their heads like sunfire, like fierce, beaming halos. Others dark shadows that lumbered in their wake, dragging them down, threatening to swallow them whole. None seemed aware of it in the least.

He rubbed his eyes and turned to the interior of the SUV. *Meds must be wearing off.* Only thing he could figure. He'd seen some interesting things while he was on them—that pit of bodies, for one, also waking visions of creatures he couldn't now describe; once he swore the mist in the painting next to his bed was talking to him. But all that was nothing like this. He glanced outside again. The colors, the incandescence. It was beautiful. So glorious. Stan had to turn away.

Abigail sat between him and Lilith. Arms pulled close to her sides, hands folded on her lap, knuckles white. She brought a fist up before her lips and coughed politely, once, then twice, and shot a furtive look at Lilith. Who didn't notice. Or, more likely, didn't care. Stan didn't know the blonde behemoth, but her personality wasn't difficult to figure out.

"How much longer 'til we get there?" he asked, for some reason wanting to calm the air between these two. He already liked Abigail, that he was sure of. She was quiet but steadfast, supportive. He sensed no greed behind her desire to help him, just sincere interest. Concern. Some subtle form of…affection? He wouldn't go that far. But it was something like that. Abigail acted like a doctor—professional, clinical, objectively curious—but underneath that thrummed a thread of something much stronger. Much more personal. She had a passion for helping people but a tendency to hide it, a deep sense of caring and respect for her fellow man. Stan could see that in her eyes, feel it in her touch when she laid a hand on his shoulder, felt his forehead for fever. And she had a particular soft spot for him.

"Ten minutes if the traffic moves," Lilith answered, exhaling a billow of smoke and tossing her cigarette out into the street. "Who knows if it doesn't."

Stan nodded and sat back. Lilith, he wasn't so sure of. Not like he was with Abby. Lilith seemed okay; she was polite, well-spoken, and very obviously gorgeous. Legs for days, smooth skin, crystalline eyes. As flawless as a body could be. But she had an edge. Stan felt that too. When she'd put her hand on his back to usher him out of the hospital room, hurrying him along to the nurses' station to sign his discharge papers. She was pushy, bossy. Things would be done her way—there was no choice in the matter. Part of Stan liked this, especially given the state that he was in. Unsure of who he was or what he should do from minute to minute. He needed guidance, and suddenly there was Lilith. Telling him he was an artist, living in the East Village and about to debut his new show at her popular gallery.

He was famous, she said. People loved him. They'd be thrilled by his comeback.

Stan thought about that now. He leaned forward to peer around Abigail. "How long was I missing, Lilith?"

She looked at him for a moment, blinking her eyes slowly. "A few weeks. I don't know exactly. We don't speak every day. You could have been gone a while before I found out about it." She flashed him a quick smile, her eyes darting momentarily to Abigail. "I sure won't take my eyes off of you now, though. You won't get away from me again."

As if feeling the glance upon her skin, Abigail turned her head, looked at Lilith, and smiled back.

"Don't worry," Stan said, again trying to diffuse things. "I don't think I'll be taking another leap anytime soon." He put a hand on his shoulder and rotated it a couple of times, his face in a grimace. "I have bruises in places you don't even want to know exist."

That drew a laugh from both women. Insincere on both parts, but at least they made the effort. Satisfied he'd broken the tension, Stan turned back to the window. Pushed the button to roll it down. A blast of heat hit him in the face, and he closed his eyes, breathing deeply. The air stung his nostrils, his eyelids, his cheeks. He liked the sensation. It felt like something he could get used to.

Finally, they reached their destination. The driver pulled over in the middle of a block, in front of a plain building. Four stories tall, gray concrete outside, like an old forgotten factory.

"This is where I live?" Stan asked, standing on the sidewalk, staring at the edifice.

Lilith spoke to the driver for a moment, then joined Stan. "And work." She looked up at the building, too, then back at him. She pretended Abigail, on his other side, didn't exist. "You like to be with your work twenty-four/seven. You've said it keeps you…what was the word?"

As she thought about it, she strode up to the building's door and pulled a set of three keys from her clutch purse. She stuck one in the lock and turned, then shouldered the door open. It hit the wall inside with a bang, the scrape of metal on cinderblock.

"Immersed. That was the word you used. It keeps you *immersed* in your work. You prefer the world you create to this"—she circled her hand in the air as she backed into the dark hallway—"*reality.*"

Stan followed in silence. Abigail right behind him. The interior of the building was, if it were possible, more foreboding than the exterior. Dimly lit, dusty floor. The walls were scuffed and chipped. Stan trailed his fingers lightly along them en route to the elevator. No wonder, he thought, he didn't like the world he lived in very much.

On the fourth floor, Lilith led them through another catacomb, stopping finally at another metal door. Stan looked up and down the hallway as she keyed its lock. No one around, no noise but the humming of the fluorescent lights hanging overhead. None of the doors were numbered. He wondered how anyone knew where they lived.

Once inside, Lilith flicked a series of switches, and the room became illuminated. Stan wandered slowly to the middle of the loft. Twenty-foot ceilings, poured concrete floors, easily more than two thousand square feet. The walls, he imagined, had been white once but were now a variety of hues. One gray and black, like ash; another splattered with crimson, like a crime scene. Another was as yellow as the sun, and in front of it stood a statue. A bird that looked like a woman. Or maybe the other way around. It had a human's legs stuck up to the shins in solidified black tar, but the torso was entirely covered in feathers.

Snowy white, with black, gummy handprints marring their purity. The creature's arms reached heavenward. Talon fingers curled into themselves. Its eyes were black holes, its beakish, tongueless mouth hanging open in mid-scream.

"*This* is what I want to be immersed in?"

"What? You don't like it?" Lilith asked, striding confidently ahead of him. As if she were comfortable here. Stan watched her as she patted a statue—some sort of man-dog—on its head, then headed to a huge, gilded mirror to reapply her lipstick.

"This art has made you lots of money, Stan," she continued, eyeing him in the reflection. "You and me both. So I wouldn't be too quick to disown it if I were you."

"I'm not disowning it," he replied quickly, moving toward the bird-woman. He didn't recognize the piece and certainly didn't remember working on it. But something about it *made sense* to him. He couldn't explain why. "It's just so…dark."

Lilith laughed at that. "And jumping off the George Washington Bridge was what? An act of optimism?" She snapped her clutch closed and walked over to where he stood. She looked at the statue for a moment, an interesting expression on her face. The most warmth Stan had seen her convey since he'd met her.

"Besides, this isn't *dark*," she said, running a hand over the thing's face. Like a mother caressing her child. "This is what's inside all of us. Good and bad. The choices we make. She reaches up for the spiritual, but she can't get her feet out of the physical mud. Or maybe she doesn't want to. Maybe she wants both at the same time. Do you think that's possible, Stan? Can we be faithful to God and to ourselves at the same time?"

By then he was touching it too. The woman's face. The skin was dark and ashy but soft, like real flesh. He wondered how he'd done that, made an inanimate creature feel so lifelike. "I…I'm not sure." His eyes glazed over as he stared at it.

"Well, I'll tell you what I think." Lilith snapped her hand back and walked away briskly. "I think we're stuck on this mortal plane when all we want to do is fly. Besides, who ever said life is all sunshine and lollipops?"

"Connie Francis." Abigail, from across the loft. She stood behind a table, one of many covered in sketches. Humans, animals, gargoyles, demons. Stan could see them from where he stood, all bold lines and hacking, stabbing strokes.

Lilith stopped in her tracks, turning just her head back to Abigail. Her red lips smirked. "Actually it was Lesley Gore, and that's not even the point, my dear." She paused, then headed over to Abigail. She looked down at the sketches, moving them around with her long, slender fingers. "The point is that darkness is a matter of opinion. One man's sin is another man's unrepentant pleasure, his greatest joy in life." She looked Abby up and down. "Not all of us walk the straight and narrow. Nor are we sorry for it."

Abigail looked at herself as well, running her hands over her cream-colored shirt, her pastel skirt. Crew neck and tea length, her heels neutral-colored and entirely sensible. She didn't even have earrings in, a necklace on, a ring on her finger. Looking up, she caught herself in the golden-framed mirror. Washed out and pale, boring and plain. Standing next to Lilith, in her shadow, like she didn't exist.

"Well," Lilith announced, resuming her march to the other end of the loft. "Stan, take your time getting reacquainted. I have some calls to make, lots of people to notify that you're back. And we should really do some media too—*ARTNews*, the *Voice*, the *Times*… Can you do interviews? You think you feel up to it?"

There was no reply. Cell phone to her ear, she stopped and turned. Stan knelt at the side of another figure. A woman on the floor in a fetal position, her glittering, winglike arms wrapped around her body like a cocoon. Flesh black and flaking, as if seared by invisible flames.

"Stan." Lilith snapped her fingers in rapid fire. "Stan. Are you with me, darling?"

He glanced at her, his hands still on the statue. "I just can't believe it." He looked down at the woman. Touched her feathers, the hair on her head. "They all seem so real. *Feel* so real. It's like I made actual people." He surveyed the room again, the lines of models running along the wall. "I can't believe I did all this."

"Well, believe it," Lilith said, walking back over to him. Crouching down next to him, flashing that thigh again. "You're a brilliant artist. One of the best I've ever known, certainly the best I've represented. Your artwork is aesthetically beautiful, technically flawless, and philosophically? Deeply, *deeply* challenging. I've never seen anyone come to one of your shows and not be moved by the experience."

"Then how did I end up jumping off a bridge? If I have so much going for me... If everyone loves me so much..."

"You lost your way, Stan. It happens. And now you don't know who you are anymore."

Stan almost laughed. "Yeah, they call that amnesia."

Lilith leaned in, grabbed the back of his neck with her cold hand. Brought his face close. "That's not what I mean. You're not who you used to be. You don't have that *fire* anymore. But you're going to get it back. I'll help you. You'll be what you once were."

And, for a minute, it flashed in his mind: Lilith as the bird-woman. Eyes solid black, red lips parted wide, screaming up to the sky. But her feet weren't stuck in the mud. And she had glossy, black wings that were ready to soar. A whirlwind surrounded her, blowing her golden hair every which way, tangling it in her crown of blackened flowers and dead leaves. She laughed into the storm, welcoming the chaos.

Next to Stan, the real Lilith straightened up suddenly. Pulled her hand away and stood up quickly. "I'll get you back," she said, then headed off again to make her phone calls.

TEN

Stan was alone with the beasts. That was what he'd come to call his works of art. Not animals, not humans. Not hybrids. Their forms were grotesque to him, not leaning toward the light as Lilith suggested but stuck for all eternity in the dark. Stan spent hours examining them, from the wiry masses of hair on their heads to the stiff spines of their feathers. None of it connected. He had no memories of creating these things. He felt no innate bond with them in his mind.

With no one else around, the loft was too silent. He almost wished for the two women's bickering again. Abby had bowed out early. Reminded him of their follow-up appointment at St. Luke's in a week, then gave him an awkward hug. He'd felt the uneasiness in her touch—about the art, about Lilith, about this new insight into who he really was. But it didn't stop her from wanting to know him. He felt that just as strongly, if not more so.

Lilith had taken her time in leaving. Making her phone calls, pacing, and smoking. Her voice sometimes loud and aggressive, other times a whisper. Stan had paid her little mind either way. It was her job to run the business end of his career, and he was happy to let her do it while he figured things out: Who he was. Who he'd been. Who he was now supposed to be. He'd walked around and touched things: the human-animal models, the frenetic drawings, the paint-spattered canvases. All the colors so dark, grays and blacks, with only occasional stabs of yellow, orange, red. He looked for meaning, for themes,

for the message he'd been trying to get across. All that came
through was suffering. Lilith had seen striving, redemption in
these pieces, but in their anguished faces, their mutated bodies,
all Stan saw was damnation. Deep inside he knew this reading
was right.

"I thought you said I do a lot of good-versus-bad stuff,"
he'd said to Lilith as she'd rummaged through her unbelievably
packed date book. Stuffed with papers and receipts, magazine
clippings shoved between the pages. "I'm not seeing the bright
side here."

She'd pulled out a wad of business cards and shuffled
through it like a deck of cards. She hadn't looked up at him. "It's
there, Stan, and you'd better see it soon. You have a show in two
weeks, and I need at least four new pieces from you. All these
are slated for galleries or sales already."

So far nothing had come to him. No ideas. No idea where
to start. Should he make another statue? It didn't seem possible.
What were they made of? How did he model them? Running
his hand over the shoulder of a woman on all fours with enormous, blue plumage rising off her back, he tried to guess its
composure. Latex, rubber, silicone? He knew nothing about
these materials or the casting process. There were no molds
anyway, no written instructions. Apparently he'd kept it all in
his head. The swim in the Hudson must have knocked it out.

Stan gave up. Wandered to the other end of the loft, where
the kitchen was. Opened the refrigerator, not surprised to find
nothing in it.

Up a flight of stairs he found the bedroom area. It was an
open space, overlooking the loft down below. Nothing more
than a mattress and a huge flat-screen TV wall-mounted at the
foot of it. On the floor on the far side were scattered DVDs and

cases. *The Exorcist, Rosemary's Baby, The Omen.* Documentaries about Jonestown and the Holocaust. *The Last Temptation of Christ. Constantine.*

Stan lay down on the bed as he perused the collection. The mattress was nice and soft, so different from his hospital bed. The sheets smelled worn-in, as if they hadn't been changed in a while. This was his smell—Stan's smell. Even that wasn't familiar to him. He put a hand up to his head, ruffled his hair as he thought. Or tried not to think. All this figuring out, trying to remember, was taking its toll. Stan curled up under the warm down comforter and quickly fell asleep.

When Stan awoke, darkness lay beyond the skylight above the bed. He rolled onto his back and stared up at it for a while. There wasn't a star in the sky—never was in New York City. Too many tall buildings with too many lights. It drowned them all out. He contemplated this sadly, wishing for just one pinpoint. A speck of hope. He wanted that goodness, that reaching toward the godhead that Lilith had described.

Instead he felt nothing. No good, no bad, not even some middle ground. Since the day he'd jumped off the bridge it had been like this: no clue who he was, no idea what he stood for. What he believed in. Was he a decent man or a real bastard? A genius or a hack? How could he create great art if he didn't know these answers?

Throwing back the blanket, he got up to use the bathroom. He washed his face and headed back downstairs. The whole place was quiet still, all the figures and drawings seeming to stare at him. Had the old Stan felt this pressure? And what had he done about it? Maybe he'd been like God—able to create something out of nothing. But this new Stan wasn't like that. He needed guidance. Inspiration.

He needed to get the hell out of here.

Still in his suit pants and white shirt, he took the keys Lilith had left and the iPhone she'd given him, and he headed out. Banging the metal door closed, pressing the elevator button about a hundred times. It couldn't get there fast enough to deliver him to the street, where salvation awaited.

Outside he stopped and took in deep lungfuls of tepid air. It had cooled off some but not much, and sweat quickly formed on his brow. Looking left and then right, Stan decided to head back over to Houston, where more things were happening. Cars, people, lights. They called to him, more than this sleepy block did. He wanted action and movement, that shininess again. Anything to jar him out of this rut.

As he walked he took out the iPhone and some earbuds he'd found in a desk in the loft, then turned the music player on. The library was loaded, the device almost at its capacity. Stan ran a thumb over the screen, scrolling through lists of artists. Sisters of Mercy. Christian Death. Marilyn Manson. Nine Inch Nails. Heavy stuff, then moodier bands like Bauhaus, Dead Can Dance, Cocteau Twins, and Chopin's nocturnes, Bach's "Toccatta and Fugue," Mozart's "Requiem." Whoever Stan was, he liked the dark stuff. That was for sure.

But how did he feel about the light? Stan mused as he hit the corner of Houston and set the iPhone's playlist to shuffle. Siouxsie and the Banshees' "Cities in Dust" burst out at ear-splitting volume. He left it that way. At least it made him feel something, even if it was pain.

On Houston the world was ablaze. Illuminated bars and bodega awnings, lines of headlamps as cars came and halted at traffic lights. And people were everywhere. Laughing, smiling, arguing as they bustled down the sidewalk in twos and fours. Jeans and sneakers, dresses and high heels. Young and fresh, faces painted for a night out on the town. Whenever Stan bumped into one, he felt a zing of electricity, the thrill of human touch. It was just what he needed—to feel like part of the crowd. This anonymity that kept him from having to think.

After a few blocks the song on the iPhone changed. Manson's "Long Hard Road Out of Hell." Stan paused at a corner, listening to the pounding bass, the singer's groaning, wretched voice. A cab whisked past, barely missing his toes sticking out in the street. The "walk" sign turned on. But Stan was oblivious to all of it, too lost in the music.

Then someone shoved him hard from behind.

Not expecting it, he had no reaction but to fall forward, his arms shooting out reflexively to break his fall. He grabbed the first thing he touched: the shoulder of the young man in front of him. Maybe twenty years old, walking with another man. Their arms around each other's waists.

Pain shot through Stan's skull, and his free hand went up to his head as an image played inside: The young man badly beaten. So bloodied he was almost dead. All dark bruises and swollen flesh. It made Stan's stomach turn, and he let out a moan and tore his hand away.

"Hey, are you okay?" the kid said, half turning to face him. Another jolt shot through Stan's head. He waved the young man away, then turned on his heel. Going out had been a big mistake. He wasn't ready for this. He had to get back to the loft. To the quiet and the empty.

But as he about-faced, he ran directly into the man who had shoved him. Easily a foot taller and a hundred pounds heavier, he was an angry man. Stan could tell from his face, all screwed up and squinting down at him. He also saw it when his fingers brushed against the man's bulging bicep. There was a gun, and a terrified woman behind a cashier's counter.

"Give me the money!" the big man yelled, hooking the barrel against the woman's nose. She held up her hands and whimpered, her whole body shuddering. The man laughed so hard he shook.

Stan withdrew his hand and stepped aside, right into a tide of pedestrians. They spilled out and around him, flooding the crosswalk, making headway impossible. He attempted to wade through, but his head reeled, and his feet slipped. He grabbed whatever he could to keep from going under:

A girl with a baby she didn't want growing inside her, deciding on the best way to end her own life. She would overdose on her mother's sleeping pills.

A middle-aged man with a gun in his pocket who'd just slept with a hooker and shot her in the head for payment. He'd kill three more before the cops would find him.

A homeless man with a scarred face, set on fire by some kids who'd wanted to see how fast an alcoholic would burn. They were never caught. Neither would he be when he retaliated.

An older woman slumped drunk over a steering wheel, the only one in her car—or the one she hit—to get out alive. She'd done her time, but her soul would never be rid of the guilt.

This was some serious shit, and Stan didn't know what to make of it. Nor could he control it. The images came unbidden every time his hands touched another human's skin. As he whirled around, just trying to stay afloat, he thought of that old pedophile in the day room at St. Luke's. At arts-and-crafts time. Stan hadn't thought that was real, what he'd seen the man do, just a side effect of the meds. A vivid hallucination. Maybe caused by the injuries from his jump.

But now he knew it was true. He saw it here; he felt it all around him. These visions were no trick of the mind, no cruel chemical joke brought on by a little white pill. Maybe he was psychic. Intuitive. Hell, maybe he was psychotic. But whatever it was…

He smiled. Stood up straight and steady. *This is fantastic.* He hadn't felt so alive in—well, since he'd washed up on the bank of the river after trying to kill himself. Something about these other people's suffering lit a fire in him. He was energized, inspired.

Immersed.

He headed back to the loft knowing just what he had to do.

ELEVEN

The old Stan was back. Or at least a version of him. Call it New Stan's interpretation. After listening to his music, looking through his closets and drawers, even getting into his computer and checking his browsing history, reading his e-mails, Stan felt like he had a pretty good hold on himself, on this person Lilith claimed he used to be. Old Stan was a dark dude. Fascinated by death, in love with destruction. These weren't just themes for him, gimmicks he used to make sellable art. He believed in the dark side. Stared into the abyss until it stared back at him. And he liked what he saw. Above all he was comfortable with evil.

Did that mean Old Stan was a bad person? Not necessarily. In his search of the loft and his own psyche, New Stan didn't find any indication of it. Yes, he made this profane art, these creations that defiled the precious human form. But he wasn't a serial killer. Or a nihilist. Or even particularly negative in his personal views. For all the web pages about autopsies and suicides he'd bookmarked, there were also instant messages with friends about baseball games, movie showtimes, random sexual conquests. Stan was an average man in many ways, driven by mundane desires.

But Stan the Artist. He was different. Elevated. To something greater, to the sublime. What Lilith had said was right: Stan's art was a challenge. To the status quo, to human sensibilities. To the senses. To the consciousness. The more time he spent in the loft—touching the models, moving them around, even talking to them—the more he understood this. Understood them. And himself, or at least who he had been before his freefall.

He wasn't that man anymore. Lilith was right about that too. Stan was different now. And his artwork had to be different too.

When he'd come home from his walk out on Houston Street the previous night, he'd immediately started sketching. Stood at the table where Abby had been and swept all the old drawings off, then picked up a stack of fresh paper. A set of charcoal sticks, a rainbow of colors. Some—the reds, blacks, grays—worn down more than others. Stan had never drawn before, at least not that he had a memory of, but it came to him easily. As soon as the charcoal touched the paper, an image emerged. First a woman—stick with what you know, right?—but not with her skin blackened. This one was pure white, not Caucasian but gleaming like mountain snow. An otherworldly pallor. The silhouette of her body fluid, the lines of her legs, her arms at her sides. Fingers pressed into the flesh of her outer thighs. Eyes closed, chin neither raised nor lowered, though it might be interpreted as either from different angles.

And all around her fire. Flames that reached up to the sky, the heat blowing tendrils of her hair all around her like a halo. Flames that licked her feet, spreading out across the floor like a carpet, a pathway toward something unseen.

Second sketch, another woman. This time her fire came from within, bursting from her navel and spreading up across her breasts, around her shoulders, creating a mane that flared out behind her head. Her eyes were downcast, a hand on her belly—the typical pose of the expectant mother. She looked upon the flames as though adoring them, the corners of her mouth shifted in a Mona Lisa smile.

From there he went on and on, one sketch after another, until the stack of papers was exhausted—and so was he. He took his iPhone again and headed outside, going straight for the all-night convenience store he'd seen around the corner. Bought himself some bottles of water, a six-pack of beer. Went back to the loft and drank one after another of both while he looked through his work. At daybreak he sat in the middle of the floor, a hundred papers in a circle around him: most promising to the left, ones he wasn't sure about yet to the right.

So this is the artistic process, he thought to himself with a laugh. Maybe he did remember something of his old life after all. He'd spent his time in silence, the only sounds of papers sliding across the hardwood floor, another bottle opening, his gulping as he swallowed. But he pictured his old self doing the same thing in utter chaos. Heavy metal music blaring. Not drinking beer but whiskey straight from the bottle. Old Stan was a smoker too—he'd found old, stale butts all over the place, spilling out of ashtrays, on the floor as if just thrown there. And the loft fairly reeked of smoke. Another thing the jump must have cleaned from his system. New Stan was sickened by the stench.

Over the next few days, he'd sorted out the sketches again, finally narrowing it down to his favorite twenty. Then twelve. And from there in half again. Lilith had said he needed four new pieces for the upcoming show, but he figured he could do six. Why not? The drawing had come so easily. It gave him confidence. Probably once he started on the pieces, whatever he needed to do would make sense to him as well. At least that was what he hoped. What he was banking on.

He figured he should call Lilith to run the idea by her. She'd already programmed her number into the phone she'd given him—and only hers. As if he had no one else to contact.

But he did. Before calling her, he dialed information and got the number for St. Luke's.

"Dr. Petrus." When Abigail answered the phone, she sounded tired, annoyed.

"Hey, it's me," he'd replied. "I mean it's Stan Foster. How are you doing?"

"Stan," she'd repeated immediately. As if she'd been waiting for him to call. "Is everything okay? Do you need—"

"Everything is okay." He laughed. Amused by her panic. "Everything is good, actually. I'm getting things in order. Even starting to work again."

She sighed. "So soon? You've been home for less than twenty-four hours. Did Lilith put you up to it?"

Stan looked out the panoramic windows on the south side of the loft as he talked to her, a bottle of Brooklyn Lager in his hand. It was only 10:00 a.m., but he had to have a vice, right? All good artists did. Pollock was a drunk. So was Gaugin. Basquiat had his heroin, and those rumors about Kahlo overdosing on painkillers? Totally true. That hack Kincade did the same more recently—*painter of light, my ass*—but that was a much less tragic loss for the art world.

How did Stan know all this? He had no idea. But it was all in his brain, these little facts he could call up at a moment's notice. Like a shopping list. Maybe not everything had leaked out of his skull when he'd submerged himself in the Hudson. Or he'd just picked it up while reading through Stan's stuff. He couldn't be sure.

"No. Well, yes. Sort of. She booked a show for me in a week. I guess some sort of comeback thing. I have to have some new pieces ready."

"What are you going to do?" Abigail sounded worried. "You know, you really should be resting, Stan. Your body just went through an enormous trauma, and your mind too. You don't have to throw yourself back into things right away just because she said so."

He smirked and took another swig of beer. Abigail sure didn't hide her feelings about Lilith. And though Lilith didn't say a word, it was obvious she felt the same about the doctor too. God forbid they ever ended up in the same room again. The fur would fly.

"I know. I'm not overdoing it, I promise. I've barely done anything yet." He glanced over at the table where he'd neatly arrayed his final sketches. Felt a pang. He had to get started. "Listen, I just wanted to say hi. I don't want to keep you. Sorry I—"

"You didn't bother me," she finished for him. Her tone all kindness and warmth. Stan wished she were there. To do what? Hold his hand? Tell him everything would be okay? Yes, something like that. "Remember we have our follow-up appointment on Wednesday. You'll make it, right?"

Stan smiled. "Wouldn't miss it for the world."

In the silence that ensued, he felt her grinning too. "Take care of yourself, Stan. And call me if you need anything."

Another minute of small talk and reassurances, then they hung up. Stan hit Lilith's number on the speed dial. She was much less supportive than his shrink had been.

"I think you're full of shit. Six pieces in six days? In your condition? Get real, Stan."

"No, I can do it." He wandered to the kitchen, threw away the empty beer bottle. Opened the fridge and got another. Pondered how to get some food in there. "I'm feeling good. I'm ready to work. I can do it."

Wherever Lilith was—Stan guessed in the back of her Escalade; she always seemed to be shuttling between one place and another—she clicked on a lighter. A moment, then he heard her blowing out a chestful of acrid smoke. "You're at the loft, right? Stay there. I'm coming over to discuss this."

"No," he protested a little more forcefully than he'd meant to. "I mean I want it to be a surprise. I don't know how I used to work, but I'd really like to be by myself for this. I know what I'm doing. At least I have a good idea. I just want to run with it and see where it takes me. I think it'll come out good."

Silence. She flicked the lighter on a few times. "Fine. You've never failed me before. Except for that whole suicide thing, but I guess I can forgive that. As long as the work is good. Is there anything you need from me? Supplies of any sort?"

Stan took a long pull on his beer. Thought about what he'd need to accomplish this. He didn't want to ruin the suspense; he didn't want Lilith to see his creations until they were done. But he had to admit he had no idea how to procure the necessary equipment.

"Fine," he said, aware that he was mimicking her. Loving that she surely picked up on the sarcasm too. "I'll give you a list. But I need it all here today. Do you think you can do that?"

Lilith really came through. Within an hour she had an army of delivery people at the loft's door. They brought dozens of bolts of cloth, bags and bags of thread, pins, needles. Thin metal piping, big sheets of window-screen mesh. Everything he'd asked for and more. Must have cost Lilith thousands of dollars. Obviously she expected a big return on investment.

Not long after that entourage left, the main ingredient he'd ordered showed up. Stan had found it hard to ask Lilith for it. He didn't know how these things were done, how transactions worked in the art world. If it were even possible to obtain this most crucial part.

"Ask and you shall receive," Lilith had prompted when he'd faltered on the request, and, lo and behold, she'd been right. By noon he had six female models lined up across the loft. Not the women he used to use, the dead forms molded out of silicone and magic. These were real people. Living, breathing humans. With limbs he could move and bend, pose and arch. He looked each of them up and down, evaluating them as if this were a casting call. Which it was, he imagined. Just another job for them.

But for him it was more than that. It was the next step—no, the leap he had to take in order to immerse himself. In the art, in this life. In what he was supposed to be. Not the Old Stan, with his death fetish and dark overtures, but a new entity. A new being with a new purpose. All the time he'd spent sifting through his things, that terrifying scene when he'd gone out in public. All those souls he'd touched, the pain they'd experienced or inflicted on others. The suffering, the horror. All of this had brought the big picture home to him, and suddenly he'd understood why the old artwork didn't speak to him. Because there was something missing from it: the spark. The one New Stan felt inside himself. The one he knew had to come out.

With these models, he had exactly what ne needed to get started.

TWELVE

Abigail worried about Stan. Not just now, as he sat right in front of her. But when he wasn't there. Between patients at work, eyes glazing over the paperwork she should have been filling out. At home, on a second bottle of wine and three replays of a Radiohead album. When she walked the streets, alone among her eight million neighbors. She always seemed to be thinking about him. Where he was, how he was doing. If he was making art. If he'd figured out yet who he really was.

"Do you have much contact with Lilith?" she asked him now. He'd come in a good hour early for his follow-up. As if he were eager. To get it over with? To see Abigail? She didn't know, and denied herself the urge to think it was the latter. This was still a professional relationship. Despite her emotions, she had to keep it that way.

Stan smiled at her. Sat back in his chair and crossed his legs, an ankle propped up on a knee. "Only as much as I need to. I see her maybe twice a week. But I've been busy too. Not much time for socializing."

"Oh, really." Abigail picked up some papers from her desk and straightened them. She glanced at Stan. "Busy with what?"

"Making art."

Now she looked directly at him. "Art like you were making before?" She thought of the sketches she'd seen at the loft. The ragged lines, the animal faces and human bodies. Sometimes it was hard to tell which was which. Stan's talent was amazing but terrifying, beautiful but monstrous. She wanted to hate it but at the same time couldn't tear herself away. If Lilith hadn't made her feel so small that day, she would have stayed much longer to investigate.

Stan looked up at the wall behind her, pushing his mouth into a frown. Thinking about it. "I wouldn't say it's the same. There are similar themes, but it's like…what I *was* doing taken to the next level. By the way, I like the new print. Whose is it?"

Abigail spun in her chair a little to see the picture on the wall behind her. The silhouette of an angel, one wing dark, one translucent, as if backlit by a blinding, heavenly glow.

"Alex Cherry." She turned back to Stan. "I don't know. I saw it online and fell in love with it. I really like the use of light. And the feathers."

He nodded slowly. "Me too. But I guess I have a thing for those. So it's a giclee print?"

"Yes. How did you know that?"

"Been doing some homework. Figured if I have to make a go of this art thing, I might as well know what I'm talking about."

Abigail smiled at him. Relieved that he looked more relaxed than the last time she'd seen him. That he'd taken an interest in something. "Sounds like you're settling in okay. Are you having any problems I should know about? Any headaches, hallucinations, voices telling you to do things?" She clicked on a pen, ready to take notes. The appointment had officially begun.

"I have that dream about the pit a lot." Stan looked down as he said it, his voice low. "Maybe a couple times a week. I still don't know what I should make of it."

"We decided that was just a dream, right? Back when you were admitted here. Remember Freud, the unconscious mind—"

Stan waved a hand in the air. Dismissing the interpretation. "Freud doesn't explain this. It's more than a dream to me. It feels real. And every time it's different. Once it's a woman. Another time, all men. Sometimes the pit is full of children, and they're—" He looked away, toward the door, the only way out.

"But it *is* a dream, Stan. You only see it at night, right? Or whenever you're asleep?" Abigail kept her voice gentle. She hated that this tormented him. And that he couldn't discern the line between reality and imagination. He was otherwise so sharp, so intelligent, she felt like he should have a hold on this.

But then she scolded herself. That wasn't how mental illness worked. It could strike anyone at any time, no matter how smart or well-read they were. And as Stan's doctor, it was her responsibility to believe him. If he said it wasn't a dream then she had to take his word for it—and try to get to the bottom of what it actually was.

"I'm also seeing other things." As he said it, Stan chewed on his thumbnail. Bit off and spat out a piece.

"In your dreams, you mean." Abigail wrote on her notepad: "Recurring nightmares. Believes they're real. Psychosis?"

"No, I mean when I'm fully awake. When I'm out in public. Whenever I touch someone."

"Possibly re-medicate," she added in her notes, then said, "What do you mean, Stan? What do you see when you touch people?"

At this point most of her patients would have gotten up and paced the room or waved their arms and screamed. Or done something to show her just how crazy they were, how unreal their thoughts. Stan, on the other hand, remained entirely composed. He uncrossed and recrossed his legs, sat up straighter in his chair. Cleared his throat calmly before he began.

"I can see what's happened in the past. Tragedies they've been through or harm they've caused other people. Murders, rapes, crimes of all kinds. Selfishness. Greed. Then I see the price they'll pay for it all in the future."

Abby kept her gaze steady. Her tone even. "Maybe you've seen them on the news or in some other media, so you've heard about what they've done and their punishments. You can find anything online. Maybe you used to troll the mug-shot sites. They're open to the public, you know. Maybe somehow you used them for your work."

Stan shook his head. "Abigail, this happens with everyone I meet. Do you really think it's possible I've seen them all on TV? Or on some website?"

A lump formed in her throat when he said her name. She never let patients take that liberty. Would have corrected him if he were anyone else. Inside these walls she was Dr. Petrus; Abigail did not exist. Not usually. Not in a normal case.

"There has to be some explanation," she pressed, as if trying to convince herself. "Maybe it's—"

Suddenly Stan lunged toward her, stretching his arms across the desk and taking both her hands in his. Their roughness surprised her, the calluses that scraped against her palms, the cracks across the knuckles. For a moment he clenched her tight, his eyes locked onto hers.

"Both your parents are dead." His words were seething and hot. "You were there when it happened."

Abigail shoved her chair back as hard as she could, running it right into the wall. In the process her hands came out of Stan's, and she held them close to her chest. Rubbing them together, working out the pain he'd caused. She looked at him, shoulders slumped, forearms still on the desk. He squeezed his eyes shut, then opened them again but didn't raise them.

"How do you know that?" she asked.

"I told you. I see things when I touch people." He looked at her now. "I'm sorry. I just wanted to prove to you I'm not making it up. Or that it's not a dream."

Abigail stiffened her back, raised her chin in the air. Trying to stave off the memories his statement had brought to her. Mom lying lifeless on the kitchen floor. Dad's greasy work shirt on the bathroom tiles. She swallowed hard, pushing it all back down again.

"So then, what's my future? You said you can see that too."

Stan shook his head. "Didn't see one for you. Besides, would you really want to know?" Seeing the alarm on her face, he quickly clarified. "I don't mean you don't have a future. Just that it's not written yet. Whoever decides these things hasn't gotten to yours yet." He gave her a tentative smile. "Sorry. I wish I could tell you more. But that's all I saw this time."

Abigail let out her breath. Pulled her chair back in. Crossed her arms one over the other on the desk in front of her. What if Stan was telling the truth? That he really did *see* things? It wasn't beyond the realm of possibility. Plenty of studies had been done on mental illness and paranormal capabilities. Nothing conclusive, but the possibility was there. Abby tried to keep an open mind—she had to in this line of work. The things her patients told her regularly pushed the boundaries of believability.

However, this was unlike anything she had ever heard. And her gut told her not to believe it. In fact, it told her to run the other way. Officially discharge Stan, no more follow-ups, no more assessments. No more worrying about him like a lost puppy whose home she had to find.

And with that thought, a small voice within her gave another choice. *Believe him*, it said. *See where it takes you. See what you learn.* And that was all she needed to hear.

"It's okay," she said. "You don't have to have all the answers. We'll figure it out together." She clicked on her pen. "Now, tell me. When exactly did you figure out you could do this?"

THIRTEEN

Never trust an artist.

Lilith had lived by this creed for a long time, and it had served her well. No matter how much they flattered you or swore they'd pay you back as soon as the check came in from their last sale, no matter how attractive they were in that scummy, stubbly way they all seemed to have. No matter how many times you'd worked with them, drank with them, slept with them. Never trust any of them. Whether they were at the top of their game or just starting out. And, though she hated to admit it, even if they were Stan.

"All the pieces are there, yes?" she said into her cell on speakerphone, sitting in the back of her SUV. Her voice in automatic bitch mode, ready to rip this guy apart if he said something she didn't like. In her hand she held a compact, mirror open so she could examine herself. Makeup was perfect. Not a hair out of place. Nothing unusual here.

She snapped the compact shut. "And all of them are in place? What about the lighting? This was supposed to happen yesterday. I shouldn't have to ask you about it now."

"Yes, ma'am," said the man on the other end of the line. One of her assistants, a groveling boy whose name she didn't care about enough to remember. "They're, uh—they're getting into place now."

Lilith lit a cigarette. "What do you *mean* they're *getting into place now*?" That was it; the fury in her tone unleashed all by itself. "What are you talking about? The doors open in one hour. We have five hundred on the guest list. Why isn't everything set up already?"

On the other end, she could almost hear him cowering. Wincing. She often had that effect on people. Usually she did it on purpose.

"Ma'am, I'm sorry. Mr. Foster told me not to tell you anything."

For a moment Lilith simply looked at her phone, propped up on the bar against a fifth of gin. Then she growled deep. A rumble that began in her core and worked its way up through her red lips.

"Put. Him on. The phone." Her teeth clenched, her hands curled into fists, pushing into the seat cushion.

The assistant cleared his throat. "I'm sorry, but he's not here. I mean he *was* here. He stepped out for a moment. I—I'm not sure where he went."

Lilith grabbed the phone, threw it against the back of the driver's seat. After a moment the partition between them slowly made its way open.

"Something I can help you with?" the driver asked. Same man she'd been using for years. Had no idea what his name was either, but she liked him well enough. He minded his own business.

"Yes. Put your foot on the fucking gas pedal. I need to be at the gallery *now*."

"Yes, ma'am." The partition went up again, and the Escalade sped away.

Lilith liked a man who did as he was told.

"This." It was all she could get to come out of her mouth. She stood in front of Stan's model. The one with the fire trails reaching up from her head and trailing out from her feet. Fabric flames stretched across metal framework like a carnaval costume. The girl had been painted white, a chalky mixture slathered onto her tan skin, then dried into whorls around her joints, caked onto her pubic hair. She was completely nude. She blinked her eyes, the only thing she could move at the moment.

"This?" Lilith repeated, and she turned to Stan. He stood next to her, gazing at the model, a beatific expression on his face. Like the sight just made him so goddamn pleased with himself. Proud of what he had done.

Finally he looked at Lilith. "Can you finish the rest of your sentence? I'm not sure what you're asking here."

She shot her hands out, palms up, gesturing at the piece. "I trust you to work alone, with no supervision, and *this* is what you give me?" She shook her head and marched away. She couldn't believe she'd let him do this. Especially in the state he was in. Half psychotic, hearing voices. No idea who he's supposed to be. If she weren't so incapable of it, she'd almost blame herself for this debacle.

"I can't even look at it." She reached into her clutch for a cigarette. As she lit up, the meek assistant from earlier raised a finger at her. About to admonish, she knew. There was no smoking inside. Before he could say it, she shot her own middle finger in the air at him. He put his hand back down and slinked away again.

"What are you talking about?" Stan followed her to the front of the gallery. She stood in the doorway. "This is the best work I've done. I'm sorry you can't see that, but..."

He looked back again, taking in the long view of the space.

His models lined up three per side, taking up at least ten square feet apiece. Given their accoutrements and all. The woman in the maternal pose. Another on a throne of flames. Toward the end, a man. Arms up, palms toward the ceiling. Fire washing down over him like a shower. Like goddamn Niagara Falls. At least he was naked too. Full frontal. Gave Lilith something to look at.

She sighed at Stan, a stream of smoke releasing from between her lips. "What is it I'm not seeing? Explain it to me. I really want to understand." Took another drag. "I *need* to understand if I'm going to sell any of these for you."

"Well, you said my other work was a dichotomy. It showed the struggle between godliness and humanity, between our own goodness and evil. The way we want to give in to our carnal desires, but at the same time we want to appease—I don't know, some higher power. Either up in the sky or somewhere within ourselves."

She nodded impatiently. "Yes, yes. Nothing I haven't read in your reviews. Get on with it."

Stan went to the nearest model. Perhaps the most grotesque of the bunch, and the only one Lilith sort of liked. A woman so thin she appeared anorexic. Bony as a camp survivor. All hips and shoulder blades, a pointy nose, stringy, dirty hair. Her fire vined around her legs like a snake, binding them together, its head disappearing into the gap between her skinny thighs. She reached one hand down into it, as if running her fingers through her lover's hair. The other hand splayed across her breasts. Eyes closed, face slack, an imitation of ecstasy.

"You can look at this two ways," Stan began, sounding clinical. Like a college professor. He pushed the ends of the girl's hair back over her shoulder. Assessed the change for a moment then put it back the way it was. He crouched down to gesture at the fire on her feet.

"Here the flames sear her to the ground. Now this can be seen as something from the underworld—eternal hellfire breaching the crust of the earth to drag her down inside. Punishment for the sin of lust. For succumbing willfully to the pleasure of the flesh."

He stood again, circling his hand in front of her nether region. "Or you can see it as her giving in to the temptations of the earth itself. The physical excitement of being human, the pleasure of the senses. And the rapture of sexual union, of course—our most basic animal function. But she's not being burned for it. Rather she's simply consumed by the joy of the act. By the heat. By the passion. Still she maintains her white skin, the symbol of her purity."

He paused. "What she has is hope, Lilith. She has life inside of her. I've never explored this before. Not in my old work. Not in my old life. Not that I remember."

Behind him, though he couldn't see it, Lilith rolled her eyes. Anything positive she'd felt for this piece suddenly fizzled out. "Hope." She practically scoffed at the word. Crossed her arms over her chest, made her way over to Stan. Wearing all black as always—tight pencil skirt with a high back slit, silk button-down blouse and patent-leather Louboutins—she was the model's antithesis. All dark against all light. In the contrast, she could almost see what Stan meant. The purity stood out like a sore thumb.

That didn't mean she liked it, though. Just because she could see it. This new art—it just didn't have that *spark* to it. Not like Stan's previous work, which had been weighted much more heavily toward the dark side. Which was, inherently, much more interesting. No one wanted goody-goody art. They wanted pieces that made them question themselves, their motives, their roles in the universe. Difficult images and figures that made them think, that challenged their conceptions.

What would these installments make people wonder? If they'd left the stove on at home? Where was the inspiration in any of this?

"So is this a new phase for you?" She couldn't keep the tinge of loathing out of her voice. "If this is the direction you're going, I need to know. So I can figure out an angle for you."

Or a way to get rid of you, she wanted to add, but she knew that wasn't an option. Not yet anyway. She had unfinished business with Stan, longstanding commitments they both needed to honor. She'd been through a lot with him, more than he seemed to know. They'd ridden the highs and the lows, fought battles she thought they'd never manage to come out of. But they still had a lot more to do. Worlds to conquer, so to speak. She hadn't told him any of this; no, she knew it wasn't time yet. He could slip back into life first. Get himself comfortable, find out who he wanted to be. Then she would hit him with the hard stuff. The real story. And see where he would go from there.

"I don't know." Stan rubbed his chin, looked around the gallery again. "I think it might be. I'm sorry you don't like it, Lilith. But I'm asking you to give it a chance. See how the reception is. I think it will find its audience. I think it will speak to someone." He looked back at her and shrugged. "It certainly speaks to me. Isn't that a good thing? That I'm figuring out what my voice is?"

She gave him a close-lipped smile. A reassuring pat on the shoulder. Such niceties didn't come naturally to her, but at times like these—when an artist needed his bruised little ego stroked—she had to force herself. Perform the expected act. Like the emaciated girl and her pitiful fake orgasm.

"Sure it is."

The brief approval seemed to appease Stan. Or at least made him shut up. That was good enough for the moment. Lilith was glad he'd found his muse—that was an important thing. She just wished he'd looked a little harder to find one that was more fitting. More interesting. More like the one he used to have when he was Old Stan. Maybe with some guidance he could be that person again—that was what Lilith hoped. No, what she needed. This wasn't a game for her. And it was about so much more than just helping him become a good artist again.

She had to stay on top of this. As she lit another cigarette, she swore she would never leave Stan to his own devices again.

FOURTEEN

The guy who drove Lilith's SUV—his name was Jake. Stan found this out because he asked. By the way the guy reacted to the question, Stan was pretty sure Lilith never had. Such menial things as people's names were apparently beneath her. Stan would have laughed at the thought if it weren't so blatantly abhorrent.

"So where does she live?" he asked as Jake made a right turn onto Avenue of the Americas. They were both in the front seat. Jake had opened the back door for Stan when he'd come down from the loft, but something didn't feel right about being sequestered back there. At the first red light Stan had gotten out and hopped in front.

"Upper East Side. Big penthouse. Corner of Park and Eighty-Third. What, you don't remember?"

Jake didn't pull any punches. Stan sort of liked that. "No, I don't remember," he said, wondering just how much Jake knew about his situation. Had his bridge jump been on the news? Was Stan that important? Or had Jake simply overheard Lilith on the phone with him? God knew she brought it up enough. Every time Stan talked to her, she went on and on about how he used to be. Before the jump. Before he almost died. Before, before, before. She had a hundred ways to phrase it, but it always sent the same message: the man he was today simply wasn't good enough for her.

Which was why this invitation had surprised him. About

an hour earlier she'd texted: "Sending car for you. Come over to talk about the show." Actually it was more of a command than a request. Still, he'd thought it a nice gesture. He didn't know what to expect at the opening the next day. All of the pieces were done, all of the plans for their installation laid out. He'd gone to the gallery and seen to it himself with Lilith's assistant, Brad. Another name she probably didn't know.

At any rate, if she wanted to give him advice he would take it. Even if he had to go to her place at midnight to get it.

"Sounds good. See you soon," he'd texted back, and now here he was in the Escalade. He rolled the window down and hung his arm out. It had rained earlier, and the night was almost unbearably humid. Stan closed his eyes and listened to the hiss of the car's tires on the moist asphalt. He wondered if his senses had been so keen before he'd died.

"Here we are, Mr. Foster." Jake had a voice like a movie thug. A Queens accent like a bag of rocks in his mouth.

"Call me Stan, please." He opened his eyes and looked out the window. The drive had gone so fast. Maybe he'd fallen asleep. He shook Jake's hand, thanked him for the ride, and got out.

At the door another man in a uniform greeted him—by name as well, which left Stan with an eerie feeling. Again he wondered what sort of coverage his little accident had gotten. He sure didn't seem famous; no one on the street recognized him, even when he walked around his own neighborhood. But then, this was New York. Home of the terminally unaffected. The chronically unimpressed. Even if people did know who he was, they probably wouldn't say anything.

"Evening, Mr. Foster," said the man behind the concierge's desk. As did the man who operated the elevator. Stan started to tell him where he was going—to the top floor, to Lilith's place—but the man simply smiled and punched in a code on a keypad. The doors closed, and up they went.

Stan heard the music when they were still three flights away.

"Oh, shit," he said as the door slipped back open again, revealing an enormous, open-space apartment. Lilith's penthouse. Packed from wall to wall with people.

The lights were off, but strobe lights flashed all around the place. There was a DJ with an impressive setup—old-school vinyl and two turntables, surrounded by massive amps. People were dancing, shouting, laughing, all holding drinks in their hands.

"What is this, some sort of joke?" He spun around to the elevator, but the operator was already gone. When he turned back, Lilith was standing in front of him.

"Oh God, you scared me," he said. "What the hell is going on here, Lilith?"

She turned her head toward the party, a slight smile playing on her glossy red lips. Heavy black kohl rimmed her eyes, her yellow hair slicked back against her head. Tonight's outfit: a vinyl cat suit and six-inch platform heels.

"We're having a party," she said, returning her gaze to him. Her eyes were dark and glassy, her movements slow. She took his hand in hers, and her hot skin almost made him flinch.

"Stan Foster, everyone!" she shouted, whipping him ahead of her into the room. Her voice carried impossibly over the deafening music, the din of the crowd. At her announcement everyone hollered and clapped. Stan looked around in the low light, trying to make out faces. Didn't see one he recognized. Just leering stares, gaping mouths, glassy eyes. Like the art he used to make. Could these have been his models then? His inspiration for the tortured, seething faces, the pain and despair they depicted? These people, and those pieces in his collection, were nothing like the creations he was working on now. The difference was like day and night. He worked with light now, and here was nothing but darkness.

He pulled back on Lilith's hand. Dragged her into the foyer. "What are you *doing*?" he asked her through clenched teeth.

She retracted her hand hard. Stan felt his elbow crack as it shifted out and back into its socket.

"I'm reintroducing you to the world, *Stan*. One would *think* someone in *your* position would appreciate the help. You're not just going to jump back on top overnight, you know." She glanced over her shoulder at the crowd, all of whom had gone back to writhing and spilling their drinks on one another. Looking back at Stan, she glared down at him, towering above his head in her high boots. But then her eyes softened. And she smiled at him, her crimson lips spreading greedily across her face.

These moments confused Stan. The ones where she seemed to like him. They didn't happen often, but enough that they made an impression on him. She'd be riding him as usual—about deadlines, money, interviews, whatever her sore spot was that day—and then she would just stop talking. And look at him like this. Almost as if she felt affection for him. Or at least didn't hate him. These seconds were fleeting, but Stan couldn't help but be impressed by them.

"Come with me," she said, grabbing his arm just as forcefully as last time. Again he tried to get away.

"Stop!" she shouted at him. "I'm not taking you back in there. Just follow me."

She turned and headed up a staircase at the rear of the foyer. Lilith's heels pounded on each step as she dragged him up. At the top she let his arm go and kept walking.

They were in her bedroom. Stan turned in a circle, looking all around. The entire place was made of windows. All the walls, the ceiling, everything was glass. At one end a set of French doors led out onto a manicured garden—geometric hedges and chaise lounges, a fish pond and fire pit. Inside the bedroom everything was white and gold. Like a palace. A big, gaudy palace. It was perfect for Lilith.

"Ugh, I have to get out of this thing," she said as she unzipped her catsuit, exposing a sliver of skin from her neck down to her waist. "I think it's starting to chafe. I wouldn't be surprise if I have a rash already."

Stan was only half listening. He wandered around the room, touching things as he went along. The gilded dresser. The pure-white bear-skin rug, complete with head and teeth. The mirrors, the artwork, the down quilt on the enormous, plush bed. At the head of it hung a painting. Of Lilith, larger than life-size. She sat on a throne, a gleaming golden crown sitting atop her head.

"One of your best works," she said, coming up from behind him to sit down on the bed. She had her suit half off. Her torso exposed. Her breasts. Stan looked only for a moment then back at the painting again.

"I really did that?"

"For my birthday last year. Do you know how many offers I've gotten from people who've wanted to buy it?"

Stan didn't find that surprising. She probably entertained frequently in this room. With a body like that—all soft curves and strong legs, full breasts and lean thighs leading up to—

He caught himself staring. He looked at the painting.

Lilith laughed at him, a sexy, throaty sound. "It's okay," she said, patting the white duvet.

Like an obedient dog, Stan went and sat down next to her.

"If I didn't know better, I'd say you were trying to seduce me," he said, still trying to avert his eyes but unsure where to look.

Lilith reached over and grabbed his chin. Turned his face roughly toward her. "It's nothing you haven't seen before. So don't go acting all shy around me now."

He let that sink in for a moment. "You mean you and I…"

"You and I have done a lot of things." Lilith lay back on the bed. The blanket puffed. She looked like she was in a cloud. She stretched her arms up over her head and let out a languid moan. "Help me with the rest of this, will you?"

She raised her leg, indicating her catsuit, and Stan, without even questioning, reached over and began to pull. When that yielded no results, he got up on his knees and grabbed the suit by its waist then peeled it down. Finally it came off.

Lilith wore nothing underneath. And as she lay there, running her hands over her freed body, Stan finally let himself look. And touch. He passed his hand up her leg, across the front of her hip. Her side. Her breast. She let out another moan, then grabbed Stan by the waist and pulled him in. She pushed her painted lips hard onto his open mouth.

And that released the flood gates. Images flooded his mind: Lilith with her golden crown, sitting nude upon a throne inlaid with blood-red rubies. A flock of crows perched atop it, all hard beaks and black, meaty breasts. They cawed and flapped as Lilith raised her hand. They perched on her. Squawking and bowing, flapping their weighty wings.

Then she was out on a deserted plain, below her the pit of souls—the one Stan had seen while he was in hospital. Lilith looked down at those lost souls, her crown now a ring of thorny brush. It cut into her scalp, blood running in rivulets underneath her fair hair. Again she raised her arm, and her murder of crows appeared. A whirlwind of feathers and dust. She laughed—derisively, as she had at Stan's shame over seeing her undressed—and pointed down into the pit. The birds descended. The cries from the pit flew up in one solid, screeching pitch.

Stan pulled away from Lilith and scrambled back on the bed until his feet hit the floor. He stood up unsteadily, checking himself for—what? Injuries? He didn't know. But he couldn't stop running his hands over his arms, his chest, and through his hair. Like something had contaminated him and he couldn't manage to wipe it off.

"I—I have to go," he said, then ran toward the stairs. He didn't want to give Lilith a chance to try to make him stay.

FIFTEEN

By the time Abigail got to the gallery, there was a line stretching out the door and down the block. She stood across the street, eyeing the crowd. Wondering if she should go in. Was she doing the right thing? She'd sworn to stop thinking about Stan so much, to keep their relationship professional. Now she felt like she was stalking him.

Granted, he had invited her. She looked down at the card in her hand. An announcement of the show and a note saying she'd be on the guest list. It had arrived at the hospital for her just a day earlier. Which hadn't helped her any in keeping Stan out of her thoughts.

She'd propped the card up against the framed picture of Lily on her desk and glanced at it through the afternoon. Found herself not paying attention to her patients, her thoughts drifting back to the bright-white card, its stark black words. At the end of the day she'd slipped it into her bag and brought it home. Set it next to her on the sofa and stared at it while she ate Chinese take-out.

Death/Birth was the title of the show. She had wondered if Stan had chosen it or if it was Lilith's idea. Abby knew she'd put him up to this. Forced him to get back to work too soon. Compromised his healing, both physically and emotionally. Thinking about what he had been through—the suicide attempt, the hospitalization, the amnesia—Abigail's stomach ached. Her appetite was gone. She put her barely touched pint of lo mein on the coffee table.

Lying back, she closed her eyes, then put an arm over her face to block out as much light as possible. *Breathe in, breathe out. Focus on the darkness, on the absence of light.* Meditating, like she'd learned in that class she'd taken a year ago. A freebie at the hospital. Thought it might help with her stress level. And it did, to an extent. She did find meditation relaxing and sometimes used it in between sessions at work to bring her mind out of the craziness.

Now all it brought her to was Stan. The one topic she was trying so hard to avoid. What was it about him? He'd really worked his way into her psyche, though she didn't for a minute believe it was on purpose. Stan had been nothing but appropriate with her, no suggestive behaviors or wandering hands. Not like some other patients. She was subject to groping and leering on a regular basis at the hospital—both came with the territory in her line of work. She'd long ago grown numb to it, as she had to her patients in general. She had to be objective in order to diagnose and treat them effectively.

But with Stan she couldn't be impartial no matter how hard she tried. Maybe—if she was being honest—it was his good looks; maybe it was his better-than-average intellect. Maybe it was just that he was so broken. Didn't know who he was or where he had come from. If he had family, friends, anyone he loved. Who loved him. Even his own name meant nothing to him. His own face.

Throwing her arm off her eyes, Abby had rolled onto her stomach. Buried her head in a pillow and let out a scream. The whole situation was frustrating. There was nothing she could do for Stan, just listen when he talked and offer him advice. For the first time in the near-decade she'd been a psychologist, she felt inadequate at her job. At her ability to help people. And that made her feel inadequate at life.

Maybe *that* was what drove her on. Her own incapacity. Her ego. Its need to prove she could do the thing she was supposed to.

In the end, did the reason really matter? Either way she couldn't stay away. And now here she stood across the street from the gallery. She stepped off the curb, then marched over and straight up to the door. There was a beefy bouncer, a velvet rope, just like a nightclub. If it were, she never would have gotten in. Plain old Abigail, with her pastel clothes and bland hairstyle. She wished she'd at least brought some non-work clothes to change into at her office.

The guy at the door took the card from her and looked her name up on a list. Then he nodded her inside. She stepped across the threshold, into the throng. She'd never been to an opening like this. Actually she avoided them. She didn't care for big crowds in general; in specific, packed art galleries were their own special circle of hell. Too many bodies moving around, too many voices in the air. It was all so distracting, she couldn't appreciate what she was looking at. When she experienced art, she liked to be immersed in it.

Immersed. That word had not been lost on her when Lilith had said it to Stan. Abigail remembered that feeling. She'd been the same way as an artist, all those years ago. She hadn't had a fancy loft or even a humble studio to paint in, just a corner of her bedroom with canvasses leaned against the wall. Old towels as drop cloths so as not to stain the carpet, paints mixed in Styrofoam egg cartons and on cracked dinner plates. She'd sat cross-legged on the floor, headphones on, Billie Holliday, Aretha Franklin, Nina Simone singing to her. She let their energy and emotions pour through her and into her paintings: a long series of self-portraits, still lifes of objects in her bedroom. Studies of the everyday life of a teenage girl. Back then her mind, her spirit were so open, she'd experimented with everything. Realism, abstract, oils, watercolors. She read up on all the techniques, spent hours choosing and buying materials. One day she would find her style, the medium that spoke to her.

At least that was what she'd thought at the time. Thanks to her father, she hadn't been an artist long enough to find her niche.

"Abigail, so good to see you." As if out of nowhere, Lilith was at her side. Her voice flat, not truly welcoming. She leaned down and air kissed Abby on both cheeks. Smelling of smoke and slightly rotten roses.

"You too," Abby replied, returning the taller woman's fake smile. "And congratulations. Looks like the show's a success."

"Yes. Everyone wants to see the great Stan Foster's return. See what he can do after his *near-death experience*." Lilith laughed, low and rough, making Abigail uncomfortable. "Why don't you have a look around? I'd love to hear your opinion on his new work. You used to be an artist yourself, didn't you?"

Abigail's brow lowered. "How did you know that?"

Lilith set her blood-red lips in a smirk. "Stan must have mentioned it. I have to mingle, darling. Enjoy the show."

She disappeared into the crowd. People milled around Abigail, closing in the gap. Drinks in their hands, talking too loudly, not even about the art. She reeled, Lilith's words repeating in her mind: *You used to be an artist.* Abby was sure she hadn't said anything about that, not to anyone she knew. Certainly not to Stan or Lilith. Just like she hadn't told him what had happened to her father.

Abigail ducked away, moving toward the first piece of art. The model with flames coming out of her belly. Abigail was stunned. Captivated by the piece. She stood still in front of it, holding her breath, eyes wide. The other guests continued to move around her, but their sound was muted, their actions in slow motion. The world had stopped around this model, her mane of blonde hair, her skin so pale it bordered on translucent. Thin body but soft, feminine curves in her hips, her waist, her thighs. The woman's blue eyes looked down at the fiery bloom around her midsection, her lips turned up into an almost-smile. Abigail smiled too. The resemblance wasn't lost on her. Not just in the model's physical attributes but in the sentiment as well. She wasn't a mother, but she'd always been aware of her nurturing side. The one thing her father hadn't beaten out of her. The force that had driven her to pursue a career as a therapist.

The difference between this show and Stan's older work was clear. Before, judging by what Abby had seen at his loft, all he created was darkness and despair. Pain and terror. This room, in contrast, was full of brightness and light. The white bodies, the vibrant cloth flames. The eyes, arms, hands facing upward, not forever aimed toward the tar-covered ground. There was life here, real, breathing humanity—a genius move, by the way, using actual models for the installments rather than a bunch of lifeless mannequins. Abby was impressed by Stan's ability to pull the endeavor off, and in such a short time.

Over the next hour she made her way around the circuit of the gallery, taking her time with each piece. Examining details, deciphering themes. Overall she saw the whole thing as a puzzle, each installment a piece, a clue to sort out. Each was a side of Stan: the nurturer, the champion, the man, the deity. Figuratively, of course. Abby might have been secretly worshipping at his altar a little too much lately, but Stan was no god. He was a flawed human, and he'd struggled since he'd returned to this earthly plane.

And that came through clearly in this new work. The figures he created were emerging from hell, dragging fire up with them, reclaiming their lives in bursts of flame and glory. Or, seen another way, the fire held them as they tried to move upward. Crushing them, incinerating their souls. Devouring their redemption. Stan must have felt both ways: freed by the experience but also chained by it. Hopeful for the future but unable to forget the past.

Aren't we all like that? Abby knew she was. She'd held on to the past for so long it felt like a part of her. Like a useless limb, like a vestigial organ hidden inside her body. She wanted to be the other way: breaking free, flying away. Wanted it more than almost anything. But it always seemed so impossible. Life didn't work that way, not for her anyway.

Abigail shook her head. She didn't want to go to that place again. The one she'd seen at the loft. She had to believe Stan had put himself on a different tack here—a more positive path. That he had chosen to break free from the darkness, not let the black consume him.

She made her way through the crowd again. It was time to leave; she'd had enough of the people here. All their self-centered chatter, their blank stares at Stan's work. Most of them hated the show, Abby had surmised that from eavesdropping on their conversations. They wanted the old Stan with all his goth gloom, his tortured women kowtowing to some unnamed evil.

Well, maybe he should go back then, she thought as she shouldered through a pack of girls in Doc Martens and bondage pants, certainly not old enough to be holding the cocktails they had in their hands. If Stan's fans wanted darkness, maybe he should give it to them. Suddenly she was furious with herself for getting so hung up on a perfect stranger. And a patient, no less. How could she have been so foolish? Building Stan up in her mind as some great misunderstood genius, a victim of his own misplaced self-loathing. Maybe he was just a bad man in a nice suit. Not the angel in disguise she wanted him to be.

SIXTEEN

Stan felt frenetic, scattered. He couldn't make his mind focus. He glanced around for Lilith, saw her blonde hair over the rest of the crowd on the far side of the room. He ducked down a little, hoping she wouldn't see him, and made his way through the sea of people. Hands grabbed him; voices called out for him. To stop, to chat, to explain the meaning of his work. If these people couldn't see it, he thought, that was their problem. If they didn't understand his message, nothing he said would explain it to them.

"Abby," he whispered, spying her across the room, heading for the door. He snaked his way over to her, catching her arm just before she reached the threshold.

"You've got to get me out of here!" he hissed at her, realizing how crazy his own voice sounded. This place, this show, these people, all of it was doing something to him. Changing him, dragging him down. If he didn't find a way to keep himself afloat, he would drown in it, in the negativity that hovered throughout the space like a storm cloud.

"Stan, what?" Abigail asked, then laughed nervously and grabbed his arms. He still crouched, trying to keep himself hidden from Lilith.

"I'm fine, I'm fine." He straightened up a bit and put an arm around Abigail's waist. He glanced at Lilith talking to a group of critics. They stood around her in a half circle. Staring at her raptly. She the queen, they her minions. Ready to print anything she told them to.

"Just get me out of here." Stan repeated the plea, whispering it into Abigail's ear. His lips close and hot so she couldn't refuse.

And she didn't. Within a moment she'd grabbed his hand and pulled him the rest of the way through the gallery. Out to the sidewalk, where the line still stretched for several hundred feet. They ran down along it.

"Where are we going?" she asked, still gripping his hand and hustling him toward Astor Place.

"I don't know." Stan looked at the faces of the people who waited to see his show. Some looked familiar, though of course he couldn't quite place them. Something in the eyes of this one, the downturn of that one's lips. One group glared at him so hard, he swore they gave off a palpable coldness as he passed.

At the corner he stopped short, jerking Abigail back. The streetlight had just turned green on Third Avenue, and a flood of cars began to pass by. Stan stuck his arm in the air, hailing a cab. One pulled over. He opened the door and helped Abby into the backseat.

"Just take me somewhere," he said, then quickly looked behind him. Expecting to see Lilith tearing down St. Mark's Place, coming to get him. To drag him back by his collar, heels dragging on the ground. Once she saw he was gone, he was sure, she'd be furious. For now, he seemed safe. He stepped into the cab. Abby was talking to the driver. Stan settled himself, angling his body toward her. When she was done, she sat back too.

"I'm sorry," he began. "And thank you. I just couldn't stay there."

A light pink blush came into her cheeks. "No problem. Did something happen? Why'd you want to leave so fast?"

Stan liked the color of Abigail's face. Filed it away in his head for future reference. "Nothing happened. Everything's going great. Did you see how many people showed up?" He looked out the back window of the cab, at the gallery and the line outside it receding in the distance. "Guess I was a pretty popular guy before…well, before."

Abigail looked too. "Yeah, it sure seems that way. Who would have guessed you have such a massive following? And—" A thought hit her. She hesitated. "And yet no one knew you were missing. How could—"

"Well, most of them hate my work." Stan looked back at her. "Maybe they just didn't care."

"How do you know they hate your work?"

"Oh God, wasn't it obvious? Did you see their faces? The way they eyed the models too. If looks could kill… They loathed the whole experience. I could feel it rolling off the crowd like a wave of heat."

Abigail tilted her head. Put on her sympathetic psychologist face. He'd seen it many times at the hospital, usually when she talked to other patients. The ones who really needed her help. "I'm so sorry. That's a tough thing to take."

"Are you kidding?" Stan let out a short, sharp laugh. "It's fantastic. I couldn't be happier."

"What? Why is that wonderful? Don't you want people to like you? And, more importantly, your work? Especially now, when you have so much to lose. This is supposed to be your comeback, Stan. Your reintroduction to the art world."

Stan scoffed. "You sound like Lilith. What am I coming back from? Trying to kill myself? Not a reason to party, as far as I'm concerned. I wasn't even gone that long. And, like you said, nobody even noticed." He paused here too. "Which is odd, right? Now that you mention it." He shook his head. "At any rate I'm not the same person I was. So I'm not going *back* at all. If anything, this was a coming-out show—an announcement of the new me and my new message."

He hadn't really thought of it that way before, but it made

perfect sense now. Lilith kept going on and on about how he used to be, how she had to help him return to his former glory. She raved about Old Stan like he'd been some kind of mythical creature, a god among mortals. Part of Stan appreciated her dedication. Part of him just wanted her to let it go and see him for the person he was now.

"And what is your new message? Wait, hold that thought a minute." Abigail tapped on the partition to get the driver to pull over. They'd arrived at their destination, wherever that was. Some sort of parking lot, mostly empty, and a big, old stone building. Abigail paid the guy, and she and Stan got out. The building's door was open. They walked inside, Abigail leading the way.

"What is this, a museum?" Stan looked up at the high ceiling of what appeared to be a lobby. There was an admission desk to the left, information to the right. Brochures about exhibits, maps of the premises. But no people around. His voice rang off the hard walls, no soft flesh to absorb it.

Abigail walked to the middle of the room and stopped. Turned around to face him. She held her bag low in front of her with both hands, her ankles crossed, shoulders relaxed. An innocent, unpretentious pose. Late-evening sun came down from the skylight, bathing her in gold. She smiled as if enjoying the warmth. Stan had never seen her so radiant.

"You haven't been here?" She looked around as if searching for someone. Though they were obviously alone. When she spoke again, her voice was softer. "Did you grow up in the city? Every fifth-grade class comes here for a field trip at one time or another."

Stan just smiled and shrugged. Maybe he had grown up here, maybe not. He had no idea.

Abigail blushed again, realizing her mistake. "Sorry. Yes,

it is a museum. Religious art and artifacts mostly. Called the Cloisters. It's really an old monastery."

Stan moved closer, taking her cue and speaking quietly. "And you can just come in any time you want? Even after it closes? What, do you own the place?"

Abigail laughed, putting her fingers over her lips to hide it. "No, I'm on an advisory board here. We have a meeting tonight, but I skipped it to come to your opening. Come on, let me show you around."

She walked toward a staircase on the far side of the lobby. Stan had no choice but to follow.

The steps brought them down into a small room with a stone sarcophagus in the middle. Two more on each side by the walls. Statues of Mary and Jesus, the sort seen in old churches. Sad eyes and pointy noses, doughy cheeks and flowing robes. The baby held his hands out to Stan, reaching for him, beckoning. Stan moved closer. Brought his face in near the child's until they almost touched. Its unmoving eyes locked on his, looking through him. Into his mind, his heart. His soul. It knew what resided there, the fight that raged inside Stan. To be good, to do good. Or to be the man Lilith told him he used to be. Stan knew there was something dark in that, in how he once was. He fought against it but was curious too. How had he been before? Had he been happy that way? He'd certainly been successful. People had loved him. Not like they did now, all the people at his show looking at him like he'd personally offended them.

Ridiculous, Stan told himself. The statue was just a piece of stone, the eyes dabs of paint. It didn't know a thing about him. About anything. He backed up. From a distance, the baby Jesus seemed lifeless again.

"Come on," Abigail prompted, then led him through a hallway, bringing them out into a room lined with windows made of stained glass. Yellow and white mostly, small panels depicting scenes from religious life. Monks performing house-hold chores. Jesus's stations of the cross. All rippled and warped with age, making the scenery outside waver in Stan's vision.

"One more turn," Abby said, leading him to the end of the hallway, then to the right. At a set of doors—old and wooden, metal handles smooth and dull with age—Abigail opened one side, and hot air poured into the cool corridor, swirling around the musty floor, the damp stone walls.

Stan shielded his eyes and stepped out into a courtyard garden. Tall grasses, lavender and daffodils, a large weeping willow tree. Its leaves swaying and swishing in a warm summer breeze. The whole scene was like the setting of a fantasy novel. He turned to Abigail behind him.

"This is beautiful. So peaceful. How do you not want to spend every minute of your life here?"

She walked past him to a stone wall on the far side. Leaned against it with her back, then hopped up and sat on it. "Some-times I do. On weekends when the weather's nice I'll bring a book and stay all afternoon. This place is like a second home to me."

Stan went over too. Did the same, sat next to her on the wall. Swung his legs around to the opposite side, where they dangled above a steep drop-off. Beyond, the Hudson River. The George Washington Bridge in the distance.

He nodded toward it. "Nice view."

Abigail looked alarmed. "Oh, I'm sorry. I didn't think—"

Stan held up a hand, stopping her. "It's okay. Don't worry. It doesn't bother me."

Abigail looked at it too, her gaze lingering. "I can't imagine it, Stan. Jumping off a bridge. So much time to think about what you're doing before you hit bottom." She turned back. "Do you have any idea what made you want to jump?"

He shrugged again. He'd given this a good amount of thought since he'd washed up on the river's shore, particularly since he'd been released from the hospital. Nothing he'd found at the loft—at home—had given him any sort of clue as to why he might have wanted to kill himself. No notes to loved ones, no journals in which he poured out his heart. Not even a bottle of antidepressants in the bathroom cabinet.

"I wish I could tell you." He watched the boats making their way up and down the waterway below. Sails and smokestacks, cutting through en route to who knew where. "My memory only goes as far back as the fall. That I remember really clearly. Something happened before that, but it's fuzzy. I'm not even sure it has anything to do with my suicide attempt."

"What was it?" Abigail brought her feet up and sat cross-legged on the wall. "What do you remember? You didn't tell me that before."

Stan thought about the memory. An argument, an ultimatum. A casting-out. The images were unclear: Whom had he fought with? Who had been exiled? He had a feeling it was him, though he couldn't be sure. All he saw were shades of light and dark, and the world turning around and around as he fell. And fell. And fell. He remembered the sensation of tumbling through the air that day. The weightless feeling returned, almost made him reel again.

"Whoa, be careful there." Abigail reached out and grabbed his arm. "What's going on? Are you feeling faint? Maybe it's too hot out here. I'll get you some water."

She began to get up, but Stan put a hand on her leg to stop her. She looked at it, and he did too. All around them the air stilled, the weeping willow's leaves falling into a hush.

"What did you mean in the cab?" Abby asked quietly. "Why don't you want people to like you?"

He loosened his grip on her leg but left his hand where it

was, just above her knee. "I wanted this show to make a statement, Abby. I want to make people uncomfortable. Shake them up a little. Just like my old artwork did but in a different way."

"It certainly was different." She raised her eyes to his. Stan liked the way the setting sun reflected in them. Like fire. Like the spark. "Not at all what I was expecting to see."

"But did you *like* it?"

"I did." She smiled, and it was like a new world opened up. He was surprised by how much he found her opinion mattered to him. "I liked it a lot, Stan. You're amazingly talented. And the pieces in this new show..."

She looked out over the water, as if searching for the right words. Looked back at him, her face serious. "They felt right to me. I didn't know you before, but I saw your art, and to me that was a glimpse into your soul. At least how it used to be. Today I saw what's in here now." She put her hand on his chest, over his heart. "And what I saw is *good*."

Stan looked out at the water too. At the bridge, the place where it had all started. The beginning of his journey on this earth. "Since the day I jumped, I've been able to realize something: I'm at a point where I truly can choose wherever I want to go. What I want my life to be. So then I had to decide: Should I continue on the same old path, making depressing art for people with no souls? Or should I try something new? Bring a little light into this dismal world?"

He looked at her, deep into her eyes. "Abigail, which would you choose if you had the chance?"

Her answer was immediate. "No question. I'd choose the brighter path every time."

Hearing that, Stan couldn't help himself. He leaned in to kiss her.

SEVENTEEN

"Artist Hits Strange New Heights at Gallery Opening."
The headline sat atop a grainy photo of one of Stan's pieces—the nude man, his genitals blurred out, his arms raised skyward.

"Couldn't think of a more creative lead?" Abigail asked as she scanned the article, the newspaper sitting on the blotter of her desk. Outside her office the halls were silent—just after med time, everyone either zoned out or sleeping. This review of Stan's show was the same as all the others she'd read—the critic didn't understand the work, compared it too much to Stan's old stuff, but it was obvious he'd been charmed to death by good old Lilith. The woman had done her job, Abigail had to give her that. Not even twenty-four hours had passed and Stan had write-ups in all the city papers, not to mention all the online reviews.

Most of them, like this one, were obliquely positive. The critics didn't like the show, but none of them could bring themselves to say anything bad about it. A strange and puzzling phenomenon across the board.

So much like Stan himself.

Abigail closed her eyes, sat back in her chair, pushed away from her desk. For a moment she remembered the feel of his hand on her thigh. The brush of his lips against hers. He'd barely made contact when she'd pulled away.

"Stan, we can't do this," she'd said. Feeling for all the world like the heroine of a bad romance novel. "I'm still your doctor. It just wouldn't be right. And I could lose my license."

"I won't tell if you don't." He'd tried again. This time she'd let him go on longer before pushing him back. She could have kissed him all night, could have spent the rest of her life sitting on that wall at the Cloisters with his hand on her leg. She remembered his warm, soft lips. The feel of his tongue on hers.

Opening her eyes, she wheeled her chair up to the desk. Willing away the tingling feeling growing in her thighs.

"Okay, you have work to do," she said, focusing on the pile of papers before her. New cases to review. Medications to prescribe. But after a few minutes of trying, she couldn't keep her mind on it. Stan kept coming back to her. The sound of his voice, the way his eyes squinted when he smiled. His devotion to his art. How happy he'd been that the people at the opening had seemed to loathe his work. Abby had never known a man who was like Stan.

Or a patient like him. She had to keep reminding herself of where they stood. As long as Stan was officially in her care—and he was, at least for two more scheduled follow-up sessions—he had to remain off limits. That meant no kissing, no touching, not even lingering eye contact. Certainly no thoughts like the ones she had about him. About how hot his breath had felt against her flushed cheek.

Abigail grabbed her head with both hands and let out a frustrated moan. She turned, opened up a drawer in her filing cabinet, and flipped through the manila folders. Pulled out the one marked "FOSTER, S." Opened it up on her desk. Rummaged through to find her handwritten notes from their sessions.

The first day they'd met, she'd called him delusional, bipolar, possibly even autistic and schizophrenic. Truth was she didn't know his diagnosis. Not then and not now. Perhaps he wasn't mentally ill, just eccentric. He was an artist, after all. How stable could she expect him to be?

She looked through the rest of his file. His intake forms, his med signoff sheets. Nowhere had anyone called him psychotic or noted any odd behaviors. Words like *talkative*, *clear-headed*, and *rational* jumped out at her. The policemen who'd found him, an ER nurse, her own notes. Everyone agreed he'd seemed almost completely normal.

"Then how did he end up here?" She paged through the file for the name of the doctor who'd referred him to the psych ward. She didn't find it.

No signoff, no anything.

Paperwork mistakes happened—all the time, actually; the hospital-going public would be shocked if they knew the truth—but that didn't explain this. Stan, it seemed, never should have been in her care.

Which meant he didn't need to be in it now, Abigail thought with a bit of a gleeful surge. He didn't need a diagnosis. He didn't need follow-ups. Which meant...

"Abigail, don't do this." She sighed, looking down at Stan's mug shot clipped inside his folder. Knowing what she thought was wrong. As his doctor, she had a responsibility to complete the routine management of this case. To ensure the patient was adjusting to being back in the community, back in his regular life.

But as a woman at the mercy of her body and emotions... well, that was a different story.

The question was which side would win this fight.

The doorbell rang at exactly eight o'clock. Abigail hurried from her bedroom, hopping down the hallway as she pulled on her other shoe.

"Coming, coming," she called, yanking down her tight, white T-shirt as she got to the door. Checked her outfit: green velvet miniskirt, opaque black tights, patent-leather Doc Martens. She hadn't worn any of these pieces in a while. Felt good to be back in her old skin again.

Reaching up, she undid the door's three locks—two deadbolts and a chain—and pulled it open. Stan leaned against the jamb with one arm up over his head. Looking for all the world like he was in some chick flick, the romantic lead coming to sweep the reluctant heroine off her feet. Cool and sexy, charming to boot. They'd be in bed together by the end of the scene.

Abigail cleared her throat. "You're very punctual."

Stan stood up straight, checked his wristwatch. Who ever wore one of those anymore? Another quirk for Abby to add to his long list.

"Look at that, I am." He smiled at her. Not like he did in the hospital, in that shrugging sort of apologetic way he'd had. His grin had grown brighter now, more relaxed and more full of life at the same time. As if Stan had shed the mantle of amnesiac psych-ward patient and come into his familiar self.

"May I come in?"

"Oh." Abigail stepped aside and let him enter her home. Trying to remember how long it had been since she'd had company. A man, no less. Then decided it didn't matter, really—man, woman, dog, cat, no other living thing had graced the threshold of her tiny apartment since God only knew when.

Stan walked through the kitchen and into the living room, where he turned in a circle. Looking at the art on the walls.

John August Swanson's "Festival of Lights." Carlos Cazares's "The True Vine." A Pieta. A Last Supper. Abigail felt exposed, like she'd left her underwear out on the floor. Like the art she'd hung on her walls was some sort of dirty secret.

But Stan made no comment. Whatever he thought of her Christian fixation, he kept it to himself. For now, anyway. Abigail had a feeling it would come up between them at some point. She remembered their first session in her office, when he'd asked why, as an estranged Catholic, she'd sought work at a religious hospital. These pictures had to seem strange to him. Hell, they seemed strange to her. So many nights she sat there in silence just looking at them, the sorrow in Mary's eyes as she cradled her dying son, the hopeful glow of the candles in Swanson's procession. These images spoke to her in a way she couldn't even put words to. Maybe, somehow, Stan could help her describe it.

But that was for another night. "I'm glad you called this afternoon," she said, holding out her arm to offer him a seat on the sofa. The only place to sit in the room. The only thing that fit besides an old dresser with a TV on top of it. She'd had this apartment forever—in the Village, Bleecker and Thompson—and never noticed anymore how cramped her quarters were. She marveled at how the things we see every day become invisible to us.

Stan sat down. "Me too. Though I'm surprised you accepted my invitation."

"Okay." Abigail joined him. "But I told you this isn't a date, right?"

"Right. Not a date," he said, his eyes wandering up to "The Last Supper." "It's just dinner. Maybe a couple of drinks. So we can talk about art." He turned back to Abigail, looking amused. "And it looks like *you* might have some talking to do."

"It's so we can talk about your recovery too," she said, standing up quickly. Moving his focus away from these images that loomed around them. "I think it's important that we keep up on that. I'm really interested in how you're feeling now that you've been home for a couple weeks, and especially since you're working again. And at such a quick pace."

"Blame that on Lilith. She's quite the slave driver."

The two of them just looked at each other. The other woman's name hung in the air between them. Did Lilith know he was here tonight? Abby wondered as she tried not to look him up and down. He looked good in his T-shirt, his ripped jeans, his big boots. The two of them looked good together. As if they'd planned how to dress. Like a couple—

Abigail stood up quickly. Yanked the hem of her skirt down just out of nervousness. "Just let me get my bag," she said. "Then we can be on our way."

She turned to leave the room, then glanced quickly back at Stan. Sitting on her sofa, arm draped over the end cushion, looking like he lived here. Too comfortable, she thought, but it gave her a rush at the same time. It had been too long since she'd let anyone into her home. Or into her life.

———

"So how does this rank so far in your history of dates?" Stan propped his elbow on the bar and held up a finger. "Wait, I meant non-dates. How does this compare to all the other *non-dates* you've been on?"

Abigail smirked at him. Reached for her glass of merlot and took a big mouthful. They'd already had dinner—Caffe Dante, a little Italian place around the corner—and moved right on to drinking. Stan stuck to his gin and tonics with extra lime; Abby had moved her way around the wine spectrum glass by glass. The more they drank, the more she felt herself loosening up, and the more she was able to crush that still, small voice in her head. The one that kept telling her this was wrong. That she should go home—without Stan—and forget she'd ever met him. Unless he needed a psych consult or a prescription. Then she could help him. But any of the dirty thoughts currently racing through her brain? Those were all out of the question. She hated that little voice.

"I'd say it's going well." Abigail didn't know quite how to answer him. Not just because her mind was fuzzy from the wine but because she'd never done anything like this before. Not dated a patient. Not pretended there wasn't this painfully strong attraction between them. "And what do you think?"

Stan smiled, his lips loose, his tired eyes squinting almost until they were closed. He put a hand on her knee and squeezed. "I think it's going fabulously."

He slurred the word, and they both laughed. Then Abigail pointedly removed his hand from where it traveled up her inner thigh.

"Let's talk about your show," she said, straightening up on the bar stool where she sat. "Did you get any feedback?"

Stan straightened up, too, and waved to the bartender for another round. "Well, you said you read the reviews. You tell me what they thought."

"No, I meant from the people who were there. Or from Lilith."

Again that name. Abigail said it like it didn't bother her. But it did—*she* did. Lilith bothered her a lot. Her air of superiority, the way she talked down to Abby. Most of all the way she treated Stan like he was some sort of trained seal. Churning out artwork to make her money, to keep her in black high heels and cigarettes, in gas for that monstrous car of hers.

And Abby wasn't the only one who was bothered. She could

tell by the look on Stan's face. He gazed off across the bar, eyes scanning the rows of bottles. Mouth set, eyes hard. His hand went unconsciously up, and he began to chew on his thumbnail. When his fresh drink arrived, he downed almost half the glass in two long gulps.

"Stan," Abby said. Now she put a hand on his leg. "What is it? What's wrong?"

When he turned to her, his eyes were afire. Dark and burning, like embers at the bottom of a pyre. "The night before the show, Lilith called me up and said, 'Come to my place. Let's talk about how things will go tomorrow.' I figure this is good, right? I've never done a show before." He laughed a little. "Well, not that I can remember. And she's an old pro at this whole art thing, so she can really tell me how it'll go down. Get me prepared."

He paused to take another drink, and Abigail watched him. His anger didn't ebb, as she'd thought it might if he started to talk about what was bothering him. His eyes still glowed, his body rigid. As if every muscle were tense.

Suddenly he stood up, taking Abigail by surprise. He reached into his pocket and pulled out a few twenties, then threw them on the bar. He picked up his glass and emptied it.

"I've gotta get out of here," he said and grabbed Abby by the wrist. Pulled her off the stool and through the crowd that packed the bar. He shouldered his way in and out, shouting at those who didn't get the hint the first time. Instinctively Abigail held back, frightened by his outbursts, straining against his tight grip. Still he led her on until they broke free onto the sidewalk outside. He let go of her.

"Stan," she said but didn't know how to continue. She grabbed her wrist and rubbed it where he had held her. The skin there was red, raw. As if his fingers had burned into her, leaving his mark like a shackle. She'd never seen this side of

Stan. Assertive. Aggressive. It worried her, but at the same time she couldn't help but be awed by it. At least he was feeling something.

"When I got there it was full of people!" he shouted, continuing his story. "All these drunk assholes, dancing and... I didn't know any of them. But I knew I didn't like them. You ever just get a feeling about someone? Like you know you can't trust them?"

Stan threw his hands in the air and let out a frustrated cry. The sound made Abigail cringe. Deep and slow, tinged with malice. A tone she never would have imagined coming from his throat.

"She just wanted to show me off. Parade me around like some circus monkey on a leash. Come see the amazing Stan Foster! Jumped off the George Washington Bridge and lived to tell the tale! I guess she knew I never would have gone if she'd told me about it. So she lied to get me there. And that was why I left the opening yesterday. I can't stand to look at her."

He seemed finished now. Deflated. But still on an emotional edge. Abigail watched him pace in front of the bar, one hand on his hip, one running back and forth through his hair. He didn't look at her, only at the ground or at the passing cars. His breath came in short rasps. Abby bet his heart was racing a mile a minute.

"Stan, come on." She kept her voice calm as she took his hand. They went west on Houston for half a block, then down Sullivan, back toward her place. She had to get him somewhere quiet, somewhere safe. Somewhere without people. She wondered if the crowds set him off—maybe he was agoraphobic or had a panic disorder. Maybe he really did hear voices, or see people's pasts, or whatever it was he claimed he could do since he left the hospital.

As they trudge along, Abby in front, Stan shuffling along

behind her, she ran through diagnoses in her head just to keep herself composed. In reality she was terrified. Not of Stan; not that he would hurt her or anything like that. She was more scared *for* him. Obviously this wasn't some passing thing brought on by the trauma of surviving a suicide attempt. No, Stan had something real about him. Something that had made him flip so quickly. Who knew what he might do next? He'd jumped off a bridge once. Maybe next time he wouldn't be so lucky.

"Come on," she said, ushering him into her building. She led him up the first flight of stairs, then the second, then they were outside her door. She put the key in the lock.

"Wait." Stan slumped against the doorframe. The same pose he'd had when she'd opened it for him several hours earlier. But this time he didn't look so good. Defeated. Sweaty. Eyelids drooping. As if the anger had taken all the fight out of him.

"Stan, you need to sit down," she said, continuing to open the lock. "And some aspirin and some cold water." Abigail opened the door, threw her bag on the kitchen table. Then she turned around to catch him as he stumbled in behind her.

"Sorry, sorry," he mumbled as she led him to the couch and set him down gently. She turned him around, pressed on his shoulders until he lay back, his head sinking into the end cushion.

"Don't worry about it." When she noticed he was looking at her, she smiled and blushed a little. "Maybe next time we'll skip the bar. Just go to a movie or something."

Stan grinned and pushed himself up a little. "So there's a next time? You'll go on another date with me?"

Abigail pushed him back. "This isn't a date, Stan," she said, though she had trouble making it sound convincing. They both let it go at that.

She went to get him that glass of water and the aspirin, hoping they'd at least fend off the massive hangover he was headed for. She sat down on the floor next to the sofa and made sure he took it all.

"Abigail, you were right, what you said." Stan handed the empty glass to her. He laid his head back down and let out a long sigh. He put his arm over his eyes, blocking out the dim lamplight. "It isn't right. You're my doctor."

Abigail didn't know what to say. But she knew she should agree with him. It wasn't right—hadn't she told herself that a thousand times already?

"I'm sorry I pushed you into this," he went on. "I know I shouldn't have—"

"Stan, I found you a new therapist."

Slowly he drew his arm away from his face and looked at her.

"It's not written in stone yet," she went on before he could say anything. "But this afternoon, after you called, I got to thinking. Stan, you need help. You have a lot of issues to work out—probably stuff you're not even aware of yet. Surviving a suicide attempt, amnesia, these are big things to deal with alone."

"But I'm not alone." He took her hand. "I have you, Abby."

The touch almost made her gasp. How long had it been since she'd felt another human's skin? Not the patients who grabbed her or the strangers who brushed by her on the street. But someone she cared about. Some contact with meaning. Abigail felt pressure building behind her eyes.

"Yes, you do have me," she agreed, laying her hand on top of his. "But you need professional help too. And you can't have me both ways. So if you want to do this… If you want to be involved with me…you need to see another doctor. I asked around, and I made some phone calls, and I found someone I think will be a good fit for you. I don't know him personally, but he came with some very good recommendations. I'd like you to give him a try."

In the silence, Stan nodded slowly, looking around again at the prints hanging on the walls. Finally his eyes came around to her again. "So I'm not your patient anymore?"

Abigail blushed again. God, if the hospital board knew what she had done, they'd probably fire her. Get her license revoked. "Not as of tomorrow morning, when I go in and file the discharge papers."

Then she leaned in to kiss him. What could it hurt? No one there but the paintings to see them.

EIGHTEEN

L ilith was taking off her clothes again.

"Do you have to do that here?" Stan turned away, focusing on his computer screen. Checking his e-mail. Accolades were still coming in about the show, but he didn't read any of them. Didn't even know the people sending them, so why bother? Their enthusiasm was fake, their congratulations meaningless. He focused instead on a web page about the Cloisters, something Abby had sent him about an upcoming event there—a gallery talk on gender and sanctity in medieval art. She'd thought it would appeal to him. It did. He hit "reply" and let her know he would go with her.

"Well, where else am I supposed to get changed? In my car?" Lilith spat as she slipped into a new black dress, which looked to Stan exactly like the one she'd just taken off. Heels back on, she strode over to the gold-framed mirror and checked on her hair and face. "I can't go to two meetings in a row wearing the same thing. People will talk. I have an image to uphold."

"Who are these people you're hanging around with?" Stan laughed. He couldn't imagine anyone caring about a dress so much.

"People who adore you. Investors." She shot him a look in the mirror as she snapped her lipstick shut. "Very wealthy investors. The people who are buying your work and putting money in our pockets."

"Oh." He shut up and went back to his web page. Stan hadn't

known Lilith long, but he knew not to argue with her about money. Or deadlines. Or anything, for that matter. She'd made it clear from the beginning: she was always right, on all matters. Stan had to admit she did know more about the art world than he did, but still. It would be nice to feel like his opinion was valued once in a while.

She stomped to the table where she'd left her planner. Opened it to the week's page, which was already scribbled over with notes. "Let's talk about the next show." She said it to Stan as an order, not a request. She tapped her foot while she waited.

He got up slowly and went over to her. Picked up the bottle of beer he'd left on the table and took a swig. It was warm, but he wouldn't let it go to waste. Not with that evil eye Lilith was giving him. That was too good to pass up.

"Since all your pieces from the opening sold," she began, her gaze lingering on him as he drank, then sliding back to her date book, "you've been invited to show at the Brooklyn Museum in three weeks. The title is…" She riffled through some papers and came out with a Post-it note. "*Redemption and Punishment.* Right up your alley, and you'll be in good company. Luis Francisco and Jenny Rickson signed on too."

Stan only half listened. He didn't know these people. Didn't even know the museum. He was thinking instead about his models from the *Birth/Death* show. Imagining them posing in someone's living room. Next to a lamp or a sofa. Or in a posh office with a CEO behind a mahogany desk. Of course whoever purchased the art didn't get the people with it. They only got the costume pieces—the flaming plumes, the trails of fire— arranged on some probably less-than-satisfying mannequins. Stan had nothing to do with that process. The paperwork and legwork, the arrangements and payments, that was all Lilith. For that he was glad to have her around. For everything else—

"Who bought my stuff anyway?"

"The same people who always buy your *stuff*." Lilith closed her date book, then shoved it in her oversized purse. "I know you don't want to accept it, Stan, but people like what you do. You have fans. A following. And many of them have money to burn, quite literally. These are the people I'm meeting with. And I'm going to be late if I don't get out of here right now. Time is money, friend. Don't ever forget that." She paused, looking him up and down. Shook her head as if pitying him. "There was a time when I didn't have to remind you of such things. Would be nice if you could be that guy again."

Leaning across the table, she kissed his cheek, leaving bright-red lip marks, then made her way across the loft and out the door. Stan got another beer from the refrigerator and went to the window to watch her. She exited the building, got into her Escalade, and took off—no looking back for Lilith. She was always like that: a handful of steps ahead of everyone else, focused on her goals, impatient to get there.

So why was she so bent on making Stan go back in time? This wasn't the first mention she'd made about how Stan used to be—far from it. Every time he saw Lilith or talked to her on the phone, she had something to say about Old Stan. How driven he'd been. How *immersed* in his artwork. How much money he'd made, how respected he was. How good he'd been in bed.

But shouldn't he be progressing? Artists grow; their work changes as they age, as their lives change, as the world changes. They're supposed to reflect the society and culture around them, not choose one topic when they're seventeen and stick with it for the rest of their lives. God, if that were true, Stan would still be painting nudes of his friends' sisters—

He dropped his beer. The glass broke against the cement floor, and the cold, amber liquid pooled around his bare feet.

He remembered.

Not everything, but that one thing. Buckets of house paint, the canvases hidden in a crawlspace at the back of his parents' basement. The girls' soft thighs and young breasts. A redhead with a crooked smile. A brunette with small feet. Reclined on his living room sofa while Mom and Dad were out. Lying in a field of grass, somewhere out in the countryside. The paintings weren't awful, but they weren't good. No wonder he'd moved on to installation art.

His laugh rang off the walls of the loft, coming back to his ears sounding empty and strange, with a hard edge he didn't recognize. It wasn't his own voice. It jarred him into silence, where he replayed the images he'd seen in his mind of his younger days. It wasn't much to go on, and he doubted it was the period in his life Lilith wished he would return to. Still, he would take it. A little glimpse of something was better than nothing at all. At least this gave him somewhere to start.

NINETEEN

At one fifteen that afternoon, Stan sat in his new therapist's waiting room, leafing through a copy of *Good Housekeeping*. He was alone, just him and all the plants and a charcoal drawing of a gargoyle. Odd choice for a psychologist's office, Stan thought, but a good sketch nonetheless. He got up to look at it more closely and saw the artist's signature underneath: M. Uphir.

"No shit." The therapist himself.

He put the magazine back, then paced the room for a minute before the door opened. A man came out to greet him—short, wearing a gray three-piece suit. Hair black as night, with silver streaks like lightning, and a dark, well-groomed, and perfectly pointed goatee. Dr. Uphir smiled at Stan, revealing a gold tooth on the left side of his mouth and wrinkles around his eyes.

"Good to meet you," the older man said, moving back into the doorway and ushering Stan into his office. Stan had never seen a private-practice therapist before, only Abigail at St. Luke's. Not that he knew of, anyway. But this was what he imagined all their inner sanctums looked like. Comfortable chairs, a coffee table with a box of tissues. Windows with opaque shades half drawn, letting in just enough daylight that the room needed no further illumination. Uphir gestured to a comfy-looking leather chair, then put a hand on Stan's back.

Stan stopped short as his body jolted. Electricity surged through him at this man's touch, leaving in its wake a wave of heat and ghastly images: Uphir surrounded by black. Engulfed in it. Around him people fell to the ground as he passed by. Twitching and crying, bleeding from their eyes and ears. Then lifeless. In an instant, gone.

Stan gagged as bile rose in his closing throat. He staggered to the chair and dropped into it, massaging his neck. Uphir sat across from him, his face placid, as if he hadn't noticed Stan's sudden change, his obvious discomfort. Did he know what Stan had seen? Could he somehow tell? Stan couldn't be sure. He didn't really understand this…this *power* he had. And he wasn't so sure he wanted this doctor to help him with it.

"So Dr. Petrus sent me your file." The older man's tone was slow and unguent. Patronizing. "You certainly have quite a history. Would you like to tell me about it?"

Stan shifted in his chair. He already disliked this man. The way he talked did nothing to help that. He thought about what to say. How much to reveal. Best to stick to the main facts—the things that would be in his chart—until he knew if he could trust Uphir or not.

"Sure," he began, sitting back in the chair. Trying to look unfazed. "Well, apparently I tried to kill myself. I don't remember much of it. I don't know why I did it. I only remember washing up on the shore of the Hudson River."

"Do you remember your life before the attempt?"

Stan shook his head. "Not really. I mean no. I've been piecing things together, but—"

He broke off as Uphir caught his gaze. The older man's dark eyes glittered like a faceted gem. Just for a second, just a flash, and then the brilliance retreated. Stan stared, glassy-eyed, his mind clouding over with doubt. His apprehension melting away. Suddenly he couldn't remember what he'd felt so uncomfortable about. All he knew was he wanted to tell Uphir everything about himself.

"A memory did come up earlier," he heard himself saying as if he had no control over his words. His mouth moved on autopilot, his voice strangely calm and even. "When I was a kid, a teenager, I used to fool around with my friends' sisters. Get them to take off their clothes, saying I'd paint them. You know, paint pictures of them. And I did, but they were pretty bad. I just did it to get in their pants. But then…I started to enjoy it. The painting. And the more I did it, the better I got at it."

"And that's the only memory you have?" Uphir wrote notes about Stan on a legal pad, his silver pen scritching as it rolled across the yellow paper.

"Yeah, that's it." Stan just looked at him, the daze he'd felt wearing off.

Uphir sat with his legs crossed, his pointy, black shoe dangling between them. Who was this guy? How had Abigail found him? Stan wondered if Abby and Uphir were friends, but it didn't seem likely. Abigail was pure of heart—another thing Stan had seen when he'd touched her. It was part of his attraction to her. A big part. People like Abigail were hard to find.

But Uphir…he was nothing like that. Evil and suffering— that was all Stan had seen when the doctor touched him. There was no way this creature was a part of Abigail's world. In fact their two worlds couldn't have been farther apart.

So why would Abigail choose this guy?

"Tell me about your visions."

The doctor said it like it was just any other fact, not a delusional secret, an embarrassing and completely impossible admission. For a moment Stan raged silently at the comment, blood rising to his face, his hands gripping the arms of the chair.

So Abby had written that down. He'd thought that was between them. Not an official piece of information for his diagnosis.

But then he reeled himself in. Abigail was trying to help him, he had to remember that. If she wrote it down, it was for a reason. At least she'd believed him. "Yes, sometimes. At least I think that's what they are."

"Do you want to tell me about them?"

Uphir smiled at Stan, his golden tooth glistening. He wanted to know. Looked eager to hear it. Stan looked around the room, wondering if he could make a break for the door. He didn't want to be here. He wanted to call Abby—

"She can't help you with this."

Stan's head snapped back to Uphir. Immediately his mind stopped racing. "What did you say?" He knew he'd heard the doctor, but he couldn't believe it.

Uphir uncrossed his legs, put his notepad down, and leaned forward on his knees. He folded his hands and stared at Stan. The doctor blinked slowly, and his eyes returned to their normal stony gray. He was a picture of calmness.

"I said Dr. Petrus can't help you with this problem you're having." He cocked his head to one side. "Come on, Stan. You know what I'm talking about. The dreams, the visions, whatever you want to call them. The pit of bodies. Seeing people's deepest, darkest, dirtiest secrets. You're disturbed by them, but you're fascinated too. You have to admit that." He grinned again and leaned in closer. He dropped his voice. "And you know they're real, Stan. Everything you see is *real*. How does that make you feel?"

Stan stood and jabbed a finger in the doctor's direction. "Who the hell are you? How do you know all this?"

Uphir gestured at him to sit down. Calm as ever, as if this

were just another day at the office. "Let's talk about this like civilized gentlemen, shall we?"

Stan glared at him for a moment. Curiosity and horror boiled in his veins, fighting it out. He wanted to know what the doctor knew, but at the same time it terrified him. What if it *were* true? Everything he'd seen. The things he thought he'd done. On the one hand he had to know. Had to put this missing piece of his puzzle finally into place. But then, maybe it would be better just to live and let die. To let Old Stan go and work on who he wanted to be from now on. Forget the past. Concentrate on the here and now.

With a sigh, Stan sat down again. His curiosity won out—that and the remote chance that Uphir might actually know something. Maybe he could explain all the strange things that were happening to him.

"You're no gentleman," Stan began. "I saw what you did. What you do. Who the hell knows?" He threw his hands in the air, admitting defeat, then let them fall with a slap against the arms of the leather chair.

Dr. Uphir sat back again and crossed his legs. "So then you know who I am. Or at least where I'm coming from. Are you ready to find out who *you* really are?"

"First you tell me how you know so much about me." Stan leaned over and snatched his file off the end table where Uphir had set it down. He flipped it open roughly, tearing through the pages. His mug shot, all of Abigail's notes. Nothing surprising here, and no details about his visions. Not one word, in fact.

He tossed the folder back at Uphir and waited for an answer.

The doctor straightened out the papers, then put the folder on the table again. "I know what you see because I know that trick too, Stan. When I touch people, I can see their thoughts.

Not their hopes and dreams but their biggest fears. Their most gnawing worries. Yours is that you think you're crazy. You think you tried to kill yourself, and somehow you came back wrong."

Uphir let out a low chuckle that raised the hairs on the back of Stan's neck.

"But that can't be further from the truth. You didn't come *back*, Stan. You just *came*. You aren't from this plane of existence, and you didn't jump off any bridge. You fell from heaven itself. The real Stan Foster—well, he just happened to be in the right place at the right time. You could say he met you on the way down, and only one of you came back up."

Now it was Stan's turn to laugh, so hard he threw back his head to let it out. "That is some crazy shit, Doc." He looked at Uphir. The little man's face soured. The corners of his mouth turned downward.

"I'll tell you what's *crazy*," the doctor suddenly hissed, leaning forward almost right out of his chair. "It's crazy that you decided to come here in the first place. Oh, God's prodigal child, his eternal rebel, his black sheep. I don't know why you're always looking to get back in his good graces. As if what you have isn't enough. As if this—"

Uphir raised his arms in a flourish, and the room disappeared. The deafening roar of flames filled Stan's ears, and searing heat burned his eyes. He raised his arm, shielding his face from the scorching air. All around him was a vast desert, red dirt and dark sky. At his feet was the pit of bodies. Writhing. Calling out in agony and despair. Those who lived clawed and climbed over those who had already died. Flesh torn and bodies burnt. Slick with blood, they tried to get out. But they never would.

"This kingdom isn't enough for you." Uphir's voice sounded sad, almost defeated. Stan blinked his eyes hard, and when he opened them again, the room had gone back to normal. The doctor sat across from him. "I never understood that, my lord. How, with all of hell under your command, you could be so unsatisfied. How could you ever want any more than that?"

Stan laughed again, this time short and hard. In disbelief, not amusement at the doctor's words. "Are you saying—" But he couldn't complete the thought. Couldn't even comprehend it in his mind.

"I'm saying you are the prince of darkness," Uphir said in a low voice, bowing his head reverentially. "You are Satan himself. And I, your humble servant for so many centuries, I have come here to bring you back to your rightful throne."

Stan laughed again. Loud and long, but this time out of fear. Confusion. Disbelief. A mix of emotions he could not get a hold on as they bubbled and roiled around in his brain.

"The prince of darkness!" Tears leaked from his eyes, from the laughter and from the sheer horror of the situation. He didn't want to believe what Uphir said, but the idea pushed its way in. Forcing him to open up, to consider the possibility. That he was what, a demon from another world? The devil himself, exiled on earth?

He had to stand up. Move his body, work these feelings out. He paced the floor between the chairs, stumbling as the absurdity of the situation threatened to pull him down. Stan stooped, hands on his knees, and took a few deep breaths.

This isn't real, he told himself, raising his eyes to look out the window. Letting the bright, hot sunshine soothe him. *Don't believe a word he says. He's tricking you.* The thought didn't ring true, but he clung to it nonetheless. It was all that kept him from opening that window and jumping again.

He stood up again, ran a hand roughly through his hair. Ready to bolt out the door, leave this place, and get as far as possible from the doctor. Stan opened his mouth to speak, but when he looked at Uphir, when he saw that damning fire in his eyes…no words would come to him. His body immobilized. All his conviction gone.

"Why am I here then?" He sat down. His voice sounded distant and weak. "If I'm…if I'm really *Satan*, why am I here on earth?"

Uphir sat back and sighed. "You were arguing with the Almighty. Telling him mankind doesn't need him anymore. Doesn't love him. Claimed you have more influence over humans than he does, that they're all evil creatures by nature."

"And?"

Uphir shrugged. "And he cast you out for your insolence. As punishment, he made you human."

Stan recoiled as if he'd been hit in the gut with the force of mankind as a whole. Breathless, he lifted his knees, instinctively curling to a fetal position. Head spinning, tunnel vision. An old, familiar blackness looming right behind his eyes. None of this made sense. Even if he could accept the doctor's story, there were too many loopholes in it.

Finally his lungs filled with air. "What about the memory I had this morning? Of painting those teenage girls and hiding the pictures in the garage?"

"That was a lie." Uphir leaned forward again. His voice took on the therapist tone, soft and sanguine. "A vestige of the other soul who once lived in that body. He was a real person, remember, with a life before you came along."

"And I took it away from him?" Stan swallowed hard. "Would he have lived if I hadn't—if I hadn't taken over his body?"

Uphir shook his head. "He was a troubled soul. If it wasn't the bridge, it would have been something else. Booze, women, the shotgun he kept in the bathroom under the sink…"

Stan's mind flashed to it. He'd been looking for a towel and found it in the back of the cabinet, rolled up in an old flannel shirt. He'd left it there. Hadn't told anyone about it. Decided it would be a little secret between Old Stan and himself.

"How do you know about that?" he asked but didn't really want a reply. He was getting really tired of this game, of this so-called doctor messing with his mind. He closed his eyes and let out an exasperated moan, then looked back at Uphir. "And who are you anyway? You never answered that."

The doctor lowered his gaze again. "I was your army's doctor. Your medic, if you will. I have fought by your side for eons, my lord."

"Then why were you killing people? I saw you. You walked by them, and they fell down dead. If you're a doctor, shouldn't you be helping them, not making things worse?"

Uphir sat back and folded his hands in his lap. "Things work differently down there. Almost as if they're in reverse. Light and dark, good and evil…healing and hurting…it's all in the contrast, Stan. As an artist you should know how that works."

"If what you say is true then I'm not an artist. I'm…I'm nothing. I'm a black hole. A destroyer. An entity of evil with no hope." The words felt strange as he said them. He hung his head. "Ah, hell. I don't know what I am."

"You are not *nothing*, my lord." Uphir's face lit up like a child who's caught Santa leaving presents for him under the tree. "You are a *king*. A *ruler* of all you survey."

"I don't feel very regal right now." Stan sniffed, blinking back tears again.

Uphir shook his head. "Well, of course not. Not in that human body." He made a *tsk* sound, showing his distaste for all things humankind. "But in your true form, you are magnificent. Tall and grand and proud. A sight to behold. Terrifying and majestic all at the same time."

"And you. What do *you* really look like?" Stan squinted at the doctor, trying to remember if he'd seen his face in the vision when he'd first entered the office. He'd known it was Uphir; he'd felt his presence. But what he looked like in the shadowy hallucination Stan couldn't place.

Uphir sat up straight in his chair. Folded his hands on his lap and raised his chin. A very proud pose. "I am nothing compared to your greatness, though I believe my appearance is commanding of respect. At least that's how others react when they see my face." He leaned forward then and placed his fingers on the back of Stan's hand.

"What—" Stan began, but that was all he could say. The doctor's face. It had changed. The black goatee remained, but the hair spread out across his face. He was some sort of animal. Black pupils transformed into horizontal slits, and sleek, bone-smooth horns rose up from his brow, curling back along his body in loops down to his waist. His hand on Stan's felt suddenly cold and rough. Stan looked down. The hand had turned black, each nail a ball of rock embedded in hard, leathery flesh.

Stan pulled away and jumped up, holding his hand to his chest as if he'd been scalded. "What—" he said again. It was all he could muster.

Uphir simply sat back in his chair, grinning and rubbing his beard in thought. "You wanted to see me." He held out his hand, palm up. "Now you have."

"No. No." Stan was at his breaking point. Since he'd woken up by the river, he'd seen some strange things—a psych ward full of Jesus freaks, dreams of torturous death, and visions of every sin under the sun—but this was more than he could take. A man turned into beast right before his eyes. Maybe he needed medication again. Another evaluation. Glancing out the window, he thought about getting a cab uptown, checking himself into St. Luke's again.

"I told you your female friend can't help you." Uphir was standing at his side. Stan did a double take, jumping back and away from the smaller man. When had he stood up? How had he gotten there?

"You stay away from me," Stan said, holding a hand out toward the doctor. As if that could ward him away. "Whatever you are—whatever you think I am—you just keep it to yourself, okay?" As he spoke, he began to back his way toward the office door. "You've got something very wrong going on here, and I don't want any part of it."

Uphir smiled darkly. "It's a little too late for that," he said as Stan inched his way across the room. Reached the door. Threw it open and glanced out at the empty waiting room that lay beyond.

He looked back at the doctor. "I mean it. You stay away from me." Then he ran, through to the hallway and out into the fresh air. Uphir's maniacal laughter rang in his ears the whole way.

TWENTY

The feel of the sledgehammer crashing through the statue's hard, plastic core was very, very satisfying. Stan raised the heavy tool above his head again and again, letting it fall down through the woman's head and torso until they were broken in shards, then he swept her legs at the knees. For a brief moment he wondered if he'd based this one on a real person. Maybe she was Old Stan's girlfriend. Or his mother. Well, now she was a pile of scrap. He moved on to the next piece. The man-dog. He started at the tail, swinging the hammer at it like a golf club.

Within half an hour, he'd reduced who knew how many years of work to a trail of rubble stretching from one end of the loft to the other. The body of Old Stan's work, the mannequins and statues, the pits of dried tar and plumes of metallic flame. All of it demolished. A fire burned in a metal trashcan in the center, fueled by every piece of paper Stan could find in the place. Watercolors, oils, charcoals. Even his pencil sketches for the upcoming show in Brooklyn. Every bit of it gone. Reduced to cinders.

Leaning against the kitchen counter, the sledgehammer propped on his shoulder and beer bottle at his lips, Stan surveyed his work.

"And lo, he saw it was good." Chuckling, he took out his iPhone and snapped a pic for posterity. Just as it finished saving, the phone rang.

He put the speaker on. "What?"

"Nice to hear your voice too." It was Lilith, but he already knew that. She'd put her own picture in for the caller ID. Her cold green eyes glaring out at him every time she rang.

"What do you want?" Stan finished off his beer, then tossed the bottle high in the air. It almost reached the cathedral ceiling, then landed in the middle of the mess down below. It shattered on a dismembered foot.

"I want to know what you're doing, Stan. It's my job to keep tabs on you. Remember?"

"What am I doing?" He laid the hammer down across the kitchen counter, then went to the fridge to get another drink. Popped the cap and took a long swig before answering. "Just doing a little housecleaning."

Bringing the phone with him, he wandered through the maze of trash, kicking pieces of molded silicone out of his way as he went. Finally he reached the trash can. The flames had receded. His artwork lay in the bottom, a pile of gray ashes.

"You? Cleaning?" Lilith laughed at him. That was the thing about her—she never laughed *with* Stan. Only at him. As if everything he said was a joke. His very existence proof that some higher power had a rotten sense of humor. "I'll believe that when I see it."

Stan smirked to himself. Thought about sending her the picture he'd just taken but then considered the shit storm it would start. Best to let her see it for herself whenever she showed up at the loft, which she inevitably did at some point every day. Couldn't go long without checking on her pet.

"So what do you want?" he asked again, tossing his second empty bottle into the garbage can. Sparks flew up as it hit a mound of embers.

"I want to know how your appointment with the therapist went."

A cold fear washed over Stan. Squinting his eyes closed, he

remembered the doctor's face—not how he looked as a human but as that other thing. The long, trailing horns, the matted black hair. "It, uh," he mumbled, a sharp pain stabbing through his head. "It was fine."

He walked out of the pile of his demolished art. Went over to the window. Outside the sun was setting, casting pink and orange hues across the sky. Women walking by in short shorts. A busker with a guitar playing his heart out on the corner, T-shirt stained with sweat. So much life out there. So many people unaware of all the bad things that lurked all around them.

"That's all? It was fine?" Lilith's voice sounded even more grating than usual, and he wanted to hang up on her. But that would only bring her to the loft faster. Lilith would not be ignored, and the man who tried would have hell to pay. And he didn't want her there. Not yet. Not until he could think of some good excuse. He glanced behind him, suddenly feeling a flicker of doubt about what he'd done.

"I'm not sure he's right for me. He seemed..." He trailed off. Just how much should he tell her about Uphir? He remembered the visions he'd had of Lilith. Surrounded by black birds, wearing a crown of thorns. Sitting on a golden throne. Was that—what had Uphir called it—her true form? If Stan really was Satan— an idea he couldn't even think of without a surge of panicked laughter rising in his throat—was Lilith some sort of demon too? An evil queen, maybe his equal in the underworld?

"He was *what*, Stan?" she snapped, drawing him out of his head. "What's going on over there? Are you sick or something? You've got to get yourself together. Have you started on your pieces for the show yet?"

Stan breathed out hard, thankful for the change in topic. "I did some sketches, but I scrapped them. Wasn't happy with how they were turning out."

"You've got to get on this. The show is in three weeks. Do you know how hard I worked to get this for you?"

As Lilith launched into her usual tirade about money and deadlines, Stan sank down to the floor and sat there, legs crossed and eyes closed. He held the phone to his forehead. Muffling her voice, and the cool glass felt good against his skin.

What am I doing here? Not just in the loft, or in New York, but on the planet earth. No matter who he was—Old Stan, New Stan, even Satan himself—he had survived an attempt on his life. Most people would look at that and see a second chance. Find some reason why they'd been spared the agony of self-inflicted death.

But not Stan. He'd been out of the hospital for a month, and so far he'd found no good reason to exist at all. Yes, he made this so-called art. And people loved it. Not everyone but enough to make it worthwhile. Could he say he brought happiness to people's lives? Maybe that was his purpose. If it was, he didn't feel fulfilled. In fact he felt nothing at all. Or maybe too much. A jumble of emotions swung back and forth through his mind as quickly as the minutes passed.

Who am I? Who am I? Who am I? He'd thought he was making headway on that. Stan Foster, the artist. Lived in the East Village. Liked microbrews and walking the streets of New York City late at night. When all the freaks came out. He knew he was one of them. Maybe not in this life but in his previous incarnation. Whoever—or whatever—that might have been.

"I have to go, Lilith." Suddenly he couldn't listen to her anymore. Didn't want to hear her blunt demands. On his time, on his body, on his soul. He just wanted to be alone. Try to figure out his thoughts. "Talk to you later." He hung up the phone and slid it across the floor. It skidded into the mess and disappeared.

Standing up, Stan brushed dust and dirt off his jeans, the

remnants of his life's work. Or somebody else's. No matter how hard he had tried, he'd never felt a connection to this art. A mild dislike, maybe, and admiration for the technique. But that had been all he'd mustered. He felt more now, he realized, that it lay in shreds across the floor. Pity for the wasted work, but also a sense of relief. These specters that had loomed over him day and night, glaring at him with black, unseeing eyes. They could no longer haunt him now. No more reminders of his dark side. The one he didn't want to face.

At least that was what he hoped. Looking at the carnage, he swore he could still feel them watching him. Could hear them whispering. Telling him who he really was.

The doorbell buzzed, and he jumped. *Probably Lilith*, he thought then remembered that she had a key. She always let herself in. Though he didn't want company, curiosity got the better of him, and he shuffled to the intercom. Turned on the video monitor. Abigail's face appeared.

He hadn't seen her in days, and the sight of her made his face flush. She looked washed out on the black-and-white screen but beautiful as ever. Blonde hair piled in a high, messy bun. No makeup, but she looked so good. Her face relaxed and soft, unaware that anyone was watching her.

Stan turned away from the screen. With the black clouds swirling in his head and this mess he'd made of things, he knew he shouldn't let her in. But the thought of just putting his hand on her cheek. Her arms closing around him. He needed that safety now, that rock in the middle of this stormy sea. He turned back and watched her for a moment more, heart aching at the sight of her. He pressed a button, and the downstairs door unlocked. Abigail went inside.

He stood inside the loft's door, ready to open when she knocked. His stomach was a nest of butterflies, all clamoring to get out at once. He would see her again, and he would touch her, and everything would be okay. She would understand what he was going through and give him the comfort he craved.

Or maybe she would just think he'd gone completely mad.

Looking back over the loft, his heart sank. How could he have let her in? Abby couldn't see this. What he'd done here. This was no artist's whim, no funny joke. It was a visible, physical representation of the psychotic nature of his mind. She'd have him committed again, probably in a padded cell.

In a straight jacket too, a voice in his head whispered. Just in case he got any more bright ideas about smashing things.

When she did knock, he hesitated. He'd made a big mistake. In a panic he ran through the loft, picking up chunks and scraps, piling them in his arms until he couldn't hold any more. He dumped them all in the trash, paying no mind to the fire that still smoldered.

Abigail knocked again. Louder this time, and more beats. "Stan?" she called.

"Uh, coming," he replied, standing amid the rubble. The world seemed to spin around him, fast then faster, pulling his thoughts along at a breakneck pace. One moment he wanted to cry, the next scream. He felt like he could take the whole building down with his sledgehammer, then cursed himself for having the thought.

This is Uphir's fault. He remembered the doctor's gleaming eyes. The vision of the room on fire. Something had happened to Stan in that office. The doctor had hypnotized him. Planted bad seeds in his head. Balling his hands into fists, he beat his skull until it throbbed. Gripped his hair and pulled out strands. The pain helped him focus. He bent down and resumed collecting his decimated art.

"Stan? Are you okay in there?" Abigail's voice again. Muffled by the heavy door. "Please, can you let me in?"

Finally Stan stopped, delivering his last bundle into the garbage can. The floor was still covered. He'd barely made a dent. This was bad. This was all wrong. Why had he done this? Ruined all that work.

"Stan?"

He held his head again, trying to stop his mind from spinning. Stop the voices from talking. He marched over to the door, unlocked it, and swung it open fast. "I'm here, okay? I'm fine."

Abigail stared at him. Calmly, unemotionally. Just like a shrink would. "Alright. I just wanted to make sure. You haven't been answering my calls. I tried all afternoon." She paused, waiting for him to reply. He couldn't even look at her. Just leaned against the doorjamb and shoved his dirty hands in his pockets.

"I can leave if—" she began. Then Stan saw her peering over his shoulder. His body tensed, and he stood up straight. "Stan, what's going on here? What happened—"

"I said I'm fine," he spat. Inexplicable rage running through his every nerve. How dare she get involved in this? Sticking her nose where it didn't belong. Treating him like a crazy person.

Don't trust her. The voice whispered to him again. Pushing the thought deep into his mind.

Abigail took a step closer. "Stan, can you just let me in? We can talk about it."

In an instant he reached out and grabbed her shoulders, forcing her to stop. Her mouth opened, her eyes grew wide. Brows lowered in confusion, she just looked at him. Another pain pierced his brain, and in a flash he saw her again—younger Abigail, a lithe, beautiful teen girl. Sixteen, maybe fifteen. Just beginning to blossom. Fair skin and light hair, just as she had now. She was in a small bathroom. White tiles on the floor. She held her dad's shirt, his name embroidered over the breast pocket: *Carl*. There was blood on the sleeves, and it transferred to her trembling fingers. She wiped it on her jeans as she began to sob.

"I said I'm fine," Stan repeated, the words seething out through his clenched teeth. Trying to make the vision stop. "I just want to be alone."

Abigail appeared shaken to the core. She nodded. "Okay." Her voice was gentle—too much so. Stan thought she sounded meek. Vulnerable and weak. How could he have been so attracted to her? "I understand, Stan. But you know I can help you if—"

"Stop! Stop fucking analyzing me!" His voice boomed as he lifted her up and threw her across the room. Her body like a rag doll flying through the air. A discarded toy. On the other side she hit a wall, then slid down it into a pile of trash. Tears spilled from her eyes. She opened her mouth to speak, but the wind had gone out of her lungs.

Stan stayed near the door. Watching her suffer. His own chest heaving with deep, labored breath. Blood boiling. A fire igniting in his mind.

"I," Abigail began, but stopped. The shock was obvious on her face. She was confused, in pain. Bewildered. Stan got a vague sort of thrill from it. From watching her stumble to her feet, a hand on her lower back. Her black jeans were dusted white, her T-shirt slipping off her shoulder. Hair all askew, delicate face twisted and questioning.

She began to walk toward Stan. Holding a hand out toward him, as if that would keep him at bay. "I don't know what's wrong with you. But this is not the Stan I know. Please, just let me help you."

He swore he saw her reaching into her pocket. Probably getting her cell phone to call her cronies at the psych ward. Well, they wouldn't take him again.

"Get out!" he whispered, his eyes narrowing to slits. The storm in his head brewing. The voices all talking at once. He moved across the loft, head down, feet moving quickly. When he looked back, Abigail was still there.

"Get out," he roared, so loudly he swore he saw the walls shake. He laughed then, low and growling. The most evil sound he'd ever heard. Maybe Uphir had been on to something.

In the center of the loft, Abigail covered her ears, her tears beginning anew. One last look at Stan, then she ran back to the door and down the hallway. He watched her go. Happy she was gone.

At least that was what he told himself.

TWENTY-ONE

Abigail's hand shook as she spun through the Rolodex. Looking for Dr. Uphir's card. She found it, pulled it from the deck, read it over. *Specializing in suppressed memories, post-traumatic stress disorder.* He'd seemed so perfect for Stan. Now she wondered if he'd even gone to see this new doctor at all.

The thought of Stan sent a shiver down her back, and she closed her eyes. Put a hand up to her aching forehead, massaging it with trembling fingers. Willing the images that flooded her brain to go away. It didn't work. She still saw the rage in Stan's eyes as he put his hands on her, the snarl on his lips when he hurled her across the room. Heard the crack of her back as she'd hit the wall, the thump of her body crumpling onto the floor. Tears sprang to her eyes as a vise closed around her heart.

How could he do this to me? She'd asked herself the question a hundred times already in the couple of hours since she'd fled the loft, running all the way to the subway without ever looking behind her. She didn't want to admit it, not even now, but she'd been afraid of Stan. Scared he would follow her. Hurt her again. Maybe kill her. His anger had been that strong. She hadn't just seen it on his face; she'd felt it in his grip, in the heat rising off of his body in waves. Looking into his eyes, she'd seen someone there—something, maybe, down deep inside—that was not the person she had come to know. Stan Foster was a gentle soul. Confused and damaged, maybe, but who wasn't in today's world?

Or maybe he wasn't so soft. Maybe she had just wanted to

see him that way. She opened her eyes, shook her head back and forth a little. Abigail had no idea what to think anymore.

The phone to her ear, she heard the ringing on the other end before she even realized she'd dialed a number. In her other hand she flicked Uphir's Rolodex card with her thumb, the gentle snapping sound like white noise, soothing her troubled nerves.

"Hello," a voice finally said on the other end of the line. Not a question, as most people made it sound when they answered the phone. This was a statement. As if he knew who she was and that she would call.

"Dr. Uphir?" Abby asked, just to be sure.

"Yes." Again sounding sure of himself. He said no more, awaiting her reply.

Abigail cleared her throat. "This is Dr. Petrus from St. Luke's. I'm calling about Stan Foster? I referred him to you last week."

"Ah, yes." Now a warmth came through in the man's voice, but there was something off about it. Abigail couldn't quite put her finger on it, but something about the tone he used just wasn't…genuine. "Mr. Foster. I met him this afternoon. Interesting case. I'm glad you sent him to me."

She sat back in her chair. So Stan did go in. But what had happened after that? How had he ended up in a trashed apartment with violence on his mind? "How did your session go?"

Uphir paused. Abigail listened to him breathing. Slow and even, long inhales. "Stan is a complex creature," he said at last. "I think it will take a while to unwind him, to find out what makes him tick." Uphir chuckled lightly. "However, it is obvious he wants to learn more about himself. He has his conflicts, but I don't think it's anything we can't overcome eventually."

The knot in her chest loosened up just a little bit. As confused as she was about Stan at the moment, this news was good to hear. Despite what he'd done to her, she cared about him, and she wanted him to get the help he needed. This anger, this violence he'd shown was uncharacteristic of him. There had to be something that set him off, something that could be unraveled given the right approach and sufficient amount of time.

"Has he mentioned his visions to you?"

Uphir's question made Abby's heart skip a beat. The vise tightened up again a little bit. Stan hadn't mentioned them in a while. She'd hoped they had gone away. In truth she'd been too afraid to ask. "Yes, he has. But I haven't formed an opinion on them yet. I have a feeling they're stress-related. Stan's under a lot of pressure, with his work and with trying to piece his life together." Abigail swallowed hard. "Did he talk to you about them too?"

"Yes, he did. In fact I believe he had one while he was here. And judging by his reaction, he certainly thinks they're real. In fact he seemed quite scared. His response to what he believed he saw was…quite visceral."

Abby sat forward again. Picked up Uphir's card and resumed flicking it. This was more serious than she'd thought. Not just an artist's imagination run wild but perhaps a true psychotic disorder. She thought back to the notes she'd made at their various sessions. Bipolar. Schizophrenic. Delusional. She'd never decided on one, but it was clear that something was not working right in Stan's head. This Uphir just gave her objective proof of that.

"I was afraid this would happen," she said, her voice sounding grave even to herself. "I had my doubts about stopping his medication when he was discharged. The hallucinations—his visions—had started while he was a patient here. At least he didn't remember having them before. Before he jumped off the bridge, that was. I gave him Risperdal to try to counteract whatever psychosis might have been causing them, and Xanax PRN for anxiety. They didn't seem to do much even when I increased the dosages. So I didn't see any sense in his continuing to take them."

"Don't beat yourself up over that. We all make professional calls we end up questioning later. I'm sure you did the best for Stan you could at the time. Now I'm sure I can help him move toward the breakthrough he needs."

Abigail sighed and put her forehead onto her hand again. The headache was lessening, but her thoughts still felt muddy. "Do you think he should be medicated? What diagnosis would you give?" She was grabbing at straws here. Begging for an answer. A solution. All while cursing herself—again—for dismissing Stan from her care. For letting her emotions win.

"Dr. Petrus," Uphir began. The stiffness returned to his voice. As if he tired of the conversation and wanted her off the phone. "I'm afraid I've said too much already. You know in our field, we must strictly adhere to patient confidentiality. As a professional courtesy, I feel I've been more than agreeable to your line of questions. However, I'm afraid this is where it ends."

"Please," she replied before even thinking about it. She didn't want him to hang up. "I'm not asking for any privileged information here. I just want what's best for Stan. And I'm not sure what that is anymore." Her voice cracked as she finished. "I'm just wondering what your professional opinion is."

"Dr. Petrus, I know you're involved with this patient." Uphir's voice was low. Not accusatory but something else. Disapproving. No, not even that. Disgusted. "And I imagine that clouds your judgment. But I assure you he's in good hands with me. I can tell already he is on the verge of a major breakthrough. He simply needs to...accept who he is. He must confront his past and deal with the truth. Once he can do that, he can move on and be who he is truly meant to be."

Abigail knew he was right. She had no idea how Uphir had found out about her feelings for Stan—had Stan told him? Heat rushed to her face at the thought—but they clearly were a detriment. They clouded her ability to think, her usual talent for accurate diagnosis. She'd always prided herself on that, on the way she could really get inside a patient's head. No matter how complicated they seemed, no matter how obscure their ailment. She could always pull it out of them and treat them in the way that would help them most. This was the one and only thing she'd ever wanted to do for Stan—and the only thing she could never grasp. He'd been a puzzle from the start, and in the weeks she'd known him, he'd grown even more so. And the further she entwined herself emotionally, the less she could see the trees. Inside this maze she was navigating with Stan, everything was forest now.

"I appreciate that," she said quietly to Uphir. What he said made sense. But there was something about his tone that disturbed her. He seemed almost too eager. As if he had some vested interest in Stan's recovery. Was Uphir trying to help him? Or was he like Lilith—manipulating Stan into what she wanted him to be? Maybe Abby shouldn't have sent Stan to Uphir. She didn't know the doctor. Come to think of it, now that she looked at his card again, she wasn't even sure how it had gotten into her Rolodex.

Stop being paranoid, she told herself, shaking the thoughts from her head. She wanted to work with Uphir on this. Getting Stan back to himself, to the life he was meant to live. But she couldn't be involved directly. Not in a professional capacity. It just wasn't meant to be.

She took a deep breath and closed her eyes. She just had to let it go.

"Thanks for your time, Doctor," she said, then hung up the

phone abruptly. Put Uphir's card back in her Rolodex, stood up, and grabbed her bag. She had to get out of here, away from the smell of medicine, the sounds of insanity. Somebody wailing down the hallway, the faint ticking of an IV machine. The little details she had grown so accustomed to suddenly felt like a rash on her skin, irritating and itchy and persistent. A reminder of this life she'd chosen, this job she'd dedicated herself to. The work that had brought her Stan, by a twist of fate or some sort of luck. He'd jumped into the Hudson and washed up into her office, with his head full of mystery and a heart hanging on his sleeve.

Or maybe that was Abigail. Her sister had always told her she fell too hard too fast, especially for men who were uniquely unavailable to her.

"Oh, Lily, for once you're right," she muttered with a completely humorless laugh. Then she shut off her office light and closed the door, locking it with a key. Ready to go home and forget about this place and the loneliness it brought her over and over again.

TWENTY-TWO

Grief is a strange thing. All the moping about, the sadness that feels permanently imprinted on the soul. The inexplicable tears, the lack of cravings for food, the increased appetite for booze. Stan wasn't sure he'd ever felt such a thing before. And he surely didn't like it now. He spent most days sleeping and every night wandering the streets, bumping into people just to get a glimpse of their inner demons. Hoping, somehow, it would help him understand his. It didn't, of course. Suffering simply begets suffering. Seeing others' evil deeds only made him reflect more deeply on his. The things he had seen in his dreams—the pit full of damaged bodies, the torture and pain and death he'd caused. That is, if he believed Uphir. Which he didn't quite, but still the thought was disturbing to him.

In the days since he'd trashed his loft and all his work, Stan had kept himself in isolation. Not that it was difficult. He only knew two people, and neither of them was speaking to him. Abby because he had thrown her across the room into a wall, Lilith because he'd stopped taking her calls and changed the locks on his door. None of that stopped her, of course. He still had at least a hundred missed calls at the end of each day, and she would stand out in the hallway for what felt like hours to Stan, banging and shouting and calling him filthy names.

"Open up, asshole!" she'd called to him just that morning. It had been just after dawn, verging on seven o'clock. He'd just gotten in from his nightly walk and was trying to sleep. "So help me, Stan, I will get a *fucking* crane with a *fucking* wrecking ball to get me in there if I have to. Are you listening, you worthless pile of shit?"

Eventually she gave up. Like she had every other time. As he listened to her voice receding—she continued her ranting as she strode back down the hall, and even out to her car—Stan felt a pang of satisfaction. Just a pinpoint of a vaguely mean-spirited glee. So Lilith couldn't get what she wanted. She couldn't make her dog come when she snapped her fingers. There was something very right in that, Stan felt, after all she had put him through. All the lies she'd told him. Who was she, anyway? Again visions floated through his mind at breakneck speed: Lilith sitting on a throne, gleaming, golden crown entangled in her shimmering hair. Dressed in dark-colored robes, commanding a murder of crows as they blackened out the sky, the far horizon. Were these images real? Was she a thing like him, some sort of spawn of the underworld, what Uphir would have him believe?

Stan put his pillow over his head. Wishing just for a second he would suffocate so he wouldn't have to deal with this. Not with Lilith, not with what he'd done to Abigail, not with himself for that matter. He was just growing tired of it. The grief, on top of the anger, confusion, and denial—all of it wore him down. He reached for the down comforter balled up at the end of the bed and pulled that up over the pillow too. And inside this cocoon, with all the world shut out of his head, finally he fell asleep.

A blinding ray of orange sunlight woke Stan several hours later. He'd thrown off the pillow and blanket at some point, his body now splayed across the naked bed. Sweat soaking the thin, white sheet. He turned away from the light, ran his dry tongue across his lips. Thinking he should have switched on the air before going to bed.

It took him a while to get up. The lack of food and his endless nightly walking left his muscles wracked, dried out, and stretched in ways they never had been before. At least not that he knew of. Another thing he wondered sometimes: what had Old Stan looked like? Had he been thin, like Stan was now? Sort of muscular and sinewy, like a starving artist with a gym membership. There had to be pictures somewhere. Now he wondered why he'd never looked. When he'd cased the loft in those first days, he hadn't come across any—no photo albums, no cell phone gallery, no web cam selfies saved on the PC. Which was odd for an artist, Stan thought. He should have been at least a little vain. Why had Old Stan been so camera shy?

He grabbed a bottle of Cricket Hill from the refrigerator, popped the top, and leaned against the counter as he drank. This new idea churning around inside his head. Had there been something wrong with him before? Bad teeth, an ugly scar? Something that made him self-conscious. Maybe that was part of the reason why he'd wanted to commit suicide. But what happened to it, then? How come he didn't have whatever it was now?

There was no simple answer to this. The only way to find out would be to find a picture. Probably Lilith had some, if any indeed existed. But Stan didn't want to talk to her. Maybe if he Googled himself. Something he should have done already anyway. And really, why hadn't he? The thought made him stop in mid-swallow. Looking out across the loft, still a mess though he'd trashed it almost a week ago, he knew the answer: maybe he didn't want to know. What he'd looked like before. Maybe he knew, subconsciously, that he would not like what he saw. Not because he'd been unattractive, or disfigured, or in some other way hard to look at. But because maybe *Old Stan had not looked like him.* Maybe physically he had been someone entirely different…which would mean Old Stan and New Stan were not the same person.

And that meant…maybe…Uphir had been right.

He finished the bottle and tossed it into the empty sink. Turning around, he took his iPhone from the counter behind him and clicked it on. Thirteen missed calls, all from Lilith. He swiped them away, then checked the time. Three fifteen. A reminder popped up about his appointment with Uphir at four. Stan hadn't forgotten about it, but he hadn't planned to go either. He'd had enough of that strange little man, his perfect goatee and his three-piece suit. Not to mention the terrible visions Stan had when the doctor touched him. Who knew what Uphir would have in store for him this time? What revelation he would bestow?

He tapped the screen to get rid of the reminder then tossed the phone back on the counter. He got another beer and headed back upstairs. Still a few hours until sunset. He could get some more sleep before his nightly walk.

<hr>

People call midnight the witching hour, but Stan was pretty sure it was more like two in the morning. Quarter past, to be exact. Shortly after the bars closed, flooding the sidewalks with their drunken masses. Sometimes Stan would just stand in the doorway of a closing club and let the hordes rush around him, stinking like cheap beer and sexual frustration. Their sweaty faces blank, limbs rubbing up against him. Men who cheated on their wives and their taxes. Killed people and got away with it. Had sex with their own daughters and had no remorse about it. The women were usually different—their sins were much more personal, more overlaid with shame. Hitting a child. Lying. But oh, they were murderers too. And sex fiends and addicts and thieves. The female species was not immune to rage, to depravity. Men and women had more in common than they would like to admit.

They look so human, Stan thought. *But they're all something else inside.*

Walking away, he wiped his mouth as if finishing a meal. But instead of feeling sated, he felt emptier inside. All the misery he saw thanks to this gift he had, this power to see into people's souls. It ate at him like acid. He found no comfort in it. Not even a prurient joy.

Stan found a bar that was still open and stopped in for a drink, hoping a gin and tonic with extra lime would clear the acrid taste from his tongue. It didn't; neither did a double whiskey. But they helped him relax at least, to the point where he no longer cared what he saw. Walking up Houston again, he kept his head down, concentrating on his feet. Left then right, putting one in front of the other. The alcohol burned in his chest, warming him and making him swerve. He bumped into passersby, ignoring both their protests and the visions he saw.

At the end of a long block, he saw the curb at his toes. He stopped. Looked up slowly at the traffic light. Still red, and rows of cars speeding by in a blur. He stared out, only vaguely wondering what to do next. Where he should walk to. What he should think about. His body was tired, his head just as bad, his heart the worst of all three. He considered just lying down in the gutter and trying to go back to sleep. Letting the traffic take him. Or the cops. Or whatever came first.

When the light changed, the cars stopped, and automatically

his feet began to move again. As if they'd done this so much, this late-night meandering, they knew what to do by themselves. Stan still kept his eyes on the ground, hypnotized by the crosswalk: white then black, white then black, each stripe carrying him farther toward the future, putting distance between himself and whoever he used to be.

On the other side, he stopped short when he collided with a body. Full on, chest to chest. A man, and he grabbed Stan's arms. Not angrily, just steadying him.

"Whoa." The guy's voice was gentle. Funny, because he seemed to be about eight feet tall. Stan looked up at him. Pink skin, a little wrinkled, silver hair. Black shirt with a white collar.

Oh, shit. A priest.

"Are you okay, son?" The older man loosened his grip on Stan's arms, bending down to look him in the eyes. His were blue and clear. Sparkling, even. Stan couldn't look at them. Too bright, too clear. Too full of hope.

"Fine," he mumbled, staring down once again at the dirty sidewalk. "Sorry." He began to walk away but only took half a step. The priest's fingers caught on the hem of his shirt's short sleeve. His knuckles brushing against Stan's bare bicep, giving him an icy jolt.

He stopped again. Both his feet and his heart. Stan tried to gasp for air, but for a moment his lungs wouldn't fill. He raised his eyes to the man, to his kind face. A smile played on the priest's lips. Beatific and placid, not a trace of anything sinister in it.

"Is everything okay?" he asked again. His voice just as soft as before. Stan closed his eyes so hard tears squeezed out, and he sucked in an enormous breath. He held it, waiting for the images to come. The visions of this man's sins. Who knew what kind of secrets a priest could hold in his heart?

But there was nothing there. The flood Stan expected just did not materialize. No blood and gore, no regrettable, immoral acts. Just a bright, white light. So brilliant it blinded him even with his eyes closed, even though it did not shine on him physically.

"I know something ails you," the priest went on, leaning in, dropping his voice to a whisper. "You're troubled. And you feel you have nowhere to turn."

Stan opened his eyes. Pain shot through his dilated pupils as they adjusted to the night again. Yanking his arm back, he rubbed the hot spot where the priest's skin had touched him. He stumbled back. The priest reached out. Then Stan began to run.

TWENTY-THREE

Heavy shoes pounding against the concrete sidewalks, breath coming out in rasps. Barely looking sideways as he crossed the streets, ducking and turning to keep from touching other people as he passed. Down through the Lower East Side, into Chinatown, crossing Canal Street. Over to the West Village. Stan kept up the pace like some sort of ghost chased him, as if running away from the devil. He almost laughed at the thought. As if he were running from himself.

Finally he faltered. Slowed his strides, bent down, and grabbed his knees. Upper body rising and falling with his hot, rapid breath. A couple squeezed by him on the sidewalk, dressed in black, a pair of phantoms. Bumped into him as they went by. Enough to knock him over, and he stretched out his hands to break the fall. Landing on a flight of steps, he turned around and sat, then brought his head down to rest on his knees.

A humid breeze blew, feeling cool against the sheen on his skin. He calmed himself, slowed his breathing. Closed his eyes and sank into the darkness. Trying to forget the light he'd seen when the priest had grabbed his arm. No, not just seen it. He'd felt it too. A clinging, enveloping warmth, covering him and filling him from inside out. The sensation was familiar although, as with most things these days, he couldn't put a finger on it. Where had he experienced it before? That sense of safety and security and…

He raised his head. Squinted his eyes open, blinking until they adjusted to the streetlamps, the floodlight on the stairs around him. Pouring down across his back like a waterfall. Everything so bright, so harsh. Not like the light the priest had given him. A gift, so soft and gentle, welcoming him home at last.

That feeling disturbed him still. Why had it been so good? Why had there been no misery? Everyone he'd touched so far, they'd all had their sad stories. Those strangers and their evil deeds, their transgressions. Uphir a walking plague, Abigail a witness to her father's gruesome death. Or whatever his visions of her meant. He'd seen them a few times, the white-tile bathroom, the oily, bloody blue shirt. The red on her fragile hands. Stan still didn't know what to make of it. Had Abigail walked in on something bad? An out-of-hand fight between her parents? A home invasion gone wrong? Maybe she'd been threatened too. Narrowly escaped ending up like her father did. Stan wasn't sure if he had died, but he'd lost a lot of blood.

What if she'd done it herself? He hadn't really thought of that. Maybe Abigail had killed her father. A bad seed, a child's fit of rage. She'd seemed so freaked out whenever he'd brought it up. So guarded. Unwilling to let him in. He wanted to share in her life, to learn about the past that had made her the woman she had become.

He almost laughed again. Why should she let him in? Why should she trust him? He didn't even trust himself. Plus he'd thrown her against a wall. No, he'd *hurled* her. It was a miracle she hadn't been hurt, not physically anyway. Emotionally was another story. Stan would never forget the look in her eyes when she'd gotten up from the floor, as she'd looked down at her dusty jeans, her shirt askew. In shock, disbelieving what he'd done. She'd been scared of him. Not even angry, just afraid of what she'd seen in his eyes. And oh, so incredibly sad. Just thinking about the tears pooling at the bottoms of her eyes, spilling drops down her porcelain cheeks, sent a shot through Stan's heart. As if he had one in there to begin with.

Maybe you are the devil.

He stood up. Time to start walking again. To run away from these thoughts as if he could escape them. But before his feet even touched the sidewalk, a wave of nausea hit him, followed by vertigo. Knocking him off balance again. He sank back onto the steps, this time on his knees. One hand on the stair before him, the other clutching his belly.

"Oh, God," he groaned. He felt like his insides were coming out. His whole body reversing itself. Too much alcohol, not enough food. And running a marathon in the middle of a heat wave wasn't too smart either. Muscles, joints, flesh, everything ached at once, and he groaned in agony. He retched bile from the pit of his stomach, spit it out on the steps. The floodlight still on him, like this was an interrogation. He raised his head, squinting into it, and gave it the finger.

And then pulled it back quick. "Fuck," he muttered. Standing at the top of the stairs, between two sets of dark-wooden double doors, was a statue of Jesus. Life-sized, a white robe, sad eyes painted vibrant blue. Looking right into Stan. Behind the statue there was a sign: Church of the Redeemer. Mass every Sunday at ten. Everyone welcome here.

Stan dropped his head again, resting it on his arms. Hands clasped together tight. He moaned again, insides still roiling, bitterness filling his mouth. He let more bile spill out, trailing in a sticky line from his bottom lip. Mixing with his feverish tears. This was it, he thought. This was as low as it got. Puking and crying, half drunk on the steps of a church. With Jesus silently judging him.

Finally he did laugh. Low and bitter, as if coming from the depth of an abyss. In a flash he saw it again: The pit. The bodies.

He stood before it, kicking them back in when they dared to try to escape. Stepping on their fingers as they clawed at the dry, red earth around the mouth of the hole. And laughing, laughing, laughing. The same sound that came out of him now.

"No, that's not me," he whimpered, scraping his forehead against the rough, concrete step of the church. Leaving a mark there, a raw spot like ashes on the first day of Lent. Snapping his head up, he looked at Jesus. "Please, just give me a chance."

No word from the stone god. No sparkle in his somber eyes.

"God," Stan groaned as he put his head back on the step. "I can't do this anymore. I can't be this thing." He sniffled, licked his lips. Face slick with sweat and tears. "I don't want the visions. I don't want the dreams. I just want to be normal." To be an average human, a mortal man. Just Stan, whatever that meant, whoever that was.

"Just give me a chance to find out," he whispered. "I'll do anything."

As if there were a God up there to hear his cries.

TWENTY-FOUR

The visions continued. Unbidden, harsh, and terrifying but at the same time exhilarating and fantastic. Flashes of light, the blackest depths. Faces that screamed and cried, lips that begged. For mercy, for salvation. But those things were not Stan's to give. As he witnessed these glimpses into another world, into hell on earth, he felt powerless to do anything to help these poor souls, and confusion: did he really want to help them anyway? After his revelation on the church steps, he'd expected a miracle of sorts, some relief of his own from this walking nightmare. Or, if not a miracle, at least a sign. A small change in his surroundings, his attitude. Something to let him know someone up there had been listening. That his breakdown had not been a waste of time. These visions not just an exercise in psychological torment.

But so far there had been nothing. Days passed, and still he felt lost in the world. Slept all day, wandered all night. Like a starving vampire, pressing his flesh against other people's just to feel something, to bring some sort of warmth back into his bones. The visions became more intense, the images more vivid, the crying a constant echo in his ears. The bodies he saw in his mind's eye, he could reach out and touch them. Smell the stench of their darkest fear. Everything was tangible, tactile. As if he were really there: Holding the wife's hand as she plunged a knife into her cheating husband's chest. Watching a playground full of bustling children through the pedophile's eyes. Feeling the jolt of the rapist's pulse as he closed his hand over his prey's mouth.

And always, always standing over the pit of bodies. That one never went away.

As Stan's visions became increasingly visceral, his need for them became more powerful as well. Like a drug he sought them out. A junkie at three in the morning, looking for a fix. Something just to help him breathe again. When the rush ran through his veins, he always felt sated, the emptiness in his heart gone at least for a moment. No matter how much it hurt him. No matter how little he understood why.

He hated this misery, but he couldn't deny the way it made him feel. The things that hurt other people most kept him nourished and alive. Unfortunately they didn't inspire him to work, and the Brooklyn Museum show was a week away. Or maybe less, he couldn't remember. In fact he just didn't care. Either way he was surprised Lilith had not been bothering him more about it. She'd given up on calling him a hundred times a day, and the texts had dwindled too. She'd only come to the loft once more, this time trying to sweet-talk her way in. Her voice cloying like rancid honey, all fake concern and sympathy. The sound disgusted Stan. Made him roll over in bed and pull the blanket over his head once more, hiding again from the world. Eventually she'd gone away, and that was the last he'd heard from her. Maybe he'd gotten that divine reprieve he'd needed after all.

The silence in Lilith's absence felt an awful lot like relief. Something like peace at last. With her gone, Stan's sleep was uninterrupted. Filled with horrid dreams, yes. But that was nothing out of the ordinary. Aside from the bodies in the pit and the occasional cameo by Uphir in his black robe, or Lilith on her golden throne, Stan was, for once, truly alone. When he did wake he would lie in bed, listening to nothing but the traffic outside, pigeons scraping their little talons against the skylight. A door slamming somewhere below. A fire engine flying past, sirens at full volume.

But no voices—not any that existed outside his head, anyway. Which was fine because in there he had more than enough company. Women screaming, begging. Children moaning and sobbing. Men whispering all sorts of evil, despicable things. Telling him what to do and whom to do it to.

"I won't," Stan said into the dark. "What kind of monster do you think I am?"

By that point he had stopped getting out of bed altogether. Stayed under the covers into the night, half lucid, these imaginary friends surrounding him like gawkers at a crime scene. He the body, sprawled on display, limbs bent at impossible angles, or all of him curled up into a fetal ball. Making himself as small as possible, hoping somehow he might disappear.

It didn't work. And the more he kept his eyes shut, the stronger the visions got. The louder the voices screamed. Until he began to believe they were reality, not some form of psychotic hallucination. Not scenes from the underworld, the souls he'd tortured in a past life. No, that wasn't possible. In the depths of his unmoving despair, he still insisted on that. He was not what Uphir said he was. What he feared he might truly be. Whenever that beast reared its ugly head, he simply stomped it down again, back into whatever recess of his psyche it existed in. The part that made up lies, that made him feel as though he couldn't even trust himself.

If he thought about it too much, this dark, circular logic, it made him laugh until he cried. Until his tired, hungry body shook, until he sunk his teeth into his dry lips to make it stop already. There was nothing funny about this. He thought he was losing his mind. Tittering like a madman, like a pervert standing at the schoolyard gate at a minute to three. Anticipating the rush when the bell rang. Then all hell would break loose.

Stan sat up in bed. The heat was unbearable in the loft. August had ended, September underway. An Indian summer with sweltering nights and humid days. He couldn't be sure which was which; even a glance out the window gave him no clue. The sky like an eggshell, fading to a muted orange-blue over the top of the city. Could have been dawn. Or twilight. Or somewhere in between, or another world. Stan didn't really care. Stumbling to the bathroom, he tried to take a piss but there was nothing left. In his hazy state, he marveled at how the body continues to feel the urge long after the human inside gives up.

Downstairs, Stan pulled open the refrigerator. The light from inside hit his face; he pulled back, crooking an elbow across his eyes. With his free hand he reached out, feeling around on the empty shelves until he located beer. One lonely bottle left. He closed the door then popped the bottle top and took a drink.

Followed by a long sigh. Even when everything was shit, a cold beer could almost make life seem alright. *Almost*, Stan thought, that urge to cackle coming back. He opened his eyes at last and looked out over the space of his loft. Still covered in his trashed work. The piles of silicone and mesh. Feathers and glitter and hair, the garbage can where he'd burned anything that accepted flame. Since that night with Abby—her back hitting the wall, her body crumpling to the floor—he hadn't done a thing to clean up. *Why bother?* he figured. None of it mattered now. Whatever his muse had been, that bitch was long gone. And he didn't want her back. The whole artist thing—what a sham that had been. He'd never felt right doing it. Now he was happy to admit he'd failed. Happy to let it go.

"Stan."

The voice was quiet and gentle. Clear. Not like the muddled wailing he heard in his head. He smacked his temple with the heel of his palm, then stuck a finger in his ear. Trying to make the voice go away. It didn't sound like the others, and he didn't trust it.

"Stan."

It came through louder this time. And so clear it could have been in the room. He looked around the loft, frightened for a moment that maybe he wasn't alone. Someone could have snuck in while he slept. Hell, someone could have lived there. He'd been so out of it, he wouldn't have known the difference.

But no. This place had airtight security. Even a human atom bomb like Lilith couldn't force her way in. Not without a crane and a wrecking ball, like she'd threatened the last time she'd come this way.

"Lilith," Stan said, his eyes narrowing at the door. Suddenly the voice made sense. It wasn't inside his head or even in the loft. It was out in the hallway, and it was her, trying to find a way in. Didn't she know? That trick didn't work on Stan. All that fake charm, the gentleness in her words. A lie, a scam. There was nothing sweet about Lilith. Nothing good in her heart. If she wanted in, it was for her own purposes, not because she worried about Stan. To her he was another horse she could whip until his work was done. Then she could reap the rewards.

"Fuck off, Lilith!" he shouted, his voice crackling in his still-dry throat. Bouncing off the empty walls, the mounds of waste. Stan took another drink and listened to the silence out in the hall, as if Lilith had turned away. Tucked her tail between her legs and gone home. Or back to the hole she had crawled out of.

Stan laughed again. This time it sounded less manic. More like a human noise. He was surprised he could make them anymore. Shrugging, he finished his beer, then left the bottle on the counter and headed toward the stairs. Back to bed, back to sleep. Back to his friends in the deep—

"Stan, please let me in."

He stopped, feet on the first and second steps. Turned his head back toward the door. The voice sounded different again. No longer saccharine sweet, the bad mother trying to lure out her idiot child. No, there was something more. A different timbre, a lighter tone and pitch. More pleading, less scolding. In fact it didn't sound like Lilith at all. If Stan didn't know any better, he would have said it was—

"Abby?" He said it anyway. The name dangling off his lips. Filling the air around him, making it hard to breathe.

"Stan, I need to talk to you."

Oh, it was definitely her. Stan's heart thumped against his ribs. He jumped back onto the floor and ran across the loft, legs shuffling through broken papier-mâché, feet getting caught up in swaths of cloth. He reached the door in a tangle, then stopped short and put a hand on it. As if he could touch her through the thick metal. Smell her scent. See into her clear, blue eyes.

"Abby?" he said again, a little more loudly now. He pictured her wearing a thin, summer shirt, leaning her forehead against the door just like he was. Mirror images. Her blonde hair falling to her shoulders, a mess of soft waves.

It would be so easy to let her in. Just turn the lock and pull.

He reached for the doorknob. Fingers closing around it.

"Abby, I don't know—"

The door thundered open against him. Hard steel battering his head, throwing his body back into the loft. He landed on half-crushed art, the dog's broken legs, a sledgehammer-shaped hole in its dangling human torso. Stan felt his back crack over it, heard the dull smack of his skull as it hit the concrete floor. He lay there watching the ceiling spin. Listening to the voices cry. Trying to figure out which part of this—if any of it—was actually real.

"Stan."

There was the voice again. But it wasn't Abigail's now. And he knew it never had been. Just a trick of his addled mind, a wish he'd never dared to speak. That she would come back to him, forgive him, grant him a second chance. Love him like he loved her even though he was a broken mess. But this was a pipe dream, a fantasy. Stan had known it all along. Abby had no need for him. Deserved better than him. An abusive amnesiac, a half-baked art peddler, a drunk and hallucinating maniac. And maybe the devil to boot. Stan stifled a laugh and a sob at the same time. Unsure which was appropriate here. All he did know was Abigail was better off without him. It was hard to admit, but he had to at least. He should have done so right from the start and saved them both a lot of trouble.

"You know you belong with me," the voice went on. Then Stan saw the blonde hair, the red lips. The creamy skin and light-green eyes. Lilith bent over him, towering in her stiletto heels. The low-cut neck of her black shirt falling open, revealing the bare curves of her breasts. Long, gold necklace with a heavy pendant—a talon? Some sort of claw—swinging over Stan's head. Back and forth, his eyes tracked it like a pendulum on a grandfather clock. Tick, tock. Tick, tock. His pathetic life ticking away.

"What are you doing here?" he managed, though it wasn't what he wanted to ask. What are you, where are you from? Who am I, and what am I doing here? Any of these would have been more fitting, would have possibly explained things to him. But he did not have the voice. Or the strength. With Lilith standing over him, he felt like he was being flattened to the ground.

"Why, I came to see you, Stan," Lilith purred, her voice like a velvet cloak brushing over Stan's face. Straddling him, bending her knees, ass up in the air. Face impossibly close to his. Like a predator, a beast in heat. "We need to work a few things out, you and me."

The display was disgusting to Stan, yet he couldn't look away. Her hot breath, her lips that looked stained with blood. All of it excited him. He squirmed underneath her, moving his hips in a way that he really didn't want to. Damn human body. No control over its base urges.

"What do we need to work out?" he asked her, just to keep the conversation moving. To get her to move away. But she didn't, just kept slithering over him like a serpent.

She grinned, showing all her teeth. Gleaming white, and were they—did they look a little pointy all of a sudden? Maybe they had been all along, and Stan hadn't noticed it. But how could he not have? The more he stared now, the more ferocious they looked. She ran her tongue over her teeth, leaving them wet and glistening.

"You need to *snap* yourself out of this," she told him, punctuating the word with a dart of her head. Her hair brushed the side of Stan's face, and he smelled a whiff of smoke. "This little mood you're going through. This isn't you, Stan. Not like you used to be. You've always been a take-charge guy. Now you're a shadow of yourself. Honestly, it disgusts me."

And with that she stood up. Quickly, like a cat springing to her feet. Stan looked up along the length of her legs, which were clad in black leather. He felt that bad stirring again and tried to sit up. Lilith put a foot on his chest and pressed down, the heel of her shoe digging into his ribs.

"You need to listen, *Stan*," she said, grinding it into his flesh. "I've had enough of this—this—act you've been putting on. This is not *you*. This is not who you were meant to be: living in filth, wandering the streets like a homeless man."

She took a quick breath, then raised her arms slowly until her hands were up above her head. A grand gesture, graceful like a ballet dancer, a black swan unfurling its enormous wings. Stan blinked. Lilith really did have wings. As her hands raised, sheaths of feathers fell into place, filling the space between her arms and her body. Dark as night, glossy as starlight. Fully stretched, she gave the wings a little shake. The feathers rustled, making a clicking, swishing sound that made Stan's head begin to ache.

"What the fuck?" he said, squeezing his eyes closed and putting the heel of his palm up to his forehead. "Li...Lilith?" He squinted back up at her. Back at whatever she was. In the seconds he'd withdrawn his glance, it seemed she had grown another six feet. The woman seemed enormously tall. But then, she wasn't a woman anymore. The wings had taken form, filled out, and widened to their full span. Her breast became downy and puffed, her feet transformed into bony, ebony talons. One scratched against the dirty wood of the floor at Stan's side, leaving a trail of three ragged ruts. The foot that had been on his chest now settled on his neck and cinched it roughly. He tried to turn his head, to look away, but the claws held him firmly in place. Instead he simply closed his eyes again. Willing this vision, this nightmare, to go away.

"Look at me, Stan. You need to see this," she said, her voice deep, echoing as if it came from a thousand miles away.

When he didn't respond, she tightened her grip on his neck. Bent down over him again. He felt her putrid, steaming breath. Smelled the dank stink of smoke.

"Look...at...me." Her whisper seeped into his skin, his bones, sent a chill up his aching spine. It was the most terrifying noise Stan had ever heard, death and destruction behind every word. Though he certainly didn't want to look, didn't want to see this monster Lilith had become, he seemed to have no choice in the matter. He fought to keep his eyes closed, but something beyond his control made them open wide. Until he stared her in the face. Right above his, the sharp teeth, the gleaming grin. Lilith's white skin and face remained, her golden hair a towering nest, a knotted gnarl. Her green eyes had turned to black, a dark, silvery fire within.

"See what I am, Stan," she went on. "Look at the real me."

"This isn't real," he whined, his voice tiny and frail in comparison. He tried to shake his head, to topple this vision from his mind. Lilith's talons pinned him down so he was unable to move.

"This isn't real," he repeated, unable to say anything else. "It can't be. You're just a hallucination." He thought of Abby, of how calm she had been when he'd told her about the visions he'd seen. The pit of bodies. The crimes and nightmares of strangers. She'd told him they were just dreams, that he shouldn't worry. Maybe she'd been right all along. Maybe he should—

"Don't you dare think I'm not real!" Lilith's voice thundered like the wrath of God. Her wings came down to cover Stan, brushing over his head, his entire body. Lulling him into a daze. He wondered how they could be so soft. Not at all like they appeared. All hard and shining like steel.

Then he felt her hand around his throat. Her human hand but rough and scaly like her feet. The nails grown impossibly long, digging into the skin under his jaw. Her fingers closed tighter and tighter, then lifted Stan off the floor until he stood up. His legs felt like jelly beneath him.

"I am the most real thing in your life," Lilith went on, still gripping Stan by the throat. Keeping him upright, a drunk who couldn't even stand on his own. "You think that doctor girl of yours is real? You think what she tells you is real?"

She laughed, and it sounded like the squawking of crows. Ear-piercing, soul-freezing. Stan cringed away from the noise, reaching up to cover his ears.

But he stopped the gesture just as his hands crossed his face. Pulled them back a little, took a good look. The skin had turned a dark shade, almost crimson, thick and leathery and dry. The fingernails were black, some broken off. Coarse, black hair ran from his palms up his arms, which took on the same shade. At the biceps the skin grew tight with muscle, then ropy with veins.

"What the fuck is happening here?" he managed to get out, looking back to Lilith again.

"Now you know what I am," she replied. "Now you know what you are. It's time for you to accept it, Stan. You're not some lowly artist who tried to kill himself. You're better than that. You are who you think you are. You're the king, baby. Look at yourself, Stan. Look!"

And with that she spun him around. A few feet away was the mirror, and as he caught his reflection he reflexively jumped back. "No!" The dark, crusty skin on his face. The yellow teeth, the red, beaming eyes. Bony nodules on his forehead, something akin to horns. This couldn't... This had to be a dream. Another vision, something his offbeat imagination had brought to him. Any minute now he would wake up still in bed upstairs, and the sun would just be going down. He could go out and walk for a while, have a few drinks. Maybe even work on some art. Anything to get the memory of this vision out of his head.

He closed his eyes, rubbed them. Thinking about a cold

beer and a hot meal. Yes, that would do the trick. But when he looked back, everything was the same.

Stan whirled around to face Lilith. She stood in the middle of the trashed loft, preening herself, posing like a queen. Stan took a step toward her. His cloven foot landed heavily on the hardwood floor.

"What did you do to me!" he demanded, his voice outgunning Lilith's by miles. Coming out of the bowels of the earth, fueled by millennia of anger and pain. Two emotions he could feel right now. It took all the strength he had—and from what he felt stirring in his thighs, his hands, his back, that was a considerable amount—not to run over and smash her against the wall. Crush her brittle bird bones with his hands. Leave her in a pile on the floor.

"I haven't done anything." Lilith was calm as ever, her demeanor slowly returning to the human form Stan knew. The eyes turning back to green, the teeth their normal pearly white. She even reached up to swipe a knuckle at the corner of her mouth, making sure her lipstick had not smudged. "Except make you see the truth for once."

As she walked across the loft, back over to him, her feathers quickly faded from sight, her feet in the stilettos once more. By the time she reached Stan, she looked just as she always did, like a dominatrix doing power lunch. She reached over and brushed his shoulder, as if straightening him up for a show.

"Don't touch me." He reached up and grabbed her wrist. His hand was now white again. The thick, dark nails gone and the hair too. Stan dropped her hand and spun around to the mirror. He was himself again too. Short, blondish hair, a few wrinkles around the eyes. The tired face, the half-dead eyes. Too many days sleeping, too many nights up late. Too little will to live.

"I'm sorry you found out this way." Lilith was behind him, putting her hands gently on him again. One on each shoulder, her face appearing beside his in the mirror. "I would have liked to tell you another way. But it seemed like the only way to get through to you." She cocked her head, smiled. An eerie calmness had come over her. Not that Stan had trusted her before, but he certainly didn't like this new attitude.

"Found out what?" he spat. But then thought better of it. Was it really worth arguing anymore? He'd seen the proof. Felt it in his own body. It wasn't just his outside that had changed; his mind had transformed too. Whatever Stan had become, it had felt very right to him. *Fuck.* He really didn't want to admit it. But in that dark body, Stan had felt right. More like himself than he had ever since he'd woken up by the river. For a moment things had made sense. And now—

There was no use denying it anymore. He was who Uphir had said he was. Stan was Satan.

He turned to face Lilith, and he took her hand.

TWENTY-FIVE

"Daddy!"

Abigail remembered the scream. Not just the sound but the feel of it in her throat, the way it filled the small bathroom as it left her lips. Bouncing off the white tiles, coming back to her unanswered. She hadn't called him "Daddy" in years, hadn't felt that sort of affection for him since she was a very small girl. Now it was the first thing to come to mind, the only word her mouth seemed able to form.

Her father lay lifeless on the floor. Half undressed, his blue shirt in a ball next to the toilet. He'd been getting ready to shower, just home from his shift at the local Sears. He'd worked there Abby's whole life, changing batteries and tires so she and her sister had toys, and clothes, and a home. So his wife didn't have to work, so she could stay at home and be a lazy bitch. That was what Abby had heard him say whenever the two argued.

She reached down and picked up the shirt. The thick, blue fabric scratched her hands. Abby held it out in front of her, like a gift she presented as she approached her father. His head next to the bathtub, knees curved around the cabinet under the sink. Behind him the wall was red, just like the shirt. It transferred to her hands, and Abigail rubbed the color off on her faded jeans.

"Daddy?" she said again, this time in a timid voice. She inched closer, afraid he might jump up and scare her. Like he'd done all the time when she was a little girl, hiding behind some piece of furniture so he could take her by surprise. She'd always laughed but only out of nervousness and fear. Deep down she hated that game. Too much truth in it, too much glee in her father's eyes when she started and screamed.

Now, with only a foot's length between her and the top of his head, she felt relieved that he didn't see her. His face was turned the other way, toward the wall where the red splotches hung in drops and splashes, some of them sliding down. On the floor, in the crevice where the wall and the floor met, some had started to pool.

"Daddy." Abigail crouched down, then reached over and touched his hair. He didn't stir; she grabbed his shoulder and shook a little. Still he didn't answer her. Not even a grumble or a shake of his fist to make her go away. Abigail knew all his little movements, these nuances and whims of his mood. The signals for her to steer clear or when it was safe to approach. But in this situation, he wasn't giving her any clues.

She lifted her skinny leg and stepped over her father's broad chest. She had to get in front of him, just to—

But she always stopped there. Couldn't let her memory go any further, couldn't see again what she'd seen then. In the years since it had happened—always *it*; she never could bring herself to say exactly what it had been—she'd never pictured his face. Or what had been left of it. The gnarl of tissue and blood, the smattering of brain and bone. Worse than anything she'd dissected in medical school, more gory than a horror movie.

And what had brought it on now, anyway? This memory, this terrible vision. She lay on the couch, eyes open, staring up at nothing. At her paintings, at the cracks in the ceiling. The ancient light fixture that never worked and her landlord refused to repair. Earbuds in, iPod on her favorite playlist lately. She'd titled it "Depressing Shit." The Smiths, the Cure, a little Billie Holliday. "The Drugs Don't Work" by the Verve. Radiohead's

"Fake Plastic Trees." Johnny Cash singing "Hurt." All songs that made her feel, even if the emotions weren't productive or helpful at all. It was better than being numb, like she'd been since she'd last seen Stan.

That's what it was, she thought. The thing that had triggered the memory. She'd been worrying about Stan again—not about how he was but about why he had hurt her so badly. And what he'd let happen to himself. Maybe she'd been wrong all along, and he wasn't a good guy. Maybe he was evil, a psychopath, even some sort of demon. She told herself these things, and she tried to believe them if only so she wouldn't have to admit it to herself: she'd fallen in love with Stan, but he wasn't the man she'd thought. Just like someone else she knew. The vision of her father's work shirt came back in a flash. She stuffed it down into her unconscious just like she'd done for so many years.

As far as Stan went, the problem was she didn't really believe it. That he was a bad person. That underneath his intelligent, insightful, and attractive exterior lurked a hideous troll. She'd never gotten that from him. Confusion, surely, but who in his position wouldn't be confused? And definitely some anger thrown in there. But again, that could have been a byproduct of his situation, and a reasonable one at that. When it came down to it, Abby could write off every one of Stan's undesirable quirks. Even the visions he had. He had survived jumping off a bridge. It was reasonable that he'd be left with some form of brain injury, and that could easily trigger what he saw as real but were actually hallucinations.

Hadn't she told him that? She thought so. Getting up from the sofa, she went into her bedroom and pulled her work bag out of the closet. Paged through some folders until she found Stan's. Yes, she'd brought his case home. Though she didn't feel good about it. She'd been putting it into the file cabinet in her office, and something had told her to stop. To take a second look at it. No one would need it there anyway—she had officially discharged him. Back when she'd thought they would have a relationship.

Abby sat down on the bed. Opened the file on her lap and began to read. First all Stan's intake forms. Not much to read, given that he'd had amnesia. Moving on to his psych eval. A floater from the department had seen him in the ER. Very minimal notes there too: "pt hungry," "pt has amnesia," "pt wants to know when he can have his clothes back."

It was only when Stan came to see her that anything real took place. Sitting back against her pile of pillows, she got comfortable and slowly went through what she'd written. Trying to remember the context in which she'd taken these notes. Occasionally she'd noted his mood: one day he'd seemed tense, another almost too relaxed. Not once had she written "angry," or "depressed," or anything negative for that matter. Because she'd never seen that side of him.

She sighed, blowing a lock of hair away from her face. "Or maybe you just didn't want to see it," she told herself, closing the folder again. She set it beside her on the bed, then sunk down into the covers. Cocooned herself inside them, then flapped them up like a parachute and let them fall. This reminded her of her childhood again, but she didn't let her mind go. Not there, not now. Not again.

She had to find something to do. Jumping out of the bed, she paced the floor beside it. Chewing on her thumbnail, thoughts racing at breakneck speed. She peered at Stan's file on the bed. Maybe she could go in to work. Get some overdue paperwork done. It wouldn't be the first time she'd spent a Saturday night in her office, all alone, just the DSM to keep her company. When she needed distraction, it was the best thing—filling out forms and processing treatment requests. Mind-numbing, mechanical work.

But that wouldn't do it this time. She was too hyped up, too anxious to sit behind her desk. So many thoughts in her head, so much to figure out. She looked at Stan's file again.

"No." She actually said it out loud, hoping her own stern tone would talk herself out of it. "You cannot go see Stan."

But just as she said his name, her stomach flipped. As if she were seeing him again for the first time. She closed her eyes, remembered him walking into her office at the hospital. Wearing his suit pants, his white shirt. Looking so completely sane. She smiled now even though she tried not to, and reached over and opened the folder. His mug shot was still clipped inside. Even in black and white his eyes sparkled. The hint of a smile played on his thick lips.

Her stomach did that trick again. Abigail closed the folder and shoved it under her pillow.

Then she put on her boots and headed out the door. Enough was enough. It was time to put this whole issue to rest, no matter how it played out.

Abigail walked over to Houston, then down to Stan's loft in the East Village. The warm, night air helped her clear her mind and formulate just what on earth she would say to him. If he even answered the door. She had no idea what his mental state was like these days or if he wanted to talk to her. Or throw her against the wall again. She hoped for the former but tried to prepare herself in case of the latter.

As she neared his building, she slowed her pace. Stopped just before the doorway, adjusted her shirt, and ran her fingers through her hair. She knew there was a video camera Stan could see her on, and she wanted to appear nonthreatening. Happy, even, if she could pull it off. Anything that would get him to let her inside for a while.

She rang his buzzer, then just stood there waiting. Shifting from foot to foot. Looking up and down the street. A few cars rolled by, a couple of people walking. Nothing out of the ordinary. No sign anything strange had occurred.

"Hello." Stan's voice came through the intercom, distant and monotone. Abigail cleared her throat and paused a moment.

"Stan? Hi, it's Abigail." She looked at the camera above, wondered if he'd turned on the monitor. "Do you think I could come in for a minute?"

A pause again. She waited for Stan to respond. After a few minutes and no answer had come, she took a step away. Getting ready to leave.

Then the door buzzed. She jumped toward it and swung it open before it stopped, before Stan changed his mind. In the lobby she went directly to the elevator and took it upstairs. Stood outside his door. Raised her fist to knock.

It creaked open before she had a chance. Stan's face appeared. He looked exhausted, sallow cheeks and dark circles under his eyes. And no spark at all in them. The fire that had been there once, something had put it out.

"Abby." He opened the door wider, gesturing for her to come in. "How have you been." His voice a whisper, all his questions like statements. As if he really didn't want to know. Just said it as a formality, a way to fill the silence.

"I'm good, Stan," she replied gently, then stepped across the threshold. Nothing had changed inside. All his artwork lay in tatters on the floor, strewn from one end of the loft to the other. The air smelled stagnant and stale, like garbage and old beer and sweat. She wanted to open all the windows, let the breeze in, then maybe clean up the place. Bag up the remnants of his work, give the floor a good sweep. Wipe everything down, make it look better, make it feel new. No wonder Stan looked so depressed. Who could be happy living in a place like this?

"I'm glad you came," he said, wandering out into the middle of the mess. Stopping about halfway through, turning to look back at her.

Abigail just stared, trying not to let tears form in her eyes. She hadn't expected him to be happy about her showing up on his doorstep like this. "I am too, Stan. Thanks for letting me in."

"No, I mean I want to talk to you." He spoke right over her, as if he weren't listening. It stung, but Abigail tried not to let it show.

"I want to talk to you too," she went on. "I've been thinking about you a lot. Wondering if you're okay and thinking about— about what happened between us." She took a breath but not too deep. Not giving him a chance to interrupt her. To tell her to get out. She had to say this to him, had to make sure he heard it. She hadn't come this far just to get shut out again.

"But Stan, you have to know you really hurt me that night when you threw me against the wall. You hurt me physically, and even worse, you hurt me emotionally. I trusted you, and I cared for you… I loved you, Stan. And when you attacked me, it shattered all of that. I've felt broken in so many ways." She paused. When she began again, her voice cracked. "But I've also missed you. I've done a lot of soul searching, and, despite what happened, I still feel like we're meant to be together. Like there's some greater purpose for us." She laughed a little as the tears finally spilled out of her eyes. "I know it sounds ridiculous, but I can't get the thought of it out of my head. It's like something— something's compelling me to keep coming after you. So I'm doing it. I'm letting you know I forgive you, Stan. I forgive you. And I want you back in my life."

Outside, an engine roared to life. In the loft, the refrigerator kicked on. Abigail's body felt lighter, as if she'd rid herself of an enormous weight. She smiled a little as she looked at Stan, anxiously awaiting his reply. He simply looked back at her, unblinking, hands shoved in his pants' pockets.

"What do you want to tell me?" she asked finally, trying to get him to speak.

Stan took a long breath. Let it out just as slowly. Ran a hand over his stubbly face. "I think about you a lot too." His voice was ragged and dry. He cleared his throat. It didn't help at all. "And I know that I made a mistake. I hurt you, and I'm sorry."

Then he looked down at his feet and shuffled through the trash for a minute. Rubbing his chin again and pulling on his greasy hair. Obviously in a train of thought that Abigail did not want to interrupt.

So far, so good, she thought.

"But I have to tell you." Stan finally stopped. He'd walked almost to the kitchen area. He didn't turn back around. "You need to stay away from me. I'm dangerous, Abby. I'm no good for you, and you need to keep your distance. For your safety."

Abigail laughed again, this time more from nervousness than from giddiness. But Stan didn't turn around. Or say anything else. Didn't acknowledge her in any way, as if she already had ceased to exist for him. She even felt herself fading away, another lonely ghost in this city already so full of them. *So much for feeling like someone needs you. So much for giving a damn.* Silently she cursed herself—for coming here tonight, for saying what she'd felt in her heart, for having the notion to begin with that forgiving Stan was the right thing to do. She wanted to curse him out, pick up this shit from the floor and throw it all at him. Take out her anger one toss at a time. Make him feel some of the pain he'd caused her.

But then another part of her wanted him in her arms, to hold on until he took it all back. All the garbage he'd spewed. This nonsense. A danger to her safety? She needed to stay away? Who'd put these ideas in his head? Lilith, probably. Or maybe Dr. Uphir. The point was Stan was gone from her now. So far Abby wasn't sure she could ever get him back. But that didn't mean she wouldn't try.

Without a word, she left the loft and headed home. Alone, no better off than she'd been before. But certainly with a lot of new questions to think about.

TWENTY-SIX

A lone at last. Some time to think. Stan laughed at the realization as he pushed the broom into the pile of junk, the fine
powder of broken plaster puffing up into his face and covering
his clothes. When was he not alone these days? Or any other
time for that matter? Since he'd tried to kill himself—or since
he'd tried to kill Old Stan, he now figured, a task at which he
seemed to have succeeded—he'd been by himself the majority
of the time. Just him and the voices, him and the specters that
haunted his dreams, his waking nightmares. The people he saw
in his visions, their unspeakable acts against one another. These
so-called humans. God's beloveds. A fantasy Stan didn't believe
in anymore.

And why should he? What had God ever done for him? He
understood it all now: his own rebellion, the big man's casting
him out of heaven. These events existed as dank, distant memories in Stan's mind, more inklings of feelings than anything
else. Little pinpricks of searing light at the end of a long, black
tunnel. Still, they explained so much. His anger. The rage that
built so quickly. The feelings of hopelessness, helplessness he'd
been dragging around with him. The visions and dreams. The
bodies burning.

Stan gave the broom a hard push, and a flurry of detritus
shot out into the air ahead of him. It landed, and he swept
again, collecting as much as he could in a heap at the end of
the loft. Then he stuffed it into trash bags. One, six, a dozen.
He lost track somewhere after twenty-five. It was hard work,

messy both emotionally and physically. Like bagging bodies in a war. Amputated limbs, severed heads, bits of hair and feet and fingers. All this love lost, such a waste of all the blood and sweat that had gone into it.

And tears, he thought. That was how the saying went. But he had none left, not for this art, not for this life. Stan's body was hot and dry, a byproduct of all those days he had spent in bed. He'd gone under the covers as a living, breathing man and come out as a husk, a shell with nothing but blackness within. A perfect vessel for the evil he now felt surging in his blood. Or maybe it had always been there, and he had simply ignored it.

Well, that wasn't going to happen anymore. Now Stan knew his place in this world. Knew who he was and what he was doing there. He could see he'd been on the wrong path all along, and though his new mission wasn't quite clear yet, the route was beginning to take shape. Hence the cleanup, so he could get back to work. There was art to create and a show to set up within a matter of only days. He felt sure it was going to be his best yet.

Now that he knew who he was—what he was—Stan didn't mind having Lilith around so much. She didn't terrify him anymore, and her bluntness, her coldness, all of it made sense. You don't get to be one badass demon like that without breaking a few hearts, or a few bones. In truth he had no idea what she really was in her true form, and he had no intention of asking. Not yet, anyway. Baby steps, he reminded himself often. There was a lot to learn in this new realm. He didn't have to take everything in at once.

"So what is it?" she asked him now, standing behind him at

his drawing table. He bent over the surface, which was littered with layers of paper, sketches of models and patterns, designs for the Brooklyn Museum collection. He'd been working on it furiously. Still not sure what the theme was or how he would execute it exactly. But the ideas were taking shape.

"It's a woman, Lilith." He glanced back at her over his shoulder. Gave her a smirk, looked her body up and down. "I'd think you would recognize one given what all you've got to work with there."

She grinned back at him. An inside joke. *We both know we're not human. Isn't it a hoot?* "I meant what is she doing? What's going on here? Where is the *art*, Stan? You have three days until the show. Two days until the pieces have to be installed. You must get moving on this. I need to see results."

She snapped her fingers with the last word. Back to the old Lilith, just like that. Whatever she was, this must have been an innate trait. The pushiness. The inner bitch.

"I know, I know. I'm working on it." Stan stood up straight, bringing the page with him. So far it was a female figure, nude, skin covered in black designs. Tribal patterns with jagged edges, shadows of lightning and flames. Wrapping around her limbs like a vine, fingers of darkness clawing the edges of her face.

"Work harder. Let me know if you need any…inspiration," Lilith replied, going to the mirror to check herself, as she always did. The signal she was getting ready to leave the loft. Stan had always thought she was merely touching up her lipstick, making sure her eyeliner hadn't run. But now he wondered: Was she looking at this blonde-haired beauty, the flawless skin, the icy eyes? Or did she see her real self in all its raven glory? Perhaps that was why she gazed so long, so lovingly. To remind herself of who she truly was, of the vast dark behind the bright exterior.

"I'll be back in three hours." She turned to Stan again, snapping the lip of her purse shut. Her high heels sounded on the floor. "I expect to see your plans then. For what you're going to do and how you will get it all done in time."

As she passed Stan by, she blew an air kiss, then continued on her way. As usual he watched her through the window, exiting the building and getting into her waiting SUV. In the front seat, Jake hung his arm out the open window. As Lilith closed her door, he glanced up at Stan and waved his hand. Then the window went up, and the car sped off. Probably with Lilith cursing the driver out from the backseat.

Stan turned back to his table and bent over it again. Moving around the papers, leaning his chin on one hand, elbow on the tabletop, deep in thought. There were some promising starts here. The one he had shown to Lilith. Another of a man, similar markings though more violent, with more areas inked. Large swathes of black covering his thighs, his biceps. Stan wasn't sure what he was trying to get across, but he liked the look of what he'd done so far.

He picked up a pen and began to draw again. The lines came easily to him, like an innate thought, a reflex born of his unconscious imagination. He sketched the figures first, men and women in different poses. Standing upright, lying down. A man crouched, hands over his head to protect himself. A woman with her arms upraised, as if welcoming whatever was coming her way. One running, one crawling, one slithering on his belly like a snake.

Then he drew himself standing in a crucifix pose. Head bowed, feet twisted. A heavy scale hanging from each hand, a blindfold across his eyes. Because this was what he had come to see: everything was about balance. About trying to tip the scales but keeping them from spilling what they held—the world, its people, the fate of their immortal souls. The purpose was not to destroy life; humans were perfectly capable of doing that on their own. Killing themselves and each other, not just with guns and bombs but with hatred and sloth and greed. All Stan had to do was show them the way, influence their little hearts just enough to bring out their true selves. To make them do their worst. To show God this world was not deserving of all the love he showed it.

Stan dropped the pen from his hand. Staring blankly at the table before him. Was this his purpose now? As it had been all along? A vision came, and he saw himself. Not over the pit of bodies this time but on the busy street a few blocks from where he stood now. Touching people as they walked by, feeling the evil they had done. The murders and rapes, the cheating and lying and all of it, all the bad things, large and small, that made up the seamy underbelly of the world. The same visions he'd seen for weeks now, every time he left the loft.

But now he saw them in a different light. These weren't just random acts he'd psychically witnessed, some parade of suffering for which he had a front-row seat. No, these were not the humans' sins laid before him when he closed his eyes. These were his own doing. His influence. He'd been there when the mother had drowned her baby, in the seconds before she'd laid him down in the lukewarm tub. He'd been there when the driver sat behind the steering wheel and cried, afraid to look behind him at the mutilated wreck he had caused—and at the moment when the man put the car in gear and drove away. Stan had held the hand of the surgeon who had briefly wondered what it would be like to see a patient bleed out. Snapped his fingers and made a dealer show up just in time to sell the junkie his fatal hit. Put that inkling of a thought inside the CEO's head: he could take all the profits and leave the country before the company folded, leaving all his faithful employees in the dust.

All in a night's work for Stan. Or Satan, as he had been called then.

He ran to the kitchen, barely making it to the sink before releasing a rush of vomit.

When the waves of nausea subsided and his stomach ceased contracting and pulsing, trying to rid his body of the putrid bile, he stood up, wiped his wet mouth on his sleeve, and got a beer from the fridge. Washed the taste down, then leaned back against the counter. He had to sort this out. What he was doing, what he had done before. Although he had accepted who he was, and who he had been in the past, he still didn't feel it deep inside, and these revelations were bitter to him. A part of him was thrilled that he had held so much power. That he might have it still.

But could he still do the same things he'd done? Could he lead people to kill? Could he wreak so much havoc in otherwise innocent people's lives? Maybe they weren't so innocent—maybe he only influenced those who were already bad. They had the ideas, didn't they? All they needed was a nudge. But did that make it right, what he did?

Stan couldn't be so sure yet. He was still a human after all, trapped in this body as he was now. And so subject to human feelings—mostly confusion at the moment. He could go one of two ways: reclaim his power, his rightful throne, as Dr. Uphir had put it. Be not Old Stan the Artist but the man Lilith claimed he used to be before his little accident. He understood now what she meant and why she'd said it so much.

The other choice? To continue on as he was. Simply be Stan Foster, New York City artist. Decent talent, a little famous, at least on the local circuit. He could just keep on doing his work and opening shows, living this life that wasn't really his but would do well enough. And in doing so, perhaps he could make up for what he'd done. Maybe atone for the sins he'd committed in that other life, that other time.

In truth he leaned just a little bit more toward this boring life. For now, anyway. Power was good and all, but he'd grown accustomed to the comfort this existence offered. Besides, he felt he had work to be done. That there was some purpose for him here. His mind flashed on Abigail, the way she'd smiled when she'd said that they were meant to be together. Maybe she'd been on to something.

"Or maybe not," he muttered, tossing his empty beer bottle into the nearby trash. He didn't want to think about her, to tempt himself into wanting to see her face. Couldn't think about his hands on her body, her arms holding him tight. That sense of relief she brought. Her light that filled up the room. All that was gone to him now. A deep sense of disappointment and anger began to rise in his chest.

He headed back toward the drawing table. At least he could put these emotions to some good use.

TWENTY-SEVEN

Though everything in the world was based on balance, not everything was *in* balance; that sort of perfection was rarely if ever achieved. Not in this world or the next, or any that had existed in the past. The battles between good and evil, fairness and injustice, movement and inertia: these oppositions had always existed and likely always would. Stan—even as Satan, even with all the power he truly had in that form—could not overcome this fact. His vague memories told him that much. He would always be fighting against God.

It was three in the morning when he finally finished all his sketches. Lilith had come and gone twice more since her visit that afternoon. Acting like a babysitter, a watchful nanny policing Stan's every move. That much wasn't lost on him. She had not approved of the work he'd done for the last show; it had been too bright for her, too hopeful. Now he understood why. Lilith wanted who Stan had been before he'd landed in this artist's body. She wanted evil and dark, menacing, flawed. She wanted controversial art, gothic and difficult to look at.

Well, this time he gave it to her. Using the man's talent and the devil's mind, he set his hands to work. First he drew out all the forms, then penciled in the markings on their bodies. Light at first, whispery trellises of cords and belts. When he was pleased with the patterns, he set them in ink, dipping a fountain pen into a well, slathering the thick liquid on the papers. By the time he was done, the designs were the most prominent feature on every page. The humans were merely props, there to display the stories these figurative ropes and bindings told.

"They're good," Lilith said on her fourth visit, tossing the pages back onto the table. Stan leaned on the wall nearby, sipping the coffee she had brought him (black, two shots of espresso, just how Lilith liked it). He watched as her eyes lingered on the drawings. She didn't look displeased but not entirely happy either. A sentiment that doubled when she turned her gaze his way.

"But what will you do with them now? This isn't a drawing exhibition. You need more substance than that."

He smiled, stood up, and went to the table. "I'm well aware of that. I have my plans."

"Not good enough, Stan. I let you be secretive last time and look where it got us. I don't want that sort of fluff again." Drops of spittle sprang from her mouth as she dragged the word out: *ffffluff*.

Stan put his fingers on the papers. Moved them around on the tabletop. Taking in the work he'd done. It had felt so good to create, to get back to the business of making art. Perhaps he hadn't been born in this body, but something about its natural proclivities certainly appealed to him. Old Stan's talents suited him well. The perfect means to express the emotions that now clogged his mind and heart.

"Just get me the models," he said, his voice low and rough. A black cloud moving in across his brain, threatening the most terrifying of thunderstorms. He looked over at Lilith, her gleaming skin, the fire in her eyes. "You can stay and watch if you want."

Her crimson lips curled into a snarling grin as Stan reached out and grabbed the hem of her skirt.

The inking went more quickly than Stan had thought it would. Once Lilith brought in the subjects, he simply lined them up along the edge of the loft and got to work. These weren't his usual models—no, these were nothing like the beautiful, young, waifish things Lilith had brought for him the last time. These people were human and imperfect, with dimpled thighs and over-dyed hair, tired eyes and sagging muscles from years upon years of neglect. As he arranged them in the order he wanted, Stan laid his hands on them one by one, grabbing their upper arms to move them, pressing against their heads to get them to turn and look one way or the other, or up or down. And each time he saw their stories one by one. The drug addict whose children had been taken away. The separation had done nothing but make her addiction worse, and her future held nothing but more loneliness and finally death. The petty thief just out of jail, on a bond paid for by his mother, a long-suffering woman who enabled his bad deeds, who bailed him out every time, though she knew she should let him sit and rot in there. He knew it too; his self-esteem was nonexistent. Another whose light would dim out quite quickly when he met the wrong end of a storeowner's shotgun.

All of them were like this: homeless, helpless, crooked, pathetic. As Stan touched them, maneuvered them, he looked into their eyes, and most of them looked back, defiant to the last, daring him to say something about their sorry state. But he didn't mention a word. It wasn't his place to pass judgment. Whether he acted here as Stan the artist or Satan, the eternal collector of such lost souls, his effect on these people was going to be minimal. The damage had already been done, their lives and fates already planned. There was no work for him to do here other than his art.

And that he was eager to get to. What he had planned was something entirely new to him—not the medium or the message really but the way he intended to go about expressing it. Creating it. Walking along the lineup of models, he brushed his fingers one more time along their skin, feeling for the perfect spots to begin applying the designs, the tendrils and tongues of black flame, the bands of solid ink. Images flooded his brain: this one shooting up, that one crying, another begging on a corner for change to buy his next hit. Finally he stopped at a woman in the middle of the lineup—skinny and sallow, wearing a dirty white tank top and too-short cutoff jeans. Long, stringy, bleach-blonde hair and light eyes, her pink lips cracked and dry. She looked at the floor; Stan put a hand under her chin and raised her face to meet his. There was something familiar about her, familiar but wrong. Searching her features, it took a moment to come to Stan, but at last he realized: she looked like Abigail. A dirty, worn-out version of her but Abigail nonetheless. His stomach surged at the thought, his hand tightening on her jaw for just a moment, making her flinch a little.

"You're first," he said, ignoring the sweat on her brow, the way her breathing had become heavy and fast. He grabbed her wrist and yanked her out of line, then led her over to an area he had partitioned off with a great, red curtain. So none of the others could see what he would be doing to her.

"Sit," he told her once they were behind the veil, pointing to a reclining chair. Like something from a dentist's office. Next to it was a table laid out with all the instruments he'd need—a box of latex gloves, some disposable razors, a spray bottle of Green Soap. Gauze pads. A few dozen plastic pots of black ink. The needles, individually packaged in sterile wrapping. And, of course, the gun. It gleamed in the spotlight hooked above the chair.

"But—" the woman began. Stan simply pointed at the chair again. She hesitated, then sat down, slowly lowering herself onto the creaking plastic.

"You already signed the contract," he reminded her as he snapped on a latex glove, then put one on the other hand as well. He pulled up a rolling stool and sat next to her, grabbing the weak flesh of her arm. "And you've received your pay. You're not thinking of backing out now, are you?"

The woman looked at Stan, and he saw all the fight simply drain out of her. Whatever small light was in her eyes, it faded to dusk, and she sat back, her body limp. Stan smiled. "Don't worry. It won't hurt very much."

With that he turned to the table. Squeezed out a few globs of Vaseline on a metal tray and stuck small, plastic caps in them to keep the caps from moving. Filled the caps with ink. Picked up a disposable razor and shaved the fine, light hair off of the woman's lower arm. She kept her eyes closed, her breathing slow. At least she had given up what little fight she had.

Then Stan picked up the gun. A four-inch-long tube, about as wide as a cigar but much heavier. A needle at one end, a tube leading to a foot pedal on the other. Stan pressed the pedal lightly and the gun released a low buzz, the needle vibrating to a dull silver blur.

He dipped the needle in the ink. Leaned back toward the woman, holding the gun over her wrist. A painful place to start, but then it was all going to hurt. What did it matter where the skin broke first, where the numbness began? With his free hand, he stretched the already taut skin between his thumb and forefinger, then went in for the kill.

As the needle slid under her skin, the woman flinched. Stan

put his weight on her wrist, pinning it down against the arm of the chair. A swell ran through his body, a hot shiver, a primal rush as she resisted and then caved, her body relaxing, water seeping from the corners of her eyes. Crying? In pain? Stan didn't know, and only felt a mild interest in the cause of her tears. He had work to do and little time to worry about this human's inner demons. The ones he aimed to release through this primitive piercing of her skin.

Stan worked through the night, and into the next day, and then on to the night again. So different from the days when he'd slept through the passage of time. The world going on around him, spinning and whirling, a frenzy of misery and longing and rage, all the many sins of man. He channeled it, along with the images from his visions, the lust and hate he felt every time he touched another person. Poured it all into these black tattoos, these stark representations of how terrible the world could be— but how beautiful too. There was something elegant in their curves, a grace in their lines. Even his most hesitant models were entranced with their bodies by the end of the process. Touching their bleeding skin, the tender welts the tattooing had caused. As if they didn't feel pain anymore, as if they were in love with the ink. And with themselves, maybe for the first time in their lives.

So had this been a positive experience? Stan couldn't say for sure. He hadn't intended it to be, though he hadn't thought it evil either. It was simply an exercise, a function of art. A way to get his point across. Which was what? How fucked up the world could be. That he could take these poor souls, God's lost children, and bend them to his will. That they would let him permanently mark their bodies in return for a little cash. The thought was pathetic to Stan, pitiful. Just as sad as the models themselves. Each living his or her own personal hell right here in the land God created for them.

But in flashes he felt mercy for them too. Their silent suffering, even as the needle ripped their flesh, leaving only the darkness behind. Permanently inside their bodies, a shadow they would never shake. A reminder of this time in their lives, this rock bottom. The day they gave up everything and received nothing in return. The day they let their souls die. The human side of Stan felt their loss sharply, as fine as the needle's prick.

When the tattoos were done, he lined the men and women up again. All of them nude, only the black designs covering their skin. They looked at themselves and one another, faces showing awe and shock, their bodies in poses of shame and ego and simple confusion. What had they done here? What had Stan done to them? As if they couldn't make sense of their actions. Even as he posed them—this one's arms around that one, that one's leg around this one's waist—they kept on with the stunned silence. A mute puzzle, a tableau of limbs and ink. Their markings all fit together, flowing toward and into one another until the pattern meshed.

Stan stood back and looked at last. All of them locked as one, a great, dark beast rising from a sea of flesh. Exactly as he wanted it. There was no ambiguity here. None of the fluff from before. He pulled his iPhone from his pocket, took a picture, and sent it off to Lilith. Within seconds she had sent a response: *Be right over.*

Stan went to get a beer for the wait.

TWENTY-EIGHT

Tattoos have a healing process: cover the area with salve, over that plastic wrap. Wash gently once a day with mild soap. Reapply and wrap again, then repeat until the skin no longer flakes, until blood is no longer being released.

These models, though, they knew nothing of this sort of hygiene. Living on the streets as they did, or in halfway houses or shelters, they had no means for such self-care and even less inclination to follow through with it. Stan hadn't helped them out any either. He could have given them tubes of A&D, allowed them to come by the loft to wash up. A more responsible artist might have. But that didn't serve his purpose. Or the great narcissism of it all. These people existed solely for him now, and he didn't want them to look fresh and new. No, he needed them diseased and hurt. Their total lack of cleanliness only added to the power of his creation.

Evil, evil, he thought as he scanned the crowd gathered at the museum. Most of them looking at his work. The other artists—Jenny someone, and a short, roundish Spanish fellow—seemed a bit lost and alone. The girl among her sculpture angels, the man with his black-and-white photos in frames, lined up single-file along a wall. A few stragglers stopped and looked, but Stan's work obviously—almost embarrassingly—drew the most attention. Queues ten deep at times and a buzz that reached a crescendo as the night wore on. As though the audience was both repelled and attracted to his creations.

"See what happens when you follow my advice? This is how it should be." Lilith appeared next to him out of nowhere. Ravishing as usual, wearing all black, hair a swath of messy waves. Stan looked her up and down. Now that he'd joined the dark side, so to speak, there was something quite attractive about her. Before she'd seemed so hard and cold, her beauty not enticing but aggressive and fierce. Now she seemed all pliant curves, with a heat that could melt even Stan's sordid heart. He took a step closer to her, took a deep breath. The scent of her cigarette, the musky, dirty smell of the being she truly was. He just wanted to grab her and take her, to own her in every way possible. Physically, mentally. And not just her but everyone. The animal inside him wanted absolute power, and more and more he found himself wanting it too.

"I don't think you're supposed to smoke in here," he mumbled, running a fingertip up Lilith's arm. Around her shoulder and along her collarbone. She swatted him off like a fly.

"Stan, are you listening to me? Do you see what's going on here? They love this shit." Lilith regarded the spectators, nudging and lowing at one another like livestock. Trying to get a better look at the freak show Stan had created for them.

"Mm." He moved closer, trailed his lips along her cheek.

"Stan." She grabbed his face and squeezed, black-painted fingernails digging into his cheeks. She turned him toward the show. "There will be time for that later. Right now you need to see this. This is what you need to do from now on. Okay? No more of that flower-child bullshit. Agreed?"

He had to admit he'd drawn an impressive audience. Thanks in no small part to Lilith's never-ending publicity machine. Once she'd seen his work in person, seen what he'd done to the sacrificial lambs she had delivered to him, she'd set the wheel in motion. Called up her colleagues, the media, her favorite wealthy patrons. Anyone and everyone she knew. Even, apparently—

"Dr. Uphir." Stan reached out and grabbed his sleeve as he walked passed. The man stopped, turned.

"Why, Stan. I didn't see you there." The doctor flashed his gold-toothed smile, and already Stan could tell he was lying. He had seen Stan. Uphir just liked to play. One of those simpering underlings who told the boss anything he wanted to hear in order to gain favor, but he was always at the same time following his own agenda. A two-faced demon. Stan knew he should not have felt as surprised as he did.

Uphir turned his eyes to Lilith. "Or you either. Good to see you again, my dear." He stood on his toes to reach up and give her an airy kiss on one cheek, then on the other side.

Stan watched their exchange, one finger pointing between the two. "You…" He looked at Dr. Uphir. "And you." Then at Lilith. "Of course you two know each other. That makes perfect sense."

"We go back a long way," Lilith said, giving the doctor a grin. "A *long* way. And as your therapist, I thought he might like to see just how well you're doing."

"Oh, yes." Dr. Uphir glanced over toward the installation. "I'm very impressed, Stan. Really amazing work." He turned back, clapped a hand on Stan's shoulder. "Good to see you've finally embraced who you really are."

In his mind's eye, Stan saw Uphir and Lilith together, not there in the museum but in the underworld. Another realm, full of darkness and heat. Stan was there too, felt the dry air wrapping around his body like a familiar blanket. He breathed it in deeply and closed his eyes as he listened to the other pair chatter, their voices no longer human but something else. Deep and raspy, a violent, hissing language Stan could almost understand. They were talking about him, it seemed, not by his human name but in other terms: Lucifer. Son of perdition. Mammon. The father of all lies.

"Isn't that right, Stan?" Lilith's human voice brought him out of the trance he'd slipped into. He opened his eyes, shook his head, clearing out the darkness. Uphir no longer held his shoulder; the doctor now stood back with Lilith, who gestured out to the crowd as she spoke.

"Isn't what right?"

Lilith rolled her eyes at him and waved her cigarette, sending a cloud of smoke his way. It broke across his face, and he coughed. "I'm going to get another drink," he said and moved away from the two quickly, slipping into the throng before they could protest.

But instead of making his way to the already overcrowded bar, he went to his installation. Slipped between the groups of spectators to get around the back of it, though the throng was just as thick there. This was a 360 piece, viewable from all sides, every angle with something different to offer the eye. From the front the tattoos showed one scene, played out along the models' pallid flesh. A maze of black paths leading down to the earth, tying them to the ground, the lines continuing across the floor and out into the audience. You are me, it said, and I am you, and none of us can escape the earth. We all end up there in the end.

From the back, the message was no more hopeful than it was in the front. Whereas Stan's previous work had focused on the dichotomy, the battle between the higher and lower powers, the human struggle to straddle the line between the two and the longing to reach for what was above, to escape what lay below, this held no such hopeful tone. The scene on the models' backs as they pressed up against one another, this one with her arms around the other, that one with his head against his neighbor's chest, was simply solid black from waist to feet. He had tattooed them like coloring in a child's picture, back and forth, back and forth with the needle until no light flesh remained. Together, side by side, they made an impenetrable wall. A monolith and an abyss all at the same time.

"How could you do this to them?"

Stan didn't have to turn around to know it was her. *Abby.* He'd wondered if she would come. If after what he had done, and what he'd said to her, she would continue with the charade, believing somehow she could save him.

Of course she would, he thought, closing his eyes again. Just as he knew now who he was, he understood Abigail too. Saw her in a new light. Since the moment he'd met her, he'd known just how good she was. Truly an angel incarnate—a good angel, one of God's best. Even though she didn't know it. Abby saw only darkness in herself, given all that she had been through. Saw herself as damaged goods, as beyond repair, almost worse off than the people she helped on a daily basis. Giving up her life to her work, offering others salvation without a care for her own.

But now... Stan turned to face her at last. Opened his eyes slowly. Abigail stood in the shadows behind the installment, back up against a wall. She wore a pale dress, hair hanging soft to her shoulders. Tears in her eyes as she stared beyond Stan's shoulder to his work. Finally they flickered toward him.

"I get what you're saying, Stan." She reached up and dragged her fingers across her eyes. Clearing the water out. "I mean I get the statement you're trying to make." It was no good. The tears wouldn't stay away. "But why did you have to do it like this? You ruined these people's lives."

"Maybe, but they let me do it." Stan refused to feel remorse.

Maybe it was his newly unearthed identity, but he just didn't like the way she was blaming him for that. "These people ruined their own lives long before I ever came into contact with them." He turned to glance at them. "The girl on the end there. Had a baby at a motel and threw it into a dumpster out back. The man two people down from her? Sells his twelve-year-old daughter to strangers to support his meth habit." He looked back at Abigail and let out a laugh. "And you're complaining about a little tattooing? I just put on the outside of their bodies what they already carry around on the inside. Maybe it's unethical, but they signed—"

"It's not just unethical, Stan." Her voice was low and trembling. As she crossed her arms, he saw her hands shaking. "It's beyond comprehension for me. I can't believe you would do such a thing. Just because they're lost doesn't mean they can't change their lives. Don't you think people can change? What you've done to them, it's…"

She gazed at the artwork again, eyes scanning the folds and creases of the bodies as if searching for the right word. Finally they landed back on Stan. "It's evil. Is that what you are now? You're evil? Some sort of demon incarnate?"

Stan felt his blood boil, and a cold shiver shot up his spine at the same time. In the confines of his loft, with Lilith, even here with Uphir around, he felt like the king of the world. *Well, king of the underworld*, he thought with a bit of an inner smirk. But there was something about Abby saying it. About her sudden realization that maybe Stan was not all he seemed. Or that he was more than he seemed. He wondered how much she knew about him—what she could know about his true identity. Maybe she was an angel, part of this grand scheme, just like Lilith and Uphir, sent there to influence him. Maybe God had told her himself. Sent her a vision, just like Stan had, or maybe—

"What is this crazy talk?" he said, without really thinking about it. Some sort of natural reflex, an innate tendency to deny who he was. *The king of all lies.* He remembered what Uphir had called him when he'd spoken with Lilith. Deny, deny, deny. "You need to think about what you're saying, Abby."

"I have thought about it, Stan." She stood up straighter, took the defeated slump out of her shoulders. Stan mimicked her posture as if readying for some sort of fight. "I've been here for a while now, just looking at this—this—this monstrosity you've made. Watching all these people fawning over it, declaring you a genius, a master. I don't know who disgusts me more, them or you."

In a flash Stan had reared up, his true self coming to the surface before human Stan could stop him. His hands raised up over his head, mouth opened wide, he lunged toward Abby, eyes gleaming red, sharp teeth dripping with acid bile. He could feel his skin tighten, shrinking into that burnt, red parchment he had seen before, when Lilith had brought the devil out of him. Saw his long, pointed fingernails as his hand swiped at Abigail. She backed up against the wall, looking terrified, hands up to protect herself.

And just like that, he receded. As quickly as it had appeared, it vanished. Stan took a step back, shook his shoulders as if shrugging off an old coat. As rapidly as Lucifer had come, he was gone, taking all his fiery rage back to hell with him. Leaving just mortal Stan in his black suit, standing in front of Abigail. Wondering if he should apologize for scaring her or give himself a pat on the back.

"You," she began, her voice the ghost of a whisper. Stan saw the utmost terror in her eyes and wondered what she had seen in him. Could she witness his intended form? See past his human shell, peer into the chasm that lay beyond? By the looks of it, she could see. Could tell what he had become, or rather what he had reverted to. But he couldn't be sure, and how could he ask a question like that? *So, when I just jumped at you, did you happen to see a couple of horns sticking out of my head?*

Instead he took a step toward her. Reaching out a hand, wanting to touch her as he once did. Put a hand on her waist, pull her body close to his. The demon in him fought this desire, railed against it with all he had. It had been winning so far— just look at this work he'd done, at the way he'd been pawing at Lilith. The thought suddenly brought a flush to his face. The way he'd stuck his hands up her skirt that afternoon at the loft, the way he had, just moments earlier, thought about fucking her right here. In front of these hideous models and all the heathens that had come to see them.

This is not how you're supposed to be, a little voice inside his head said. It sounded a lot like his own—or, rather, like Old Stan's. Like the voice of this body he had hijacked for his demented purpose, whatever that was. The reason he'd ended up here. Maybe to prove to God how bad these humans were. How susceptible to his evil will. Well, hadn't he shown that now? Stan quickly looked around the gallery. Wasn't this more than enough?

Watching the blind herd, all the people dressed in their suits and gowns, their diamonds and plastic faces, Stan felt nothing but disgust. There was no modesty here, only vanity. They swam in the filth of this creation, this so-called paradise of God. And here Stan was in the middle of it, wallowing right along with them, but so superior to them all. The contradiction broke his mind, and suddenly he hated himself even for thinking all this. For looking down on these people. He didn't want to be that person. And as he realized this, he saw the destruction he'd done, and he hated it.

"Abby," he said weakly, turning back to her. But she was

gone. He spun around in a whirl, searching the faces around him frantically to no avail. She had simply disappeared. Run off, probably, while he'd been distracted by his thoughts. By his inner conflict. By this argument he had with himself. No side was winning yet. Just when he thought he had it all figured out, in came another facet to consider. Another piece of the puzzle. This time it was Abigail, and now that she was back, he couldn't be certain he really wanted to be so evil after all.

TWENTY-NINE

You're losing your goddamn mind, Abigail told herself as she ran down Eastern Parkway toward the subway stop. Stan was not a demon. That had been—what, a hallucination? She wasn't on any drugs. Hadn't had a thing, sadly, to drink. She'd done nothing to elicit such a sight as that. The red skin, the black hair all over his body. Yellow teeth and cloven feet, and had she even seen a tail? *A tail?* Abigail stopped and grabbed her hair, pulled at it with her fists. Hoping the pain would make the images go away, these nonsensical pictures in her head. They couldn't be real, they couldn't be real, they couldn't be—

But they didn't go away. And so she ran again until she was safely underground, on a train that would carry her far away from this place, far away from what Stan had become.

The car was nearly empty, and she found a seat all alone near the back. She dropped herself down onto the molded plastic, doubled over until her forehead reached her knees. Sobs wracked her exhausted body, great, heaving sighs of pain and fear and disgust. Brain trying to make sense of all that had just happened but without success. There was no explaining it. What had happened to that good Stan she'd known? The one who had been striving for more, to make something of his life, to pick up the pieces and put them back in a new, better order? The Stan who had sat in her office, going on about Sartre and the Roman Empire and life itself? If she'd felt like she'd been fooled before—and oh, had she ever felt like she had been fooled by this man—now it was a thousand times worse. How could she

217

not have known? There should have been some sign. All those years at Catholic school, all those Sundays at Mass. What had they prepared her for if not this—this confrontation with the devil himself?

"Oh, God, no," she whimpered, the tears beginning anew. She folded her body further upon itself, as if she could disappear completely if she simply made herself small enough. Eyes squeezed closed, she felt lightheaded, as if she were stuck out in space. In a vacuum, on the vast plains of the underworld. Somewhere she couldn't breathe. Air seeped into her lungs in ragged gasps. She sat up, trying not to hyperventilate. Grabbing the seatback in front of her, she steadied herself for a moment. Stared out ahead of her at the other passengers: an elderly woman in a headscarf, shopping cart by her side. A young man, baseball hat and earbuds on, bobbing his head from the motion of the train or from his music perhaps. Abigail couldn't tell. A mother and child playing "I Spy" outside the train windows.

These were just ordinary people. The kind Abigail saw every day on her way to work and when she returned home alone every blessed night. Nothing was evil here. Nothing to hurt her.

She took a deep breath and let her mind go blank. Freeing it of panic, letting go of that memory of Stan as he had appeared in the gallery. Then she scrubbed her hands over her face and looked out the window next to her. Brain shifting into doctor mode, where it was most comfortable. No emotions, just logic. Her preferred state.

And what did her doctor mind tell her now? That there had to be some rational explanation for all this. Not just for Stan but for the work he had done, for why she had gone to see it. Everything happens for a reason, wasn't that what people said? So what was the reasoning here? Why had she been led to see him like that, if what she had seen was true? Because as crazy as Stan's sudden change in appearance had made her feel, she couldn't deny it was real. She'd felt his hot breath on her face, stinking of death and fetid, rotting flesh. Felt the heat from his body as if it emitted pure flame. Was made up of fire itself.

She shuddered at the corporeal memory of it. Then shook it off and tried to think of nothing at all. As the train sped out of Brooklyn and back into Manhattan proper, she breathed deeply, let the scenes of the cityscape calm her mind a little. The projects and penthouses, the square parks and corner bars. The underground stations, people waiting to get on with their packages and bags and strollers. Everything bustling, stirring, full of people and life. There was evil out there, sure, but so much unseen goodness too.

Just like Stan, she thought. But then stopped herself. Given what she knew now, she had to admit that just wasn't him anymore. Silently she cried again, tears sliding down her cheeks, leaving hot trails. Maybe he had never been good; maybe she'd assigned that status to him because it was what she'd wanted him to be. At the point when they'd met, she'd wanted so badly for someone to come into her life. To save her from herself, to keep her from drowning in misery. So she had mistaken Stan's charm for something it never was and never could be: Sincerity. Understanding. Love. All of that had been a lie. Everything she had felt, all the things he had said, none of it had meant a thing. She could see that now, and oh, how stupid she felt because of it. Of all the shitty things that had happened to her in her life, this was the lowest of the low. A rock bottom she had hit at full force. With Stan up there at the top, laughing down at her.

Leaning her forehead against the window, she covered her face with her hands as the train rolled on. Bumping her skull against the glass, a dull pain she welcomed with relief. Gave her something to focus on, an ache she could wrap all her feelings around so she wouldn't have to feel anything at all. When the conductor finally announced her stop, she stood up and ambled out onto the platform, where she grabbed a column and stood for a moment. Getting her bearings, letting her rattling head clear. Finally she opened her eyes fully and took a look around.

Everything was the same. This was the subway stop she saw every day, twice a day—the same stairs and MetroCard machines and turnstiles. The same dank smell, the dirty tile walls.

Yet nothing was the same. In the space of a moment, her entire world had changed. She'd seen something she should not have, something she didn't know how to handle at all. Abigail looked around and for the first time realized it was all a sham. The trains, the concrete floors. The people waiting, laughing, arguing, holding hands. All of it a thin veneer for what lay beneath, for the evil that lurked. The one she'd spent her life denying was there.

Now she saw it everywhere. And all she could do was go home, have a drink, and go to sleep.

THIRTY

Everything went better after that little bitch ran out crying like a schoolgirl. Weak and scared, sniveling and blubbering as only a human could. Lilith had followed Abigail to the exit of the museum and watched her go, trying to hold back the maniacal laughter that threatened to rise in her throat at the sight.

Pathetic. She lit another cigarette and leaned against the doorframe, waiting for Stan's footfalls to echo down the stairs into the nearly empty lobby. She knew they would. He was tied to that girl like a dog on a chain.

Three drags on her smoke, and he was already there.

"That took you longer than I thought it would." She blew a puff of smoke out into the wet night air. Stan moved in beside her. Hands in his pockets, eyes searching the street for his beloved doctor. "I knew you'd be right on her tail."

He looked at her. His eyes a flat, dull gray. No spark, no fire. As if Abigail had snuffed it out.

"I have to let her go," he said. "It's not good for her to be around me." He looked down at his feet, kicked his toe against the stone of the doorstep. "I told her that before, but she wouldn't stay away."

Now Lilith did laugh. "You're useless. You know that? You let this stupid, *stupid* world get to you. You let it get in your head. It all makes you think too much." Lilith reached over and tapped a long, red fingernail against Stan's temple, cigarette between her fingers bobbing with the motion. Smoke rising up in a swirl, curling around his head. He coughed, and Lilith pulled back again.

"Everyone loves the show," she said, leaning against the jamb. Across from her Stan took on a similar pose, but with his head tilted out to the side, staring at the street forlornly. "I've gotten lots of new business cards. These people want to see more work from you. Gallery owners, private collectors…a curator from the Guggenheim, Stan. That is some big shit. He's talking solo show to headline their winter exhibits."

He had no response. Lilith felt her rage rising up, setting her body aglow. "Goddammit, look at me!" Her shrill voice echoed off the lobby halls, coming back again and again before escaping out the massive doorway.

Still no response. Stan even closed his eyes. Purposefully shutting her out. Lilith closed her eyes for a moment too, pinching the bridge of her nose with two fingers, taking a few deep, cleansing breaths. This wasn't how it used to be, back in the old days. Before all this heaven and earth bullshit started rattling around in his brain, making him addled, feeble, getting him tied up in all this drama and nonsense. He'd lost sight of his reason for being and seemed to have no interest in finding it again.

"You are *the* most stubborn being in existence," Lilith muttered to herself, then opened her eyes and took one last, big drag of her cigarette. Flicked the butt out onto the steps, then moved over to Stan.

She grabbed his face with her hand. Squeezing his cheeks into his teeth. "You have to get over this." Smoke leaked out of her mouth, drifted into his face. He didn't cough this time, didn't even flinch. As if everything in him had gone dead and not in a good way. Not the way Lilith needed him to be. "You need to forget this woman and focus on the work you have to do now. What you have up there"—she jerked her head toward the stairs leading back up to the gallery, where hundreds of people still milled, their buzz carrying down into the silent hall—"is impressive, Stan. I have to admit."

She let go of his face roughly, pushing his head back against the granite doorway. His skull hit it with a dull thud. She moved both hands to his chest then, pinning him with a touch. "After that last show I didn't think you had it in you anymore." A sly smile, moving a little bit closer to him. Pressing her body on his. Trying a new tack. "I thought maybe you were losing your touch, but now I see where your true heart lies."

"Lilith." He put his hands around her wrists but could not move her away. In this form he had no power, no physical strength. Not like when he went demon. Lilith grew warm just picturing it: the muscled arms, the bulging thighs. The hot, red skin that burned even to her touch.

"I'm not that person anymore," Stan said, his voice flat as he looked at her. His eyes were so lifeless, Lilith almost felt a chill. Stan released his grip on her, then slinked out beneath her arms. "Or whatever I used to be. Whatever he was. I might look like him sometimes, but that's not me. Not anymore, Lilith. That's not who I want to be."

He backed away slowly, raising his hands out beside him as if at a loss for words. Tears welling in the corners of his eyes.

The bastard, Lilith thought. Had he just been tricking her all along? Making her think, over this last week, that he had accepted who he was? What was more, that he *liked* the real him? That was how it had seemed to her, especially when they'd fucked on the floor of his loft so many times. Rolling around in the dirt, he'd let his true self out. He had to feel how free he had been.

Now she saw it was all a lie. She stormed over and grabbed Stan, this time by the collar of his button-up shirt.

"Don't you tell me what you are or you aren't," she hissed. "I know you. I know what's in your soul. I've seen what you can do. You are no special saint, *Stan*. You are no human either. You are evil incarnate, the scourge of man, the meanest thing I've ever seen on cloven feet. You are great and fearful to behold, and I have *worshiped* you for eons. For millennia, Stan! And this is what I get in return?"

She moved her body closer to his and relaxed her grip, then let him go. Snaked her arms around his back, pulled him in close again. Her body writhing against his, making a little of that old, familiar friction. "You can deny who you really are if that gets you off." She leaned in and felt his body stiffen. In fright, maybe, though possibly desire. Or maybe both. Either way was good for Lilith.

"Like it or not," she went on, murmuring in his ear, "you are a *god*. You are not *Stan* where we come from." In a dart she ran her tongue up his cheek. He jumped back, but she clutched his arms and pulled him in.

"This is what you want, isn't it?" Lilith purred, her lips back against his ear. He shivered in the hot night air. "You want love, Stan. In your last life and in this one, it's the only thing you've ever needed. You're dying for it. You'd do anything for it." She snapped her teeth together, ran her hand roughly down his torso. Into the top of his pants. His shaking turned into a shudder and she moved in for the kill.

"You want people to *accept* you." She moved her hand, and Stan's eyes rolled back and closed. He finally gave in, his body going soft as he leaned in to her touch. Lilith closed her eyes too. "You want adoration. That's what this is all about. The art. The shows. All the wandering you do at night…putting your hands on people just to feel something in this body, inside this hideous shell—"

In a moment his lips were on hers, cutting her words short. Devouring her like a starving beast. His hands moved, pawing at her face, her breasts. Reaching inside her clothes, heated skin dragging on skin.

Lilith opened her eyes, and the museum was gone. The doorway, the street beyond, the dark trees and sky. The nattering people at the show. She and Stan stood on the desert plain of the underworld, harsh, searing wind racing around them as they clung to one another. Still kissing, limbs entwined. Stan pushed her down on the hard, dark ground, a cloud of dust billowing around them, his heavy body over hers. His burnt skin, her tender flesh. Black birds circling above as if to welcome them home.

Just how it's supposed to be. Lilith smiled and raised her arms above her head, spreading out in a delicious stretch as Stan moved on top of her. Forever and ever, this was how they should be. Oh, how she had missed this fire. This heat they had always felt. Before he'd let his earthly obsession come between them. Before he'd ruined what they'd built together over so much time.

"Oh, yes," Stan moaned as he pushed himself in, crashing against her. The pain was infinite and beautiful, and Lilith wished that it would never end. That he would never stop. His rhythm made her blood rush, brought every nerve in her body to stand at attention.

"Yes, yes," he growled again, the word turning into a mantra. As he continued his pace, Lilith scratched her sharp nails up and down his back, drawing lines of blood, and bit into his hard shoulder with her pointed teeth. Stan was all hers now, as he had once been, as he always would be. She'd known it even in the darkest days, when he had met that girl, let her convince him he was a good guy. Some artist savior come to set man free with flowers and papier-mâché. Hippie bullshit. Lilith was glad that was over.

"My love," she purred, then wrapped her legs around his waist and flipped him over on his back. She straddled him and rocked her hips, her tension mounting. She threw her head back and closed her eyes as his rough hands grabbed at her bare body.

"Lilith."

His voice echoed from a thousand miles away. From another world. Then all the sounds stopped: the wind howling, the birds crying. The heat suddenly dropped away, and Lilith opened her eyes. They were back in the hall of the museum. And it was still empty. All except for her and Stan.

He stood a few yards away, breathing hard, watching her through half-closed eyes. Slowly he shook his head. "Not like that."

"What…" Lilith began but stopped and put a hand to her forehead. A blinding ache shot through it. Always happened when she went from there to here too fast. "What are you talking about? What…Stan, just what the *fuck* do you think you're doing?"

"Saving myself." His voice was low, barely above a whisper. He stood in the doorway; beyond, outside, it had started to rain. Lilith hated that sound, the patter of the drops on pavement, washing everything clean, making people think they could start anew. "I'm not that thing anymore. I'm a man, Lilith."

She threw her hands in the air. Let out an exasperated laugh. "Here we go again." She and Stan stood for a moment, each glaring at the other. Lilith didn't know what to say. Or what to do. She'd tried to reason with him. She'd talked to him and used his body to get the point across. No matter what she did, he didn't want to hear it. He didn't want to see the truth.

Well, maybe it was time for threats.

With a smirk on her face, Lilith sauntered over to Stan. Hands clasped behind her back, chin held high, all professional badass once again.

"You want to be a man?" She stood before him, looking him straight in the eyes. "Okay. But there will be conditions. You stay in this body, and you have this life. You get this redemption you think you want. But beyond that, you'll have nothing, Stan. No fame, no fortune, no talent. You will be just a mortal, another sad story wandering these city streets. No more special than a drunk sleeping on a heating grate. A loser. A nobody."

Stan held her gaze. Blinked a few times, as if considering what she'd offered him. Calculating it in his mind. "That would be alright with me."

The rage came to Lilith again in a flash, and she gripped her hands together more tightly. To stop herself from grabbing him once more and forcing him to go back home. To keep him in the underworld by force, to make him forget this place.

"You're making a mistake," she seethed, then turned on her heel and walked away. After ten paces, she stopped, though. Arms folded across her chest, an idea forming in her mind. She turned again. Stan stood in the door, face silhouetted against the night.

"But I must inform you." She kept her voice light and sweet, like a secretary informing a client of the fine print. "There's one thing you'll have to do first."

THIRTY-ONE

"Let me in, Abigail." Stan leaned his forehead against her apartment door and tried to keep his voice at a civil volume. Didn't want to alert the neighbors: *Hey, check it out! Satan in the hall!*

No reply came. But he could hear music playing softly inside. If he wasn't mistaken, it was Beethoven. Or maybe Brahms. Something classical and relaxing, if not just a little bit morbid. Stan closed his eyes and knocked on the door again, this time with his head.

"Please, Abby. Please. I just want to talk to you."

Another minute passed, and still he heard no one stirring inside. Just the cellos and woodwinds, lumbering along in their dirge. Finally he stood up straight, ran a hand through his hair. Tried not to remember how Lilith had pulled it with her hands as he'd—

He turned and went, shaking the thought off as his boots clomped along the old tile floor. Abby didn't want him there, that was obvious. And really he couldn't blame her. After all he'd done to her. After all she'd seen.

"What do you have to say?"

Her voice was small but angry, and Stan almost didn't hear it. He spun around and found Abigail looking at him through the slightly ajar door, still held in place by the chain lock. Just a sliver of her pale, tired face, a red, tear-stained cheek. One watery, blue eye blinking at him as if it hurt to look.

He took a step forward, and she took one back. Stan put his

hands up as if she were a wary animal he wanted to pat on the head.

"Don't leave," he said but didn't dare go any further. He stayed right where he was, halfway down the hall, almost at someone else's door. "I just want to know that you're okay. After—" He glanced at the door next to him, wondered who stood behind it. Peering out at him from the peephole. He suddenly felt exposed and knew he shouldn't say too much.

"I'm okay," Abby replied, but that was all. Her eye moved up and down Stan's body. Searching for clues, maybe. A patch of red skin, hidden horns, a spiked tail. Stan ran his hands over himself, checking for the same. Could he turn into that creature without even meaning to?

"Abby, it's just me," he said, holding his hands out to his sides. Hoping what he said was correct. The monster was gone, hidden somewhere deep inside him, or back on that desert plane. He wasn't sure where it had gone, but he could definitely feel its absence. The problem was Stan didn't know quite how it all worked—what provoked the beast to come out in the first place or what might bring him back. Worse yet, he didn't know how to control it when it did return. "No tricks. Only me this time."

He could see her body soften a bit. The shoulders slumped, the knees bent. She wiped her wet cheek and chin with her hand, smoothed her hair back from her face. "Then say what you have to say." She sounded more confident but still had a hard time looking directly at Stan.

Stan took a breath. "I'm sorry. For everything I've done to hurt you. For that night at the loft, for ignoring you, for cutting you out of my life. For…for what just happened tonight. Abigail, I didn't mean to scare you. I didn't want you to see me that way. I don't know why it came out—"

"What is *it*, Stan?" Abigail's lips trembled. "What…" She

had to pause to collect herself. To be able to speak. When she did, it was in a whisper. "What did you turn into back there?"

He sighed. Looked down at his feet for a moment. Rubbed a hand across his face, searching for the right answer to this. He couldn't just come out and say it, couldn't tell her what he had become. Or rather what he had been all along. Simmering underneath this mortal skin, unbeknownst to him. If he told her now, it would be just another deception, another black mark on his record with her.

But what else could he do? What was there left for him at this point but to tell the truth?

"I'd rather not get into it out here," he began, taking a tentative step forward. "Can I just come in—"

"Don't you come any closer!" Abigail backed away, farther into the apartment. An instinctive retreat, her hand held out in front of her. Pointing an accusing finger, a holy woman casting the demon out.

Suddenly Stan felt enraged. The heat rose up in his body like a furnace coming to life, like a heat-seeking missile zeroing in on its score. He flew to the door so fast, when he reached it, he wasn't sure how he had gotten there. All he knew was he wanted in. He wanted in, and he wanted her.

"You really think a locked door can stop me?" he snarled through clenched teeth as he pushed his arm in through the crack and waved it wildly. Toying with her, scaring her. Abigail skittered away and huddled against the wall on the other side of the room. Her whimpering and crying made Stan's anger grow.

"You know who I am, Abigail!" he shouted. Not caring about the neighbors anymore. His voice booming and raw. "You saw me. And I saw the look in your eyes. You know exactly who you're dealing with. If I wanted to hurt you—"

And suddenly he stopped. A white-hot pin stuck in his mind. Something about what he'd said: *if I wanted to hurt you.*

He didn't really, not when he was in his right mind. This was just the beast talking, trying to put the fear of the devil in the girl. Looked like it was working so far.

"Abby," Stan said, pulling his arm back and once again leaning his head on the door. He felt the rage drain away, seeping down through his body and out of his pores. In this more peaceful state, he could see exactly what he had meant to say. "If I wanted to hurt you, it would have been done already. I could have busted in and done whatever I wanted to you."

These words didn't seem to help. Abigail didn't move, didn't stop her sobs.

"Abby." He peered in at her again, could only see her back as she cowered. "I could have broken in and…and…and hurt you if I wanted to." He closed his eyes tight. This wasn't coming out like he wanted, but he didn't know what else to say to make Abigail forgive him. To take him back. Maybe she wouldn't this time; maybe she didn't want him anymore. He'd given up his last "get out of jail free" card. In fact he'd torn it up and thrown it in her face.

What an idiot, he thought, banging his head on the door again. But that didn't even begin to cover it. Without Abigail, who did he have here? Lilith? Dr. Uphir? That made him laugh. As if they cared at all about Stan. They cared for themselves only, for preserving their own eternal damnation. They wanted their leader back, their dark ruler, not Stan the artist, Stan the human with regrets and remorse. All they wanted was rage and hatred. Not all those other complicated feelings, like longing and loneliness and love.

"Abby," Stan murmured again as he slowly slid down, landing on his knees on the hard floor. He leaned into the doorframe, his head down so far his chin dug into his chest. "I went about this all wrong," he went on, talking more to himself than Abby. Assuming she wasn't listening to him anyway. "I shouldn't have banged on the door and yelled at you. I shouldn't have scared you so much. What happened at the museum—I didn't do that on purpose. I...I didn't want you to find out like that. I didn't want you to find out at all. That's why I told you to stay away from me that night at the loft. Not because—"

He sniffled, feeling a pressure building behind his eyes. "Not because I didn't want you in my life. I do. I want you more than anything. I need you. Abby, I don't want to be this thing, this person I've become. I want to start all over. Can I do that, Abby? Can I? Can we just forget this all and begin again?"

By the end his words were trailing off, his voice cracked and broken. His chest racked, breath coming in short gasps. Tears dripped from his eyes down onto the dirty floor, splashing, steaming, a string of saliva trailing from his open mouth.

Inside the apartment, Abigail had stopped sobbing. Maybe she'd used up all her tears for him. He certainly couldn't figure out why she would cry for him at all. Pathetic as he was. Behind the door he heard a shuffle, Abby bumping into a chair and setting it right. Then her fingers curled around the edge of the door again. Her eye peeked through.

"You're not going to hurt me?" she asked. Sounding timid but...hopeful. At least Stan thought that was what he heard. What he wished she felt.

He moved his hands across the floor until he found her feet, toes sticking out between door and frame. He grasped them, kissed them, let the water from his eyes wash them clean. "Never again," he said, sounding utterly defeated, shaking his head. "I'll never lay a hand on you. I'll never say a mean word to you. I will never, ever hurt you again in any way. Please, Abigail. I need you. I can't make it through this without you."

Abby gave no response. Stan remained at her feet. The longer the seconds ticked on, the more nervous he became. Maybe the forgiveness he wanted wasn't coming. Maybe she wouldn't want him back this time. Why should she? An abusive asshole ruler of the underworld—not exactly a catch, even in a city like this, where it was always hard to meet people. Abigail deserved better. He knew that, and he hoped she knew that. But he also hoped she could see how much he needed her.

In the thick silence of the hallway, the sound of the chain lock scraping out of its latch was like the voice of God speaking to Stan. A golden sunbeam shining down upon his tired back. Sweet salvation, a relief that was palpable in his gut.

He looked up, and Abigail was gone. But the door to her apartment stood wide open. He raised himself up and slowly walked inside.

〰〰

"So what are you going to do?"

Standing across the room from Stan, a mug of tea clutched in her hand, Abigail spoke in a tone of forced calmness. She sipped her hot drink, which Stan had a feeling was just as much a weapon as it was to calm her nerves. Just in case he tried anything. Could hot liquid scald the devil? The question flitted through his mind, and he held back a small but highly inappropriate laugh.

"Well, I told her I want to stay, of course." On the sofa, he had unlaced his boots and sat cross-legged, rubbing one of his ankles. He wasn't sure how he'd injured it, or when, or why every part of his body seemed to hurt. Maybe it had something to do with the transformation between this body and the other. Maybe it was an aftereffect of his still-disturbing romp with Lilith.

Abby had little to say. She'd stood the entire time they'd been talking, which, judging from the pale sunlight glowing over the tops of the buildings across the street, had been all night. Now she just nodded, looking down at her tea, as she had so many times already. Taking it all in. Not committing to anything. Not even to believing what Stan had to say.

Which was fine. He understood that. Because what he'd said, over the course of the last several hours, had been a lot. More than that, an avalanche of information, of confessions and promises. Stan had laid himself bare before Abby, telling her everything he now knew: his true identity, Lilith's and Uphir's too, how they had been sent here—or maybe come of their own accord—to drag him back, kicking and screaming if necessary, to the underworld. Then Lilith's threats against him, that if he wanted to remain on earth, he would be a nobody. Just as he'd started here, a man with no name, with nothing to show for himself.

"What does here have for you?" Abigail asked now, surprising Stan. "You're a ruler there. A god. What are you here compared to that?"

She looked at him, and Stan wanted to believe that her eyes had now softened a little. Perhaps she was just tired. Probably—she'd been through so much. But maybe she felt sorry for him too, and though normally he wouldn't want pity, if it was the only emotion she could give him at the moment, he would take it in both hands and run with it.

In response, he shrugged. Looked out the window again, considered how to answer. "I'm nothing," he said finally, his voice barely above a whisper. "I'm nothing special here. Even with the art, and the shows, and what I guess are my fans… None of that means much to me. It's entertaining. No, it's something I feel I have to do. I'm called to it." He looked at Abby, remembered her stories about her younger days, when she'd dreamed of being an artist herself. Looked around at the paintings on her walls, none of them done by her. What did they represent? Not just beauty to her but a longing, something missing from her life. Stan could really see that now, more clearly than he had before this all had come down. When he'd only been focused on finding out who he was. Not which version of himself he wanted to be.

"I imagine you understand that," he went on, peering at Abby once more. Almost afraid to look at her full on, too scared it might frighten her off. "And I guess it's just a remnant of—of the person who used to live in this body. Of Stan before I took over. It's not *me* really. So I think if I didn't have it…I would probably be okay."

Abigail nodded weakly, put a hand to her head as if holding it up. "So you would do that? You would stay here and give up the life you have, just to not…not to go back to…hell?"

The word hung between them. They'd both spoken it before throughout their conversation. But repetition had not diminished its weight. It still felt heavy as gold, like a boulder sinking fast to the bottom of an endless, black sea.

"Yes, I would. Not just to save myself from going back to hell but to be reborn as a real person." The statement felt so true to Stan, so right, he knew it was the choice he had to make.

"And that's it, then. You say the word, and they'll leave you alone?"

Once again she sounded skeptical, and once again Stan couldn't blame her for that. He'd had trouble believing it himself, when Lilith had first mentioned it. That he could simply renounce his throne, become human after millennia as an otherworldly, evil being. Surely he had followers in hell, much more than just Lilith and the doctor. An army, if he understood right. So many others who might come to call, to reclaim him as their own. Too many who would not give up the fight.

Stan let out a sigh, ran his hands through his hair. Wished he had some coffee or even some of that foul-smelling herbal stuff Abby pretended to drink. "Well, that's where it gets a little complicated."

Across the room, Abby's face fell, as if it were possible for her to look more morose. Stan saw it, and his own resolve wavered. He'd known all along he would have to reveal this to her at some point, but now that the time had come, he was having some trouble finding the right words. "Lilith told me there's a...*condition* to my staying on earth. Beyond the losing my talent and being an ordinary man."

He and Abby gazed at one another, just a moment longer than he'd thought they would. And in that second, there was no mistaking: the connection was there. Maybe it was buried for the time being, but deep down she felt it too. Just what he felt: that they had been put together in this for some greater purpose. Because they were supposed to be. Together, that was. A team of a sort.

"I need to find someone who believes I can. Be a normal man. A good person. Someone who believes I can be redeemed and is willing to help me find my way. Someone who is willing to forgive me."

The words came out of his mouth before he even knew what was happening. And as they did, he could feel the air change in the room. The heat of the late-summer morning turned into something dry and stifling, so much he had to reach up and pull away the neck of his shirt. Abigail seemed to sense it too; her delicate fingers scratched her throat, leaving red lines like wounds across it.

"Forgive you for what?" she asked, then let out a rasping cough. She set her tea on a nearby bookshelf and rubbed at her neck once more. She looked at Stan, her eyebrows lowered, as if he could explain this heat.

"For what I've done," he said, feeling the hope he'd built up over the hours quickly slinking away. He looked down at his lap, fiddled with a silver ring he'd found in Old Stan's loft. "I've done the worst things. I haven't killed anyone, not directly, but…but I've made people do it for me. I used the influence I had to tip the scales, to make people take advantage of their base desires."

Across the room, Abigail stared out the window blankly, at a black bird that had landed on the thin outside sill. Its head and beak bobbing and pecking, its sharp caws coming in through the glass.

"Exactly how did that work?" Not taking her eyes from the bird, her words far away. Fingers now toying with a thin, gold chain around her neck, with a cross hanging from it. Stan had never seen it before and wondered when she'd started wearing it. When she'd begun to feel the need for such protection.

"Do you really want to know?" He tried to keep the exhaustion from his voice, but he couldn't help it. He was tired, and tired of explaining himself. But he knew he owed it to her and that if he had any hope of fulfilling this criterion of Lilith's, Abigail was it. His only hope in this life. He sighed, turned back to his ring, and spun it around as he spoke.

"Don't believe all the theatrics you see in movies. It's much more subtle than that. There's this moment when people are in the middle of things, when they can make a choice. Whether it's something good or bad, something that's happening to them or something they're doing to others, there's always that one split second where it really is all up to them. They can walk away or they can stay and fight. They can put down the gun or they can pull the trigger. My job, as Satan, was to be there in that moment and tip their hand in favor of bad. To make them swing the ax, or drop the bomb, or smack the screaming child, or…or…a million other terrible, *terrible* things that humans do to one another. Hiroshima, the Twin Towers, Vietnam, Columbine, the Holocaust. Babies dying in bombing raids, schoolkids getting hooked on crack, you name the atrocity, my hand was in it. Pushing the players around. But never forcing them to do what they did, mind you. They always had their free will. God made sure of that when he made this place."

Stan stopped for a moment, looked up at the print of the Last Supper hanging on the wall opposite the sofa. At Jesus's sad eyes, his apostles' reaching hands. The confusion and tumult. Even the son of God couldn't stop the chaos that men create.

"But you made their will a little less free." Abigail looked at him now, her eyes bright and boring into him. Arms crossed over her chest, standing up straight and strong. Stan almost wanted to laugh at her; the little bit of evil that still lived inside him saw her defiant demeanor as a joke. As if she didn't know this went on. The good Catholic schoolgirl, all those years of lessons on how the beast would fuck you up if you gave him a chance.

But the Stan in him wouldn't let him ridicule her. Abigail didn't deserve that, and she had a right to be outraged. Any good person would be, and she was among the best. If nothing she had done so far had proven that, this reaction would tenfold. Only a woman like her would have the guts to show the devil that she wasn't scared.

"And you remember all this?" she asked, the volume of her voice rising. "You remember doing these things?"

"Not exactly. Not really." Stan squirmed in his seat, twisted his ring, uncrossed and recrossed his legs. "I don't remember being there or pushing people to commit these acts. I just know I did it, and I did it a lot. Like it was…my essence. I relished it, I guess. It's part of my unconscious memory. Sort of like you know you were born—it's a fact that it happened—but you don't remember the actual event."

A hush fell over the room. The noisy pigeon flew off; even the traffic outside, the honking cabs, the shouting drivers, seemed to fall away. Abigail and Stan looked at one another, and suddenly he realized how much the dynamic had flipped. She no longer looked timid and scared; in fact she seemed close to enraged, a steaming, stewing pot just ready to boil over. At the same time, Stan could feel his hands begin to shake. He stuffed them between his thighs and the sofa cushion to keep them still.

"Well." Abby's eyes grew wide as she crossed the room in three strides, pulling at the bottom of her shirt along the way. Stopping right in front of Stan, she pulled it totally off, then spun around. "Do you remember this?"

"Oh, God," he uttered and averted his eyes, but then made himself look again. Pink, fleshy streaks ran from her shoulder to the indentation of her spine, raised, angry tracts like wildfire across her pale skin. Covering half of her back or more, a pattern like spilled paint or water thrown against a wall. Stan reached up a hand but hesitated to touch, afraid he would hurt Abby. When their skin finally met, her body tensed, but she didn't pull away or tell him to stop. He ran his fingertips over the network of scars, amazed by how resilient human skin could be. The images flashed inside his head: Abby's father. His anger, his rage. Such darkness and at such a cost. The blood he took from Abby, from her sister and mother. The price of their souls. He broke them down, little by little over handfuls of years. Culminating in one bad day. This one that had left her scarred in more ways than one.

Stan snapped his hand back. Tears sprang to his eyes, and he swallowed hard to keep the bile down. Abigail turned to him, her expression made of stone, her eyes gone cold. Hair falling over her face. Unresponsive as he slipped his hand into hers.

"Please," he said, choking out the word. "Please, Abby, sit down. We really need to talk."

THIRTY-TWO

Abigail had only a handful of memories of the day her parents died. But even now, nearly twenty years later, they were vivid as the sun shining in the sky. Illuminating all around her, shrouding her life in their hazy glow. Every decision she made, it seemed, depended on how much they haunted her on any particular day. Her isolation, her depression, all offshoots of that one day, that one moment that changed it all.

As a child she'd been happy. She still remembered that too, in blips and frames. Snapshots of her second birthday, blowing out the candles with her family gathered round. Her dad, Carl, holding her on the swing set in the backyard. Her mom, Ann, giving her a bubbly bath. And always smiling, smiling, smiling. Not just her but all of them. Even Lily had seemed at peace then. So unlike how she was now.

"When I was five, everything began to change," she told Stan as she wiped her eyes for the hundredth time. The skin around them was swollen and tender from too much crying, her nose congested, her throat sore. "I started school, and that meant my mom didn't have to be home with me anymore, so she went out and got a job. At a donut shop."

Even as she spoke, she wasn't sure why. Stan had asked her to sit down.

"That must have been difficult for her. After all those years of staying home with you and your sister." Stan sat on the other end of the sofa from Abby, obviously trying to keep as much space between them as possible. Trying to show her some

241

respect. Abigail perched on the couch's arm, hugging a pillow in front of her.

"It was. It was good for her. I mean it wasn't a life-changing career, but it got her out of the house and gave her a little money of her own. Made her feel like part of the world again." She paused. Remembered how happy her mom had been to start that silly job. As if she'd been a CEO of a Fortune 500. Over time, of course, the work lost its shine, and it became just a place to go a few days a week, to pass the hours while the girls were at school and collect a few dollars that she never even spent on herself. Every penny she made went toward something for her daughters—new clothes, an afternoon at the movies, food when their father drank away his paycheck.

Ann also had a savings account. Not in a bank, but in an envelope hidden in a shoebox in the back of her messy bedroom closet. Someplace Abby's dad would never look.

"This is our rainy-day fund," she would tell Abby and Lily as they watched her count out the bills from her tips, all singles, and add them to the box. "Just in case the storm ever gets too bad. We'll always be able to find safety. This money will get us there."

At the time Abby had truly believed her mom's socking her pay away had something to do with the weather. It was only later—much later, many years after her mom's death—that Abby understood the hurricane was really her father. A tornado, a tsunami that drowned and killed everything that should have been precious to him. Leaving nothing but a wretched, gaping hole in the lives of those who had the bad luck to survive.

Abigail cleared her throat. Shook her hair back off her neck and shoulders, stroked her fingers across her brow. "It was my dad, see, who didn't like the idea. He always criticized my mom for being lazy when she was home with us. She was dealing with two babies, and still cleaned all day, and had dinner on the table every night at five when he came home. She waited on him hand and foot and never, ever complained. But nothing she did was ever enough. But then when she got a job..."

Abigail teared up again and dropped her chin to her chest. Her father's shouting ringing loudly in her head.

What the fuck'd you get a job for? Don't I support you? You think there's something wrong with my money? You ungrateful bitch. I'll show you who's the breadwinner in this house.

And then off the belt would come. He didn't discriminate when it came to beatings—any of the females in his house would do. Wife, daughters, they were all the same: freeloading, no-good sluts. If they were lucky, the edge of his leather belt was all they got.

"He didn't like that either," Stan finished softly for her. Abigail looked at him and nodded her head almost imperceptibly, the wall she'd built to keep him out lowering just a little. This only made her feel worse. Why did he have to sound so understanding? And be so perceptive of her thoughts? Why couldn't he be mean and rude, as dangerous as his alter ago would have him be? So she could just turn him away and be done with it; so she wouldn't get involved in this mess, this incredible, unbelievable situation he was in. So she could run far and fast, and get away like her rational brain was telling her to.

But then there was her instinct. Her gut feeling. That was a lot more sentimental. It wanted to give Stan a chance. Looking at his tired eyes, his messed-up hair, his clothes all wrinkled and disheveled from this night on the couch, Abby almost felt sympathy for him once again, as she had from the first time he'd walked into her office. He'd been a man then and still was one now, if appearances counted for anything. This was just Stan before her, not some devil. Not *the* devil, with a capital D.

Stan Foster, former psych patient, quasi-famous New York City artist. Potential love of her life and a damn good kisser to boot.

And Satan, she told herself silently. *Don't ever forget that part.*

Her back stiffened. When she spoke, her voice was cold. "What do you have to tell me? What does it have to do with this?"

Stan sat up straighter too. Cleared his throat a couple of times, consulted the Last Supper one more time. Abby had seen him staring at it as she'd talked, as he'd pulled the story of her early life from the recesses of her mind. She hadn't spoken of it in years, not to herself or to anyone else. She'd simply put it in a shoebox, like her mother's rainy-day fund, and put it away for safekeeping. For her own safety and everyone else's, because God knew if she let those feelings out, she couldn't do what she did. Not in life, not in her job. And so many people depended on her.

In her profession they called this *suppression*, and though she'd never recommend it to a patient, so far it had worked for her.

"I was there," he said, so quietly Abby almost didn't hear him.

"You were what?" she asked, a hollow feeling coming to her stomach. Then a wrenching, a nauseated churn.

Stan looked at her. Met her gaze and didn't let it go. He shifted in his seat to face her, bringing a leg up onto the sofa cushion in front of him. "I was there on the night it happened."

He held out a hand, motioning to her shoulder. Reflexively she reached for it, her fingers slipping in under her T-shirt. Feeling the raised scars, the hard roadmap by which she navigated her life. Abby shook her head. Softly at first, then so vigorously it made her brain hurt. Stan remained silent, watching her with pity on his face.

"Your father was on a rampage. Again. He'd been doing it a lot lately. His drinking was so bad by that point that it was affecting his health. He didn't realize it, but his liver was failing, and his kidneys weren't far behind. All he knew was he was in pain, and that added to his rage."

Abigail closed her eyes. Remembering her father in his chair, the recliner in the living room. He'd spent so much time in it, the seat had a permanent dent in the shape of his ass. Toward the end he'd barely left it, even to go to work. Just stayed there popping Buds all day and dozing in front of the TV.

"Then he got fired," Stan continued as if reading her mind. "Went in one morning, and the boss told him to go home. He'd been at the same job for twenty years. The only thing he'd stuck with aside from his marriage, and that hadn't gone too well either. He went home aiming to take both of these problem out on your mother."

Abigail's nails dug into her shoulder, clawing at the sheath of dead skin that covered it. She remembered that Saturday. She'd sat at the kitchen table, reading a book while her mom made her breakfast. Soft-boiled eggs and toast—her favorite. The radio was on, an old Elton John song. The eggs rattled and bumped in the rolling water. Mom scraped a butter knife across her toast.

"You were sixteen then, and tall—bigger than your dad. Probably stronger too, since he was so sick. And when he came in the door shouting, you stood up and yelled back. Told him to get out, to go drink his fucking beer, to leave your mother alone. He wasn't used to this. You talking back, threatening him. It only made him more mad."

She nodded absently. Remembering the stink of sweat on her father's arm as he coiled it around her neck, catching her in a choke hold. How she'd scratched at his skin until it bled. Her mother screaming, screaming at him to stop.

"*Shut up, bitch!*" Stan raised his arm and did a backhanding motion. "He swung around and hit your mom across the side of her head. You heard something crack—maybe the bones in his hand, maybe her nose as she fell face-first into the kitchen counter, then crumpled to the floor. She was knocked out."

Abigail closed her eyes, brought her head down to her knees. Hugging herself to keep from floating away. Her head was so light. Too many memories, all that pain she'd stuffed down inside herself for so many years. She reached into the arm of her shirt and rubbed her callous, scarred shoulder, as if that could make this all go away.

"You got out of his grip and went over to your mom," Stan went on, now holding his hands out in front of him as if grabbing a person by the arms. "You shook her and shook her, but she wouldn't wake up. You sobbed over her, your tears dropping onto her pale, smooth face."

"She was always so beautiful when she was like that." Abigail laughed at the morbid thought, then raised her head. She looked around the room, her vision blurred by her gathering tears. "That wasn't the first time he'd knocked her out. When she went unconscious, her body relaxed, and I could almost see how she was meant to be. Not so tense and scared like she always was but a *woman*. A human being. With little wrinkles at the corners of her eyes, and crooked front teeth, and—"

She couldn't finish. Remembering her mother's face was too much. The way her lips had gone slack, her nose cut and bleeding from where she'd hit it on the edge of the counter. Yes, Abby had seen her that way before, and far worse, and more times than she could remember by then. But that didn't make it any less shocking. No matter how often she had witnessed her father's rage, the collateral damage always stung. It always felt brand new.

"Your father didn't like that, you helping your mother," Stan said, picking up the story where she'd left off. "Because he didn't see it that way. All he saw was you going against him. He saw you taking her side. And he could not stand for that. Especially not on that day, when he'd been dealt such an ego-crushing blow. For him, losing his job was like getting castrated. It took away his manhood and his control over his family. If he wasn't the source of money, what did he have to hold over your heads?"

Abby slid down onto the sofa and sat cross-legged, facing Stan. She took a deep breath and wiped her eyes once again. "He was a real bastard." Her voice was hoarse, barely more than a whisper.

Stan went on as if she hadn't said anything. Getting himself into the story, telling it like he was describing a movie he'd seen or some salacious book he'd read. Abby didn't quite like the way he shifted in his seat, half turning to face her, or the glint she saw in his eyes when she finally let her gaze meet his.

"He was, but he was about to become a whole lot more than that. Watching you crouch over your mother, he got this spark of in idea inside his twisted mind. The pot on the stove. The water had mostly boiled away—just an inch or two remained. But it was enough. It rolled at a steady boil, the eggs dried and cracked bouncing from one wall of the pot to another. Carl reached out—"

Abigail looked away. Brought a hand up to her mouth to keep from crying out. She knew what was coming, of course. She'd lived it then relived it a million times. Dad reaching for the pot. Curling his dirty, rough fingers around its black handle. She hadn't seen him do it, but she'd heard the pot scrape against the stove's metal burner. The noise hadn't registered at the time; she'd been too busy trying to revive her mother. Smacking her pallid cheeks, raising her hands and dropping them onto the hard floor. They landed with a dead-weight *thud* every time.

"Mom. Oh, God, Mom," she'd whimpered. Afraid that her mother was dead but too scared even to think about the possibility. What would Abby do without her? Stuck all alone in the house with that monster of a man, suddenly his only target. The only female to absorb his rage. Lily, almost three years older than Abby, had moved out months ago, on the day she'd turned eighteen. Just packed up a bag and never came back. Now she stayed with friends uptown, she wouldn't say exactly where. Abby hadn't seen her since, but Lily called twice a week just to make sure she was alive.

The phone, Abby had thought, coming out of her panicked stupor. She had to call 911, get some medics to come and take care of her mother. Back then there were no cell phones, just the yellow rotary with the curly cord, mounted on the wall several feet above. Abigail looked up at it and saw something out of the corner of her eye. A shadow. Sort of man-shaped but not like her hulking, stocky father. This image was tall and lithe, slipping out of her field of view as if it had never been there at all.

And then came the searing, blinding pain. Out of nowhere the boiling water pouring over her shoulder and back. Melting her thin shirt, meshing it with her skin as the steaming liquid ate through to the bone in spots. Abby didn't know what it was, what her father had done. She only knew that it hurt like hell and then nothing more. In moments she lay unconscious in a pile on top of her mother.

"Abigail," Stan said, bringing her mind back to the present. She looked and saw the pain on his face, cheeks flushed, brow furrowed. Why did he seem so upset? "Your father didn't want to hurt you. Not like that."

A sob pushed its way out of Abby so violently, she snorted

and coughed as she cried. Immediate tears in her eyes, the pressure in her head unbearably tight. She put her palms flat on her temples, trying to make it stop. To make all this pain go away, to push it back down where it had slept for so long.

"You don't know anything about it," she hissed through clenched teeth, giving Stan a nasty glower. How dare he defend her father, after all that man had done? "So just keep your mouth shut."

At that Stan looked taken aback. He shifted in his seat and looked at the room, avoiding meeting Abigail's eyes. For a moment he closed his own, rubbing them roughly with his thumb and his forefinger.

"I know everything about it," he said, his voice just as low as hers. He blinked hard and stared at the blank TV as if lost in thought. Then turned his head back. "Didn't you wonder how I know the whole story? Abby, I was there that day. I made your father throw the water."

The stillness and silence in the apartment were like lead in the air. Abby felt her stomach drop, then the rest of her right along with it. Her limbs felt like dead weight, unable to move, unwilling to respond to her brain's commands: *Get up. Run. Flee.* Her body wouldn't do any of these things. She was rooted to her spot on the sofa cushion, hands still on her head.

"How can you say such a thing?" she asked, her voice wavering more and more on each word. Her lips trembled, then her shoulders, her hands. Her whole body. The feeling came back all at once, hot and fast like a blaze rushing through her blood. Like it had that day. The water pouring down, the scalding pain.

"How…" She shook her head, not even sure what question to ask. "Stan, what are you talking about?"

He sighed then, as if he didn't want to explain what he had

said. Not out of hubris but more with a sense of stinging, prickling mortal shame. Abby could see that very clearly: Stan was embarrassed by what he'd done, whatever that might have been. Whatever he thought it was. The idea that he'd had something to do with her father's abuse—it seemed so ridiculous to her. But it was very real to him. She could see it in the set of his eyes, the way his lips downturned. He wanted her to hear his confession. And as compelled as he seemed to say it, she felt just as obligated to listen.

"When your father reached for the pot, he had a moment of doubt. Just a split second, but it was enough for me to slip in and do my work. Or rather to get him to do the work for me." Stan shot a glance at her then returned to staring at his hands in his lap. "You see, if I could get him to throw that water on you, it would change your whole perception of the world. You'd had it bad before, but this would take your suffering to another level. It would make you not believe in God. You were already on the fence. You just needed a final shove. And that was what I did then, remember?"

"Yeah, you pushed the players around." Abigail's voice was distant. She stared at him, too numb to cry, too tired to run. "And when—" she started to say but stopped to swallow the lump in her throat. "When my dad shot my mother? And then himself? Were you there for that too?"

Stan shook his head slowly. "That one was all him. After he burned you, he lost what little humanity he had. You call him a monster? At that point he really was. By the time he stood in front of her with the pistol just a few months later, there was no Carl to speak of. Only the shadow of death."

"So why did he kill himself?" Abby's voice grew louder, and she swiped her palms down her legs, unconsciously wiping away her father's blood. Like she'd done that day in the bathroom. Her mother dead outside the door. Face blown off with one shot, another in the chest just to make sure her heart stopped beating.

"Evil isn't the only force in this universe," Stan replied quietly. "And everything must be in balance. For all the bad decisions I influenced, there were angels on the other side helping people to do what was right and good. Keeping the equilibrium, so to speak."

Abigail laughed now, a dry and brittle sound that scraped its way out of her throat. "An angel made my father commit suicide? That doesn't seem very righteous to me. If anything I'd think they would save his life."

Now Stan nodded. "There are good angels and bad angels. And then there are some in between. They switch their allegiances as often as humans change their minds. Always going for the winning team, whichever that may be at any given moment. Sometimes they just follow their own agendas."

She looked at him in silence for a minute. Taking it all in, processing this strange information. "And it was one of those that got to him. That made him turn the gun on himself."

"That's my best guess. I'm still not sure how all of it works. Being king of the underworld doesn't come with an employee handbook." When he got no reaction, Stan reached over and slipped his hand into hers. He smiled. "That was a joke, Abby."

She didn't feel like laughing, though. Not anymore. And not at any joke where the fate of humanity was the punch line.

"Stan, I need you to leave." She pulled her hand away, but his remained on her leg.

"I—Abby—don't—" He sat up straight, stuttering as he grabbed her knee. "Please, don't do this. I'm not that thing anymore. I told you—"

"I don't care, Stan." She gripped his fingers and removed

them from her leg. Trying to keep her voice steady and the hys-
teria she felt in her chest at bay. "You told me a lot of things."

"Don't you believe me?"

She could hear the desperation in his voice. Why was her
approval so important? She stood up. "I do believe you. That's
the problem, Stan. Now get out. Please."

He made no move to stand. He wasn't going to leave.

"Get out!" she screamed, her words shrill. Then closed her
eyes and covered her ears. Blocking out the sight of Stan, the
sound of his breathing. Trying to make him disappear.

"Get out, get out, get out!" she cried again, and when she
opened her eyes, she had gotten her wish. She was alone in the
apartment. Stan was gone.

THIRTY-THREE

Maybe it was all a dream. Abby tried saying it in her head a few times, turning it over and over as she lay in bed, staring at the ceiling. Maybe that visit from Stan had been a hallucination. She'd had some bad tea, or maybe someone had slipped their extra pills into her coffee at work. Stranger things had been known to happen. Like, for instance, the man you love turning out to be Satan.

She laughed but stopped quickly. Her ribs hurt, her back was sore, and her shoulders felt like she had been dead-lifting weights in her sleep. All the stress, the tensed muscles. Sleeping in fits and starts, and pacing the floors of her apartment when she couldn't get any sleep at all. None of this was good for her body or for her mind. But she couldn't stop thinking about all that had happened. Couldn't put Stan out of her head once and for all. Even though she knew she should, that never, ever seeing him again would be best for her.

The man was the devil, after all. Really, truly Satan himself. Whenever Abby thought about it, her first reaction—still—was to think it was somehow a mistake. Maybe Stan wasn't the devil but rather being manipulated by the devil. Maybe she hadn't seen what she'd seen; maybe everything Stan had told her was a lie. Maybe he was just a psychopath, an amnesiac who'd made up this twisted persona for himself. He had nothing to cling to in this world save his wretched art and the equally wretched woman who peddled it. When Stan had shown up at Abby's door last night, she could smell Lilith all over him. Her perfume was distinctive—like decaying flowers, pungent and sickly sweet. It hadn't been difficult to figure out how Stan had gotten doused in the stuff.

"That is a mental image I do not want," Abigail told herself and threw the covers off her body. She swung her legs to the floor and stood up, stretching her arms high as she looked out the window. Typical New York day, traffic rumbling, people walking everywhere. Scowling and laughing at one another, joking and shaking hands. The big brotherhood of man. If Abby had felt left out of it before, she was the world's biggest outcast now. Nothing like dating the antichrist to make you a pariah in the community.

But they weren't dating. She had to remind herself of that again. Really, they never had been. Not officially. So what was it that drew her emotions back to Stan over and over again, to love and tenderness and this overwhelming desire to make this life good for him? As if she could do that. If there was one thing Abby had learned from her parents, it was that you can't rely on another person as the source of your own happiness. That had to come from within, and if you couldn't find it there, well, then, you were basically screwed. Like her father, who had hated himself so much he couldn't even let other people love him. Not even his own family. He'd ended up killing his wife because he couldn't stand that look of compassion in her eyes. Even after all the years he'd tortured her and yelled at her until she'd broken down to nothing, Abby's mother had still felt love for her father. She had never understood that before. Now, she thought, she had an inkling of how her mother could have such an open heart.

In the bathroom Abigail brushed her teeth, washed her face, got ready for the day. She had an hour before work, so she took her time picking out what to wear and putting on some makeup. Made herself coffee, ate some breakfast, listened to music. And the whole while, kept all bad thoughts at bay. Just as if this were any other morning and nothing was out of the ordinary. At quarter to eight, same time as every day, she picked up her bag and keys and headed out the door to catch the A train uptown.

Walking to the station, dodging all the other people on the streets who were hurrying to get to work, Abigail pulled out her cell phone to check for any messages. She had been on call last night but during her hours with Stan had neglected any buzzing or ringing she'd heard from the phone. Looked liked she'd missed three calls, four text messages, and six e-mails, most of them from her supervisor. None of them pleasant and friendly. Abigail read the texts and scanned the subjects of the e-mails but didn't bother with the voicemails. There would be enough yelling, she figured, when she showed up at the hospital.

Just as she got to the subway entrance on the corner of West Fourth, she noticed one other e-mail she'd missed. From Stan, it said. Subject: "Please read."

Abigail stopped at the top of the station's stairs, blocking the way. Eyes fixed on her phone. The throng of commuters around her pushed and swayed until she was moved to the side, and she leaned on the railing that surrounded the underground entrance. Still staring at the e-mail. Trying to decide what to do.

And then she just opened it.

Abby,

I know you must hate me right now, and I can't blame you for that. But I wish you would believe me when I say I am a changed man. Or, rather, I'm the man you've known. I'm not the monster anymore, and I don't want to be him again. I will do anything to stay in this life—and to prove to you that you can trust me.

I told you about Lilith's ultimatum, that I have to find one person to believe I can be redeemed, that I'm worthy of redemption. After all I told you last night about how I hurt you and your family, I can't imagine why or how you could forgive me. But I also know you are the only person in this world who can help me. You are a pure soul, Abigail. You are made of light. No one means more to me than you do, and no one else's forgiveness and support would mean as much to me as yours would.

In the end, of course, it's up to you. And if you find that you can't do it, I will never hold it against you. I know what I ask of you is very big and very tough. I would not blame you for wanting to wash your hands of me.

Either way you decide, I'll be waiting for you on Saturday at 5:00 p.m. at the Cloisters, out in the courtyard. Lilith has given me five days before I'll be returned to the underworld, if I can't find someone to believe in me. If you can't, or don't want to, or if you simply don't show up, I'll slip back to hell and never bother you again. Though the oath of a demon might not hold much weight, this much I promise you.

With love,
Stan

With love. Abigail scoffed at the words as her eyes quickly scanned the letter again. She sure didn't feel pure or made of light. All she felt was heavy, her feet made of lead, her mind filled with a ton of bricks. How could he ask this of her? And how could she say no? Given all she knew about him, all he had been through. But she had to, didn't she? Who was she, after all, to decide it was okay to pardon Satan? To give him a pass for all he'd done, especially to her and hers. Abigail reached up and touched her shoulder, rotating it, her fingers crawling inside her blouse to feel the scarring there. She didn't want to cry again, but that old, familiar pressure began to build behind her eyes.

Closing the e-mail, she went back to her texts. Opened one from her supervisor and tapped out a reply: "Taking a sick day. Sorry for last night. Unexpected emergency. See you tomorrow."

She hit "send," and off it went. There was no way she could work today, no chance she could concentrate. Her mind raced in a thousand different directions. *Forgive Stan, don't forgive Stan. Meet him on Saturday, don't meet him. Going crazy, not going crazy.* For every troubling thought, she had a counterargument and in the space of only a moment, she'd changed her mind a handful of times. Snapping back to reality and looking around, she watched all the people run. Anxious to get to work, to sit at their desks, to answer their phones. Waiting for their paychecks so they could buy more things to fill their homes, to fill up the holes in their hearts. A lot of little birds scrabbling, cheeping at one another as they fought over twigs for their nests.

That's all we are, she thought. Animals in the wilderness, intent on putting one another down to get ourselves ahead. On killing one another. Maybe not outright, with guns or knives, but slowly. Secretly. How many different ways did people hurt others and themselves every day, so many without even knowing it? Pushing and shoving on the streets, putting each other down. Stuffing their mouths with junk food, drinking themselves into oblivion. Massacres and drugs and wars, a world undoubtedly controlled by evil. Led by the hand into a dark, dismal void from which there was no escape.

Abigail closed her eyes. Remembered her childhood days, all those Sundays spent on her knees at High Mass. No wonder she thought this way. To a Catholic we are all sinners, all of us caught in a web that only God and Jesus can rescue us from. The best we can hope for is redemption when we meet our end. On this earth, though, we're doomed, and there's not much we can do about it.

"But I have a choice," Abigail said, flicking her eyes open. The thought suddenly occurring to her. Around her everything was so bright, the sun beating down on her weary head. She raised a hand to shield her eyes and turned back the way she had come, though not to go home. She had a very different destination in mind.

The Jesus statue was still there. But it looked somehow smaller than she remembered. Abby hadn't even walked by the Church of the Redeemer in so many years, not since her parents had died. She stood on the sidewalk now and watched him for a minute, this watchdog of her youth. Remembering touching his robes as she'd rushed past, her mother's hand around her wrist. Hurrying to get inside. Scurrying to find a seat. In those days they were always rushing, it seemed. Always running away from something.

She went up the steps now quickly and touched the statue

once more. Its plaster had aged and worn, leaving rough patches and spots of green mold. Too much weather, not enough love. Like everything else in this world, she thought.

Trying the dark, wooden doors to the left of the Jesus statue, Abigail found them unlocked. She pulled one opened and walked inside. As soon as it closed, a darkness enveloped her, the only dim light coming in through the stained-glass windows of the sanctuary. A musty incense filled the air, and she inhaled it deeply. Frankincense and myrrh, remnants of the previous day's Mass.

"Let my prayer be directed as incense in thy sight: the lifting up of my hands, as evening sacrifice," she recited. Psalm 141. She used to have them memorized. Not just the popular ones—your 23, your 121—but all of them front to back. And many other parts of the Bible. While her classmates were reading *The Babysitters' Club* and braiding each other's hair, Abby had been at home, alone in her room, immersed in God's world of suffering and fear. Trying to find some redemption, a way out of the hurt in which she lived.

Walking down the middle of the nave, Abigail ran a hand along the pews. She'd spent so many Sundays here, praying and praying, begging her God relief. Sometimes on Saturdays too, and if it was real bad at home, at the late Mass on Wednesdays. Sitting on the hard pews, breathing in the incense when the thurifer passed her way. Swinging his censer three times, once for God, the son, the holy spirit. The smoke a symbol of the prayers of the faithful rising up to heaven.

"Good morning. What brings you here today?"

Abigail spun around. A priest stood behind her. Not much older than herself, it seemed. Brown hair and a gentle smile. He looked at her, eyes gleaming, waiting for her response.

"Uh." It was all she could think of. What was she doing there

after all? Why had this thought occurred to her? When she'd
stood by the subway stop, it had made so much sense: Having
trouble with the devil? Go to church to repent! Or at least to
seek some advice from the experts in the field. The Catholics
were no joke when it came to saving souls from Satan's grip. But
what could they tell her about the job of saving Satan's mortal
soul?

"Would you like to sit down?" the priest offered, his voice
as soft as his grin, then put a hand on her arm and guided her
over to a nearby pew. Abigail sat down, clutching her bag to her
chest. Still unsure what to say.

The priest sat down too, and peered at her. "Is there something troubling you, my child?"

Abigail stifled a nervous laugh. *My child*. He sounded like a
priest from a movie. Even the way he tilted his head and rested
his arm on the seat in front of them.

"No," she replied automatically. It wasn't the first time she'd
been asked. After her mother was gone, Abigail renounced the
church, but it wasn't ready to give up on her yet. The clergy
had descended on her house—or rather on her aunt's apartment, where she'd stayed until graduation. Priests and nuns,
showing up and ringing the bell. Trying to get her back. Saying
they worried about her. Not about her health or her sanity or
whether she did well in school. Just whether or not she went to
church. Confessed her sins. As if she had so much in her life to
be sorry for.

"What about my father?" she had asked one of them once,
purely out of frustration. She was tired of the strong-arming,
the way they pushed her to repent. She hadn't done anything
wrong. This mess was not of her making. In her eyes, it was
God's fault—God's and her father's. End of fucking list.

"God will judge him for what he has done," the priest had
said. He'd been a youngish man then, much like this guy next

to her now. His voice had been grim and grave, his eyes dark, downcast. "And I can't blame you for judging him too. Not just your father, I mean. The both of them."

Though it did not convince her to go back to church at the time, the priest's answer had stayed with Abby. It was the first— the only—honest thing she'd heard any of them say. Rather than toeing the party line and trying to get her to do so too, this priest, this man, had shown her that he was human too. That he suffered and had doubts. That sometimes he questioned things that were sold as truth.

"Father David," she blurted out now. That had been the priest's name. Surely he was old now, maybe even dead. Gone on to his great reward. Abby hoped he had confessed what he'd said to her before he'd gone.

"Oh, you mean Bishop Casey?" The priest grinned. "If you want to see him, this is your lucky day. Usually he's over at St. Patrick's—that's his home base now. But he's visiting us today." He stood up. "Come. I'll take you to him."

"So you're telling me...you met Satan. Or someone who says he's Satan."

Though Abigail's exchange with Father David had happened some years ago, little about him had changed. A little more gray in his hair, his body slightly thicker around the middle. And now, instead of a priest's black, he wore the white robe of a bishop. A red sort of cape around his shoulders, a satin skullcap on his head. Around his neck hung a large, wooden cross, and he'd been fiddling with it as Abby had told him the story: How she'd met Stan. What he had become. The offer that now stood before her.

"Yes," she replied, her voice sounding tentative. This wasn't the response she'd foreseen. She'd thought he'd be more under-standing. "I met him. I know him. I saw him in his true form."

Bishop Casey folded his hands. Rested his chin on them, looking at Abigail as he thought. "What did he look like?"

Abby let out a sigh and stood up from her chair. "I shouldn't have come here. Look, I know you don't believe me—"

Casey motioned for her to sit down. "On the contrary. I believe every word you've said. I'm just curious if he appears as we've been told for so long."

Slowly lowering herself to sit again, Abby kept her eyes on the bishop. Still wary, but what other choice did she have? Who else could she talk to about this?

"You mean did he have red skin...and cloven feet...and black hair? I'm not really sure what I saw. But I can say this. That he also looked just like one of us."

Casey sat forward, leaning against the desk. They sat alone in the other priest's office, door closed—but Abigail wondered if he was listening outside.

Abby hesitated to reply. What if the bishop knew who Stan was? He could have been an art buff or at least kept tabs on the more controversial stuff. Stan's work had raised more than one religious eyebrow, that was for sure. And she didn't want to expose him. Not yet. Not until she'd made up her mind.

"I understand," Casey said when he got no further response from her. His voice was just as soothing as Abby remembered from their conversation long ago. "You don't want to say who he is. That's alright, my dear." He sat back, picking up his cross again. Fingers working around its edges as his mind worked. "You said he presented a choice to you. Tell me more about that."

Abby blew some hair out of her face then settled back in her chair. It wasn't very comfortable, and neither was she. Bag balanced on her knees, pointing her feet so her toes touched the floor. The posture of a teenager, of a scared little girl with a very big secret.

"He's been given a choice, he said. He can stay on earth and renounce his throne in the underworld, but he'd be a nobody here. No talent, nothing special about him. Just an ordinary Joe like the rest of us."

"Not quite the rest of us," Casey interrupted, flashing a smile at her. "From what I remember, you were quite an artist as a girl. Do you still paint?"

Abigail's cheeks grew flushed. She looked down at the floor. "Uh, no," she mumbled. "No, I don't do that now."

"Too bad. You had quite a passion for it."

"There's one more catch," she said, wanting to change the subject as quickly as possible. "To Sta—to Satan's story. If he wants to stay here, he has to find someone to believe in him—to believe he can be redeemed. That his soul is worthy and that he deserves to start again as a man."

"And let me guess: that someone is you."

Abigail looked back at him now and nodded. "If I forgive him, he can stay in this world." She swallowed. "Then he can stay with me."

Across the desk, Casey leaned back in his chair and let out a sigh. Put his hands up behind his head and looked up at the ceiling as if something—someone—up there could possibly help. "So you want me to tell you what to do."

Abigail thought about it. Was that why she'd come here? To let someone else make the decision for her? "No. That's not what I want. I just need advice. I know what my heart says. I just need to know it isn't leading me down the wrong path. Is it true that anyone can be redeemed? Or is there a point of no return?"

Bishop Casey looked at her and smiled again, then folded his hands on the desk. "It is written that all people can be redeemed. And who am I to say what path is right? Only one knows that." He raised a finger and pointed it up. "Unfortunately, He's not saying. Not directly, anyway. But you know what your heart wants, as you said, and often that's the way He speaks to us. That's how He shows us His will. You say he told you that he—or Satan—visits people at just that moment. Well, be assured that God also makes those visits." He paused, looking at Abigail through squinted eyes. "You're sure you know what you want?"

Abby's mind reached into the past. Pictured Stan as he had been, as the man she had loved. Coming into her office, lost but well-dressed, alone but full of life. The first time she'd seen his art, his loft. How he'd taken her into his world.

And then thrown me out of it, she thought but then tried to wipe that part of it away. That hadn't been Stan then, when he'd thrown her, when he'd shut her out of his life. That had been the beast talking, stripping him of anything that was good in his life.

"I want him back. I want to believe in him," she said now, her voice cracking, her throat suddenly dry. "Is that selfish? To save him just to have him by my side?"

"And now abideth faith, hope, love," said the bishop.

"But the greatest of these is love," Abby finished. "First Corinthians."

"Very good." Casey winked at her and sat up straight again. "I'll also remind you of Paul, who said we should separate ourselves from evil. Abigail, do you know what you're getting into here? Are you strong enough to handle it? I know you're worried about this man. And with your good, good heart, you want to help him all you can, in any way that might be possible. But

I am worried about you. I want to know you'll come through this okay."

She smiled weakly. Like she hadn't thought that herself. A cynic, a depressed psychiatrist, and a lapsed Catholic to boot. Who better to fight the ruler of darkness? "What was it Jesus said? 'If your brother sins against you, rebuke him, and if he repents, forgive him'?"

"So he sinned against you personally." As soon as Casey asked the question, he put a hand in the air as if to make the words stop. "Of course he did. I'm sorry, Abigail. In probably the worst way possible. And now he asks for forgiveness from you. That is a heavy weight." He held out both hands in front of him now, palms up. "I don't envy you this choice you have to make."

Without thinking, Abby reached out and put both her hands into his. Without a flinch, he gripped them tight.

"If this man truly wants to change," Bishop Casey said almost in a whisper, "and he's asking you for the help he needs to do so, perhaps it is your duty to respond. We all owe something to one another as human beings. God tells us to love one another before ourselves. And to love not with words but with action. He may be the devil. We will never know for sure, Abby. But he is a man too. That's all I'll say. In the end, the choice is up to you."

THIRTY-FOUR

W hat does a man do when he knows he's only got a few days left on earth? Stan felt like he'd been in this position before. Waking up on the day after his confessional with Abigail, something felt familiar to him. This hint of finality, of everything drawing to a close. There was a sense of freedom in it, a feeling that nothing and everything mattered all at once, and that he could care or not and the result would ultimately be the same. Lying in his bed, staring out the skylight above at the white, puffy clouds, he thought about Old Stan. Wondered if he'd done the same thing on his last day in this loft. Slept late, pondered his mortality, and decided at last that this would be the day. Or had he just been by the bridge and thought he'd give it a shot?

Granted, now he wasn't about to die. If Abby didn't accept his proposal and grant his wish, he'd simply return to hell as ruler and never be allowed back on earth. It wasn't the same as death; maybe it was worse. At least humans who thought about suicide didn't know exactly what was waiting for them.

The sun came out, and Stan's mind switched rapidly between wanting to cram as much activity as he could into the next four days and just going right back to sleep. Eventually the middle ground won. He got up, brushed his teeth and hair, did all the mundane, specifically human tasks he had come to repeat every day by default. It was well after noon already, and his stomach growled, so he made his way a few blocks over to One and One, a pub he'd frequented during his night crawls. In daylight it looked much less inviting; most of the tables were empty, just a few lost souls nursing drinks at the bar. He ordered a burger with a pint of Guinness, then another of Bass, and finished it all off with a double shot of Jameson's. Finally he felt appropriately lubricated and ready to face the day.

But once he got outside, the bright sun overwhelmed him, and he stood on the corner of Houston and First not knowing where to go. Arm up over his head to shield his eyes, he looked up and down the block, waiting for a sign of sorts. An omen, anything that would lead him down the path he was supposed to follow. A sign from God.

Nothing came. As usual. Which only made his sudden lack of motivation worse. With a belly full of greasy food and alcohol, he began to feel sleepy, and all he could think about was his bed. With only three days and a handful of hours left, he turned back down Houston and headed home.

Stan dreamt of hell again. Or maybe he was really there. The vast plains stretched out all around him, the ash and the dust kicking up. His body in its true form, red and muscled and tight. He closed his eyes and breathed deep, taking in the scent of this place that might now be his home. If Abigail rejected him. If he couldn't stay on earth. He'd have to get used to it again, the overwhelming odor of burning skin, the ceaseless screams. Had he really felt at home here once? Maybe so, but he wasn't sure he could do it again. Though he didn't know what other choice he had.

"That's right," a voice said to him, hot breath blowing across his face. Like rotten flowers and cigarette butts. "You know this is where you belong."

Stan opened his eyes, and there was Lilith. Standing next to his bed, her face hovering just an inch from his. Her tongue licked out from between her glassy, red lips and lapped at his sweating cheek. Stan rolled over and out of the bed, clutching the sheet around him as he sprang to his feet.

"What are you doing here?"

Lilith stood up slowly. Cocked her hip and put her hands on her waist. "I came to see you, my boy." She looked Stan up and down, assessing him as usual like a piece of meat. "To see if you're ready yet."

"Ready for what?" Stan picked up his pants from the floor then slipped them on. As if she hadn't seen him without them before.

"To come home, of course." Lilith pulled a cigarette from her purse and snapped her silver lighter on, then jerked it closed. Took a long drag, sent a stream of acrid smoke into the room. "To give up this charade of yours. You know she won't forgive you, Stan. I don't know why you bother trying."

"You know nothing," he said, pointing a finger at her as he looked for his shirt. He found it tangled in the sheets and put it on too. "And you know *absolutely* nothing about Abigail. So just leave her out of this."

"Leave her out?" She tilted her head back and laughed. "Maybe that's what you should have done from the beginning. Honestly, falling in love with a human? And one like that. So feeble and weak." She shuddered.

"Did you have some point in coming here?" Stan picked up his shoes and headed down the stairs. As if he had somewhere to go.

"Just reminding you that your clock is ticking." Lilith followed him down, her heels clomping on the wooden stairs. At the bottom she followed him to the window, where he stood with his shoes in his hands, looking out over the dusky street. Her SUV was parked outside, in its usual spot. Engine running, Jake in the front, window down, awaiting whatever order she would give him next.

"Is he one of us too?" Stan asked, not turning to look at her. He pressed a fingertip against the glass, covering up the driver's head with a smudged print.

"Who, Jake? No, he's a human too. But the good kind. The kind that does what I say without asking questions. Not some stupid little girl who runs crying whenever her delicate sensibilities are offended."

"She's stronger than you think." Stan closed his eyes for a moment and thought of her—of Abby, tall and proud, her chin held high. That was the woman he knew, who stood for what was right and helped people in need. Like some kind of superhero. The image made him laugh.

"What's so funny? Don't think she won't be a target if this escapade of yours continues. You know women can find me just as enticing as men." Lilith didn't even try to hide the contempt in her voice. Not just for Abigail but for Stan as well. She knew he was losing him. That she might lose him forever. And the thought of his choosing a mortal over her plainly disgusted her.

"Get out," he said, his voice flat and calm. His eyes still closed. Behind him he heard no movement, then the snap of her purse and the click of her shoes across the concrete floor.

She paused at the door. As always, she had to make a dramatic exit. "Fine," she said, throwing her cigarette on the floor and grounding it out with her toe. "But I'll be seeing you soon enough. You are nothing without us. Once you realize what you'll lose, you'll come back to your senses. After all, you know better than anyone how easy it can be to tempt people into doing what you want."

Stan dropped his shoes on the floor, then took off his clothes and headed back upstairs to bed.

Two and a half days left. Stan dragged himself out of bed at midday again, washed and brushed, found his clothes on the floor downstairs by the window, and put them on. He wanted to see his art again, to look into the eyes of those models he'd—well, he had to admit it to himself: he'd disfigured them. He remembered the process now with a sort of numbness, like the tattoo gun still vibrated in his hand, buzzing and shaking his body until he felt almost nothing at all. As if he hadn't been the one pressing the needle into their sad, sickly flesh, blacking out whatever small dreams of their futures they might have had left.

Abigail had tried to tell him. Sitting on the subway en route to the museum now, Stan closed his eyes and tried not to complicate the day by bringing thoughts of her into the mix. But as always he couldn't keep them at bay. What had she said at the show? *Just because they're lost doesn't mean they can't change their lives.* Given his current situation, the irony of this statement was just too much and he doubled over, putting his head between his knees. Assuming the crash position. The other people on the subway looked at him—he could feel their stares burning into the back of his head, down the sides of his body. As if he were some sort of freak show, not flesh and blood like they were but the devil himself, his red skin showing through this human hide. Could he ever really be one of them? Blend in with the masses, another face in the crowd? Another simple life

form experiencing all the uncertainty each day brings, the ups
and downs, the good and the bad?

"Eastern Parkway," the train conductor announced, the
intercom buzzing, his voice muddled. "Brooklyn Museum."

Stan sat up again and took a couple of deep breaths, then
got to his feet. Like a fighter getting ready to go into the ring,
he bobbed up and down, twisting his neck, working out the
nervous energy. When the train stopped and the door opened,
he leapt out and bounded up the stairs before he had a chance
to change his mind and go back home.

Outside, the late-afternoon brightness hit him, and he pulled
out his sunglasses. For the ruler of the underworld, he thought,
he certainly was sensitive to light and heat. The streets were busy
but not crowded, but he kept his hands in his pockets as he walked
anyway, just to keep them from brushing against any bare arms.
He hadn't had a real vision in days, not since Lilith had jumped
him in the museum lobby. Or maybe he had pushed himself on
her. He couldn't remember now how it had gone down and didn't
even want to anyway. That was over and done with, that phase.
His exploration of his evil side. Now he wouldn't touch Lilith for
all the money in the world.

When he reached the museum he took off the shades and
walked into the cool, quiet lobby. Headed up the main stairs to
the gallery where his art was still being displayed. Pausing outside the doorway for a moment, he prepared himself for what
waited inside. This reminder of his darker days, his evil side.
The beast that lived within him and wanted with all its might to
be let out. Stan was afraid that when he saw his work this evil
would overpower him again. He had to stay focused and calm.
Couldn't let his emotions get the best of him.

Easier said than done. Inside the gallery, his subjects stood
posed, naked as newborns. His wide, black-ink paths running

all over their bodies. One saw him, then another and another, and in a moment all eyes were on Stan. Judging him, accusing him. All of these people had fear in their hearts, or anger toward him, or a mixture of both. Tears rolled down their tattooed cheeks. Limbs trembled. Hands curled into fists. Not just because he had put them here on display, but because once this exhibit closed, they would still bear the scars he branded them with. Now they were branded for life.

Stan felt like he should say something. An apology, an explanation of some sort. But how could he explain all this? *I'm sorry. I was the devil at the time. I didn't mean to do it.* No words could ever be enough. Yes, as he had tried to tell Abigail, they were all very bad people. They'd done their share of evil deeds and ruined more lives than their own. But Abby had been right too. They were humans above all. They wanted something better but had no means of escape, no path to the rock that was higher than the rising seas of their lives. Stan could relate to that more than he wanted to. He wanted redemption, just like them.

"The one thing I can't give them," he mumbled to himself, then turned and left. There was no use in staying there, prolonging their hurt. He wondered why he'd come at all. As he slowly walked back through the museum, a darkness came over his mind, and for the first time he felt like he might fail. Since he'd asked Abby for forgiveness, he'd felt such a lightness, such optimism that somehow it could really work. She could just say the words—*I forgive* you—and he would become a man with all the baggage, the vulnerability and uncertainty that comes along with it.

How stupid he'd been. How utterly blind and foolish. There was no way he could win this war. At least not by himself.

THIRTY-FIVE

This is what it feels like when your life is about to end. Looking over the edge of the bridge, leaning your body well past the railing. A hard wind hits your face, stinging your skin, and you close your eyes. Pretend that none of this is real anymore, the sound of the traffic, the warmth of the sun. No one even notices you, so maybe you just don't exist at all. It will only take a little more weight, a gentle lift of your feet from the ground and—

Stan, in his black suit and white shirt, earbuds in and iPhone tucked away in an inside pocket, pulled himself back before his body lost its balance and went tumbling down to the water for a second time. He'd lived through it once; didn't want to tempt fate twice. Looking down the length of the wide, winding Hudson River, New Jersey to the right, New York to the left, he thought about Old Stan and wondered where he was now—the spirit that used to inhabit this body he so rudely hijacked on his own fall from the sky. Hopefully up there hanging out with God, looking down on Stan now and having a good laugh at the mess he'd made of this life.

And why shouldn't he? In the handful of weeks he'd been on earth, what had he done? Drank too much, made some art, found out he was Satan, had sex with a harpy, ruined other people's lives. What a track record. Stan leaned his arms on the metal railing and put his head down, as if that would make the embarrassment, the shame he felt go away. *Out of sight, out of mind*. He'd been given a chance here, and he'd wasted it from day one. He could have made a difference, maybe helped some people or at least found a way to help himself. To make himself into a man. A *better* man. Instead he'd just floated from one night to the next, accomplishing little but living off of other people's misery.

He shifted, sticking the toes of his shoes through the gap between the bottom of the fence and the concrete walkway. He could see the river through the fence's slats, the water rolling and surging six hundred feet below. Ships and boats passing in silence as his music droned on: soft songs now and melancholy, not the heavy metal and goth anthems his previous incarnation had enjoyed. Neil Finn's "Sinner" ended and Bush's "Letting the Cables Sleep" began, and he watched the waves softly splashing in time against the bridge's pilings. Beckoning him to come, calling him back to where deep down he knew he belonged.

"Shit," he muttered and cranked the volume, then stood up and began to walk. Not back to land but toward the middle of the bridge, where its massive, famous cables touched down then sloped back up. He stopped when he got to the place where he had jumped. Ran his hand over the railing and stood there, trying to let his cloudy memory do its work. It was like he could remember that day and how he had felt, but then again he didn't. Must have been more of Old Stan's residuals. Just a sensory feeling in the muscles and bones. The only thing he knew for sure was he had woken up on the riverbank, bruised and sore and dripping wet. And without a clue who he was. Or who he had been.

He pulled out his phone and changed songs. Green Day's "21 Guns." He also checked for messages and the time: none and almost four thirty. Time to head back to the city and get a cab uptown. Make his way to the Cloisters, to his fate, whatever it might or might not be. Turning to the water once more, he leaned over the railing and looked down, just to make sure it wasn't where he actually wanted to be. Despite how horrible he felt, how confused about himself and this world he had been thrust into, there was a tiny spark of hope in him. A feeling of peace. That little bit of Abigail that had rubbed off on him, that lived inside him now. That he wished, no matter how things turned out, would never go away.

Turning around, he walked back to the far shore, his last mile on this long, hard trip. Counting his footsteps and the minutes that might be his last on this earth.

The Cloisters was crowded, and even in the parking lot, as he got out of the taxi, it was difficult for Stan not to touch anyone. Typical for a Saturday afternoon toward the end of summer, everyone wanted to be outside, to take in those last warm rays of sunlight while they could. Stan felt them beating down on the back of his neck as the sun made its slow descent toward the horizon, and he shook the lapels of his jacket, sending a little cool air around his body. He'd been sweating the whole way here, though he had to admit it wasn't entirely because of the weather.

Straightening his tie, he walked up to the building and went inside. The lobby was just as busy, full of parents and children and older folks clutching water bottles and museum maps, fanning themselves and talking, laughing. Stan stopped at the front desk and paid the admission fee, laughing a little at the dark humor of it all. *Twenty-five bucks to find out whether I live or die.* Seemed like a bargain, all told.

"Thanks," he said to the woman behind the counter, handing

her back the entry ticket. "I won't need it." She gave him a quiz-zical look, but he merely smiled and walked away into the throng. Hands in his pockets so as not to rub skin with anyone accidentally...but then he slowed his pace. Took his hands out and lightly brushed them against some random hands. *What the hell?* he thought. *Might be the last time.*

The flashes hit him strong and hard. He stopped in his tracks, put his hands up to his eyes as he closed them tight. These people he touched, they hadn't done anything bad. They were the rapists, the murderers, the terrorists he was used to. These were just ordinary humans. Out for an afternoon with their kids or their parents or friends. Excited about seeing art, about being in the world and surrounded by life. Stan saw the bad things, too, of course, but now they were not sins com-mitted, not the crimes perpetrated by the people he touched. No, these were heinous acts they had suffered themselves—the miscarriages, the robberies at gunpoint, one had even survived the Holocaust as a child.

Stan opened his eyes and looked. Only a few feet away, a white-haired woman stood. Skin wrinkled by time but rosy pink on this hot summer's day. She wore a dark, sleeveless dress, and on her bare arm he saw a tattoo—down by the wrist, a line of small black numbers. She glared at him, her eyes clouded by tears, but not from sadness. Only rage born of despair, of the horror that came from such intimate involvement with death. With evil. She knew who Stan was, and he felt her hatred like a dagger in his heart.

He ran past her and out of the lobby. Down a small set of stairs, into the room with the sarcophagi, with the Mary and Jesus statue that had seemed to come to life the last time he was there. He stopped to look at it again, just to make sure. See if it had any words of wisdom. The baby's lifeless eyes looked right through him, its mouth set in stone. Nothing, as usual. No help. No clue how to navigate this world.

Stan kept moving down the long hallway to the courtyard doors. He heard voices outside, but the stained-glass windows prevented him from seeing how many people were out there. Or if Abby was among them. As her name entered his mind, he slowed his steps a little, suddenly feeling afraid. He'd come so close to the end. In a minute he would find out where he would spend eternity, or the next forty or fifty years of his life if it all worked out the way he wanted it to. He thought about turning back, getting into the cab, and disappearing from New York, going somewhere he'd never be found. Across the country, around the globe. Was it possible? Could he just get lost? The thought was tempting for a moment, enough to make him stop walking altogether.

But then he thought, *Probably not.* There was no way he could just vanish. Lilith had a homing beacon on him; she would find him in this world or the next. Of that he was sure. His power meant too much to her, and no matter where he was she would always come to collect him.

Unless I'm a human. Then he would have no power at all.

He had to find out what Abigail chose.

Running down the hall, Stan turned the corner and burst through the courtyard doors. He stumbled outside, only his grip on the door handle keeping him on his feet. Skidding to a stop, he let the door go, and it banged closed. The noise drew all eyes to him. A reflex to an unexpected noise, nothing more, nothing less. *They have no idea why you're here.* He told himself not to panic but couldn't help wondering how many of them were Lilith's cronies sent there to retrieve him if this whole becoming human thing blew up in his face.

Wiping his sweaty hands down the front of his jacket, he

took a step, and most of the crowd went back to whatever they had been doing. Talking, taking in the scenery, sketching pictures of plants. And there, by the wall, was Abigail, looking out over the river at the spot where they'd kissed. He took another tentative step, mind racing, trying to figure out how to approach. Fast or slow? Loud or soft? Should he call her name, run into her arms like in a romance novel? No, she wouldn't have that. Too dramatic. And besides, Stan had no idea if she'd want to touch him again. Maybe she hated him, and if she did, she had every right to.

But she had shown up. That was something, at least. He walked over to where she stood.

"Abby." He said it softly, like a reverent prayer.

She turned around. She didn't reply, just looked at him for a long minute. No sign of emotion on her face—no happiness or relief, but no anger either. Just her sweet, beautiful eyes staring at him. He'd thought they never would again, and seeing them now made the last five agonizing days disappear. He couldn't help but smile at her, shyly, then with growing courage. Even if she cast him out, sent him back to be the ruler of the underworld, he would have this one last moment with her. A bit of perfect happiness to see him through.

Without thinking, he reached out to touch her, and though she started in surprise, she didn't pull away. He put his hand on her face, felt her soft skin and the flush of her cheek. And in that touch he saw everything he needed to know—rather, he saw nothing. Abigail's past was gone, her future still unwritten. Just a white light, so bright he had to close his eyes. In the darkness his other senses increased, and he felt the wind like a warm blanket shifting over his body, heard the murmur of the crowd like the sharp buzz of a swarm of bees. The scents of jasmine and gardenia filled the air, and as Abigail slipped her hand into his, he felt almost an electric rush.

He opened his eyes. Abby still watched him carefully, but her expression had softened. She wasn't quite happy yet, but she'd moved to understanding at least. That much he could see. To acceptance of who Stan was, what he had been, and who he still could be. Everything else, he hoped, would follow in due time.

He wrapped his fingers around hers, and she squeezed back.

"Let's get out of here," she said. Stan nodded, and they walked slowly across the courtyard together. Down the hall and up the stairs and into the lobby, where the crowd had thinned.

"Almost closing time," Abby said and nodded to the woman behind the desk as they passed. She nodded back, eyeing Stan, but he didn't let it bother him this time. As long as he had Abby by his side, he felt, he could get through anything. As long as she believed in him, everything would be alright.

Stan went through the door of the museum then turned to hold open it for Abby, giving her a flourish with his hand to welcome her through. He watched her face as she stepped back out into the afternoon light. Awash in the orange haze of near-sunset, everything about her glowed: her pale yellow hair, her pink-stained lips. She was radiant like fire itself, and Stan couldn't help but want to touch her again. He reached out a hand but stopped as Abigail seemed suddenly alarmed. Her back stiffened, her delicate brow creased. She looked over Stan's shoulder, and he turned to see what it was that made her so uneasy so fast.

In the parking lot, a black SUV idled. An Escalade with tinted glass, the back window opened just a crack. Wide enough for a thin trail of cigarette smoke to escape from within.

In his jacket pocket, Stan's iPhone began to ring.